CW00687812

THE GHOST
AND THE CHURCH LADY

The Ghost of Marlow House

The Ghost Who Loved Diamonds

The Ghost Who Wasn't

The Ghost Who Wanted Revenge

The Ghost of Halloween Past

The Ghost Who Came for Christmas

The Ghost of Valentine Past

The Ghost from the Sea

The Ghost and the Mystery Writer

The Ghost and the Muse

The Ghost Who Stayed Home

The Ghost and the Leprechaun

The Ghost Who Lied

The Ghost and the Bride

The Ghost and Little Marie

The Ghost and the Doppelganger

The Ghost of Second Chances

The Ghost Who Dream Hopped

The Ghost of Christmas Secrets

The Ghost Who Was Say I Do

The Ghost and the Baby

The Ghost and the Halloween Haunt

The Ghost and the Christmas Spirit

The Ghost and the Silver Scream
The Ghost of a Memory
The Ghost and the Witches' Coven
The Ghost and the Mountain Man
The Ghost and the Birthday Boy
The Ghost and the Church Lady
The Ghost and the Medium

HAUNTING DANIELLE - BOOK 29

USA TODAY BESTSELLING AUTHOR
BOBBI HOLMES

The Ghost and the Church Lady
(Haunting Danielle, Book 29)
A Novel
By Bobbi Holmes
Cover Design: Elizabeth Mackey

This novel is a work of fiction.
Any resemblance to places or actual persons,
living or dead, is entirely coincidental.

ISBN: 978-1-949977-68-4
A

Dedicated to Hunny, the inspiration for the character of the same name, who recently traveled the Rainbow Bridge. When on the other side, give our love to Spooky the Halloween Cat (the inspiration for Max). And to Miss Kitty (the inspiration for Bella). You are all greatly missed. Thank you for the love and inspiration.

ONE

Ten-year-old Evan MacDonald noticed the dog first. A yellow Lab carried what looked like a tennis ball in its mouth. Tail wagging, it paced back and forth in the street in front of the MacDonald house. Evan had never seen the Labrador retriever in his neighborhood, and since it was off a leash and no one in sight, Evan assumed someone had lost his or her pet.

Tall for his age, Evan had entered a gangly stage, yet he still possessed soulful brown eyes, delicate features, long dark lashes women envied, and wavy brown hair trimmed short at the sides yet longer on top, showing off unruly curls. He loved dogs, and one of his favorite pastimes was playing with Ian's golden retriever, Sadie, and Chris's pit bull, Hunny. Both dogs enjoyed playing catch and roughhousing on the beach. Some people feared pit bulls, but Evan had never been afraid of Hunny. Of course, he had known Hunny since she was just a scared pup. Evan understood Hunny had a lot of fears, Walt had told him. Walt knew because Hunny had told Walt.

Evan watched the Lab for a few more minutes before deciding to try coaxing the dog into his yard, and then he could get his dad. His father, Police Chief MacDonald, could find the dog's owner, and if the dog didn't have one, maybe Evan could keep him. Evan smiled at the idea. The smile quickly faded when he saw her.

He let out a sigh and watched as a fair-haired girl with bouncing shoulder-length curls came running toward the dog, who ran toward the girl. She looked about Evan's age, yet she didn't dress like the girls in his class. She wore a dress with a full skirt and short white puffy sleeves. Despite the October chill, she had no jacket or coat. On her feet she wore white socks trimmed in lace and black and white shoes.

The dog stopped right when it reached her, sat down, and dropped the ball at her feet. Laughing, the girl picked up the ball and then threw it. The ball flew down the street, out of sight, the dog following it. The girl stood and watched, making no attempt to go after the dog.

Evan muttered, "She shouldn't be doing that in the street." He marched to the end of his driveway, toward the girl, who now stood, her back to Evan, some three feet from the MacDonald mailbox.

"Hey!" Evan shouted. The girl did not turn around. "Hey, you! Girl! Don't throw the ball in the street like that."

The girl turned toward Evan and stared at him for a moment. Finally, she asked, "Are you talking to me?"

"Yes. Is that your dog?" Evan demanded.

"You are talking to me," the girl muttered.

"Well, is he?" Evan snapped.

She cocked her head slightly, now smiling. After a moment of silence, she walked toward Evan, stopping about six feet from him. "Yes. His name is Charger."

Evan looked down the street. He didn't see the dog. He looked back at the girl. "Where did he go?"

The girl shrugged. "He'll be back."

"Aren't you afraid he'll get lost?" Evan asked.

"I said he'll be back. He always comes back."

"You shouldn't throw the ball like that in the street. He could get hit by a car."

The girl smiled. "Oh, I'm not too worried about that."

"If it were my dog, I'd worry."

"Do you have a dog?" she asked.

"No. But if I had one, I would take better care of him than you do."

The girl's smile vanished. "I take real good care of my dog. He's my best friend. We will always be together."

"You won't be together if he gets hit by a car."

The girl laughed.

Evan frowned. "It isn't funny. And it's against the law to let your dog run around off a leash."

"A leash wouldn't hold Charger, trust me."

As if he heard his name, Charger came running from down the street, his tail wagging.

Evan smiled at the dog, who now stood before the girl, a ball in his mouth. The dog looked at Evan and cocked his head questioningly.

"Yes, Charger," the girl said in a soft voice. "He can see you. He can see both of us."

Evan frowned at the odd comment, but the girl just looked his way and giggled before snatching the ball from the dog's mouth and throwing it away from her.

WALT HAD JUST TURNED down the street to Chief MacDonald's house, Danielle in the passenger seat, when a golden Labrador retriever dashed in front of the Packard. He slammed on the brakes and, without thought, threw his right arm toward Danielle to keep her from moving forward.

"Did you hit it?" Danielle asked, pushing Walt's hand away while leaning forward to peer out the windshield.

"No. But where did he go?"

"People shouldn't let their dogs run loose like that," Danielle said.

A few minutes later, after parking the car, Walt opened the passenger door for Danielle. As he did, he noticed Evan standing by his mailbox, watching them, a blank expression on the young boy's face.

Walt glanced back to the street, checking again to make sure he hadn't hit the dog. When he saw nothing, Danielle got out of the car and walked with Walt toward Evan.

"Hi, Evan," Danielle greeted him. "Do you know whose dog that was?"

Evan nodded, his eyes darting back to the street.

"What's wrong?" Walt asked. "I didn't hit him, did I?" Walt glanced back to the street, now concerned he might have hit the poor dog, and after Evan witnessed it, the dog had run off afraid and injured.

"No," Evan said, his expression still blank.

"Do you know whose dog it is?" Danielle repeated.

Evan nodded. "She said it was her dog."

"And who is she?" Walt asked.

Evan looked up at Walt and said in awe, "I just saw a ghost dog. I've never seen one of those before."

"A GHOST DOG?" the chief asked Danielle. He sat with Walt and Danielle in his living room.

Danielle glanced to the hallway where Evan had disappeared with his older brother, Eddy, not long after entering the house. "And a ghost girl," she added in a whisper.

"He didn't realize she was a ghost when he first saw her," Walt explained. "It upset him she was playing ball in the street, afraid the dog was going to get hit."

"And she and the dog just disappeared?" the chief asked.

Danielle nodded. "That's what Evan told us."

The chief let out a sigh and leaned back on the sofa. "He seemed perfectly fine when he walked in here with you two."

Danielle glanced back to the hallway and then to the chief. "I have to give your son credit. He seems to take his gift—and what he encounters because of it—in stride. I think it relieved him not to have to worry about the dog."

"Because it's already dead?" Walt asked with a chuckle.

"Pretty much." Danielle shrugged.

"It has me concerned. If there is a little girl ghost, then I have to assume a child has died," the chief said, his tone serious.

"From how Evan described her, I suspect this child died years ago. Still sad, but not quite the same thing," Danielle said.

"How did he describe her?" the chief asked.

"She was wearing a checkered dress with a full skirt, white Peter Pan collar—" Danielle began.

"I don't think Evan knows what a Peter Pan collar is," the chief interrupted.

Danielle smiled. "He didn't say it was a Peter Pan collar, but from how he described her clothes, that's what it sounds like she was wearing. And she had on white socks and shoes that were probably black and white saddle shoes, by his description. She had curly blond hair with a big bow."

"He didn't get her name?" the chief asked.

"I believe he was too busy chastising her for letting the dog play in the street," Walt said.

"He had enough time to describe her wardrobe, from the bow to the socks," the chief returned.

"Well, he is getting that age," Danielle mused.

The chief frowned. "What age?"

"The age little boys start noticing little girls," Danielle teased.

"He is ten," the chief snapped.

Danielle grinned at the chief but said nothing.

"Just wait until your baby is born," the chief began, only to be cut off by Evan, who had just walked into the room unnoticed.

"You're having a baby?" Evan blurted, now looking at Danielle.

Danielle smiled at Evan. "Um… yeah."

Evan looked at his father and frowned. "How come you didn't tell me?"

"I asked your father to wait a little while before he told you," Danielle answered for the chief.

"What are you going to have?" Evan asked.

Danielle shrugged. "Too soon to tell."

"Is that why you didn't want to tell me yet? So you could wait and tell me if it was a boy or girl?" Evan asked.

Danielle and Walt exchanged quick glances. She looked back to Evan. "Yeah. That's why."

But it was a lie. After announcing the news of her pregnancy to a few of her close friends at Connor's birthday party, Danielle had asked the chief not to say anything to anyone yet—especially Evan. While she felt they would have a healthy baby, because of what Walt's mother had told him, she understood if something went wrong with the pregnancy, it more likely would happen during the first few months. Should the unthinkable happen, Danielle didn't want to have to explain to someone as young as Evan why she was pregnant one minute and not the next. However, the sort-of secret hadn't really stayed a secret, and if Evan hadn't just walked in on them, he would have likely found out soon anyway.

"I wanted Lily to have a boy," Evan said.

Danielle smiled at him. "Yes, I remember."

Evan studied Danielle for a moment and then announced, "But you can have a girl."

The chief laughed. "Oh, you are giving them permission?"

Evan blushed. "I didn't mean it that way. I just meant I think a girl would be okay. Girls aren't so bad."

"They aren't?" Danielle asked, arching her brows at the chief with a smug smile.

"Well, it's not like we can hang out or anything," Evan said.

"You and Connor play," Walt reminded him.

"Yeah, but he's older now. But I guess a little girl could be fun too. Not like I can play baseball with either of them," Evan said, sounding a little disappointed.

"Evan, you're almost getting old enough to babysit," Danielle said.

"Gee, you would let me babysit?" Evan asked.

Now it was the chief's turn to arch his brows. "You would let Evan babysit?"

Before Danielle could answer, Evan said, "It would be a long time before I could babysit."

"It would?" Walt asked with a smile.

"Sure. Well, I could do it if Marie were there. That way, Marie could change the diapers. I don't think I wanna change diapers." Evan wrinkled his nose at the idea and then asked his dad if he could take some cookies in the room for him and Eddy. The next minute, he was gone.

"For a kid who just encountered a couple of ghosts, my son is resilient," the chief said.

"It was the idea of changing a diaper that almost did him in," Danielle teased.

"Do I need to worry about this girl ghost and her dog coming back?" the chief asked.

Danielle let out a sigh and said, "Unfortunately, that's just part of Evan's normal."

TWO

On Sunday morning, Danielle Marlow opened her eyes and looked up to the ceiling of Marlow House's attic bedroom. Her right hand reached over to Walt's side of the bed. As Danielle suspected, she was alone. With a yawn, she reluctantly sat up and wiped sleep from her eyes. Sunlight streamed in the window, yet not as bright had the window been facing east instead of west. She was about to pick up her cellphone from the nightstand to check the time when Walt came walking into the room.

"Good morning," he said brightly.

Danielle turned a smile to her husband, but it quickly faded when she saw what he carried—two coffee cups.

"You know I can't have coffee. Are you trying to torture me?" She let out a groan and added, "Even if I could drink it, once I smelled it, I would probably puke."

"Puke is such an unladylike term," Walt said with mock primness. Danielle rolled her eyes in response.

"And so is rolling your eyes," he added.

Walt set one cup on the dresser, a distance from Danielle, and then handed the second one to her and said, "It's not coffee. It's Cheerios. No milk, dry."

Danielle frowned but accepted the cup. She looked inside.

"Lily told me to give you Cheerios before you get out of bed. It will help with the morning sickness." Walt sat down on the edge of the mattress, his gaze never leaving her.

Danielle smiled at Walt and looked back into the cup of Cheerios. "Yeah, she told me that, too. I meant to bring some up last night." Danielle picked up a few pieces and popped them in her mouth.

Walt remained on the bed, watching her. After a few minutes, Danielle glanced over to the cup sitting across the room. "If that's your coffee, it's getting cold."

Reaching out with one hand, Walt patted Danielle and said, "That's alright. I didn't realize the smell bothered you."

"It's okay. I actually feel pretty good. I think these Cheerios are helping."

Walt stood up. "Just in case, I'll sit over here and drink it."

Danielle flashed Walt a grin and watched as he retrieved his cup of coffee and took a seat at his desk. He swiveled around in his chair, his back now to the desk as he faced her. "If you're going with Lily and Heather to Melony's this morning, I didn't think you'd want to feel sick."

"Thanks, Walt, that was sweet of you. And I'll be honest, I wasn't sure I'd feel well enough to go this morning."

"And now?"

"A lot better. Not so queasy."

"Good."

"I should probably get in the habit of leaving a cup of Cheerios by my bedside at night." She took another bite.

"While I don't mind bringing them to you, that would probably be a good idea."

"What are you going to do when I'm gone this morning?"

"I plan to do some writing."

"I won't be here to bug you," Danielle teased.

Walt smiled at Danielle over his coffee and said, "I don't have a problem when you're in the house. I rather like it. But I confess, it is distracting when we have a full house. While I enjoyed Ian's and Lily's families, it's nice to have our home back to ourselves."

Danielle grinned. "I have a feeling Lily is the one who's going to be missing her privacy now that Ian's parents are living in Frederickport."

"Maybe Ian's mother will spend most of her free time over at

Kelly and Joe's. After all, they have a wedding to plan," Walt suggested.

"Only if Lily leaves Connor with Kelly."

LOOKING INTO HER BATHROOM MIRROR, Danielle wondered if she should cut her hair before the baby came or simply continue wearing a braid. Letting out a sigh, she turned her attention from her hair to makeup. She had already dressed for breakfast at Melony's, wearing blue jeans and a knit sweater. After putting the finishing touches on her makeup, she headed downstairs. Fifteen minutes later, Danielle crossed the street to Lily's house while Walt stood at the attic bedroom window, looking down at her.

Heather had made it to Lily's house before Danielle. Instead of jeans, she wore black stretch pants with her boots, and a long purple sweater, with her long black hair pulled atop her head in a messy knot. Lily had already backed her car out of the garage, and she stood with Heather in the driveway, chatting. Like Danielle, Lily wore jeans with her blouse and jacket. When they saw Danielle approach from across the street, they stopped talking and turned to her.

"Morning, Little Mama," Heather greeted her cheerfully.

"Are you going to keep calling me that?" Danielle asked, now walking down the Bartley driveway toward her friends.

"Probably," Heather said with a shrug.

Lily nodded up to the attic window. "Morning, Dani. I see Walt is watching to make sure you make it across the street safely."

Danielle paused a moment and looked back to Marlow House. She spied Walt standing in the window, looking down at them. She smiled and gave him a wave. He waved back and then turned from the window, disappearing from sight.

"Morning," Danielle said, turning back to Heather and Lily. "He brought me Cheerios in bed this morning."

"Did it work?" Lily asked.

"What, not steak and eggs?" Heather snorted.

"Yes, thanks." Danielle turned to Heather and added, "It was for the morning sickness. If he would have brought me steak and eggs, I would have puked."

"Are you going to feel like eating at Mel's?" Heather asked.

"I think so. I'm much better." Danielle grinned.

AS THEY HEADED to Melony's house, Danielle told Lily and Heather about the little girl and dog Evan had seen yesterday.

"And you have no idea who it was?" Heather asked.

"None," Danielle said.

"I wonder how often you guys see dead people and don't even realize it," Lily said.

"You mean, how often do we see ghosts and think they're living people?" Danielle corrected.

Lily shrugged. "Same thing, right?"

They discussed ghosts for a few more minutes when Heather shifted the conversation by asking, "Are your in-laws all settled into their rental?"

"Yeah. But Ian is aching today. He wanted to hire some guys to move his parents' stuff from the storage to the rental, but his parents insisted they do it themselves; his mom didn't want to spend the money, said they had already paid a fortune for movers to bring their stuff up from California. And Ian's father would never allow his son to pay for it."

"But he would let his son break his back moving furniture?" Heather asked.

"Something like that," Lily said with a shrug. "Ian tried to get them to go over to Kelly's and stay there while he and Walt moved everything. But his mother said she didn't want to ask Walt, since Walt and Danielle had let them stay at Marlow House and refused to take any money."

Heather chuckled. "I know why Ian wanted Walt's help."

"Yeah. It would have been easier on all their backs if Walt could have used his telekinesis. Instead, it was Ian and Joe who moved everything," Lily said.

"Was Kelly there?" Danielle asked.

"Yeah. I got to stay home with Connor," Lily said with a grin. They all chuckled.

"It was too bad Kelly had to postpone her bridal shower. I know she wanted your sister to be there," Danielle noted. The groom's sister had planned a bridal shower for her sister-in-law-to-be but cancelled when she came down with the flu the day before the shower.

"They haven't set a new date yet, but Laura says she's going to fly up," Lily said.

"Kelly should be Laura's sister-in-law, not yours," Heather snarked.

"Only if Ian had a brother. Laura can't have Ian," Lily said as she pulled into Melony's driveway.

When the three women got out of Lily's car, they heard loud knocking coming from next door, accompanied by a woman's voice calling, "Rachel, it's Leanne! Rachel! Rachel, it's Leanne!"

"If Rachel wasn't awake before, I imagine she is now," Heather said dryly as she, Lily and Danielle paused in Melony's driveway and looked next door. They watched a middle-aged woman scurry from the front door to one window, where she peeked in the house, before rushing to another window, while all the time calling out for Rachel.

RACHEL MOORE SAT on the rocking chair, studying the lifeless body occupying her bed. The woman looked as if she slept peacefully, oblivious to the pounding on the windows downstairs and the relentless shouting from outside.

Leanne is going to wake up the neighbors, Rachel thought with a sigh. She leaned back in the rocker and told herself that was no longer her concern. After a moment, the knocking and shouting stopped. Rachel paused and listened. *Leanne is using her key*, Rachel thought. Glancing back at the dead body, she cringed.

She hated for Leanne to walk in on this. Finding herself dead hadn't surprised Rachel. After all, she was ninety-five, and most women who made it to her age were in care homes or living with family. She had been fortunate to live out her life in her own home. She would have preferred dying a week later. Yet she was confident everything would work out—providing Larry kept his nose out of her business.

Rachel heard steps coming down the hallway toward her bedroom. "Yes, Leanne used her key," Rachel told herself. The next moment, the bedroom door opened. Instead of walking into the room immediately, Leanne stood in the open doorway, staring at the woman, who appeared to be sleeping in the bed. She called out hesitantly, "Rachel?"

"I'm sorry you have to see me like this," Rachel said with a sigh. "I'm dead, dear."

Dressed for church, Leanne wore a polyester polka-dot-print dress, its hem falling mid-calf, with black kitten-heel shoes, and a beige bucket hat with a satin bow. She slowly entered the room. Rachel watched as Leanne approached her body. Once at the side of the bed, Leanne reached down and picked up Rachel's right wrist. She held it a moment, testing for a pulse. After gently placing the wrist back on the bed, Leanne leaned over and pressed one ear against the dead woman's chest, looking for a second opinion.

After a moment, Leanne stood up straight and looked down at the body. She let out a sigh. "It looks as if you went peacefully," Leanne said in a soft voice, her gaze never leaving the dead woman's face. "Now you can be with your daughters and husband. I imagine you're happy. This is for the best."

Leanne smiled softly, reached out, and gently brushed the gray hair from the dead woman's closed eyes. She remained standing there for a few minutes, lost in her own thoughts. Finally, she opened her purse and pulled out her cellphone and placed a call.

"911, what is your emergency?" came the voice on the other side of the call.

"I came to pick my dear friend up for church, and when she didn't answer, I used my key to get into the house. She's ninety-five, and I was afraid she might have fallen or something. But she was still in bed. I think she's dead."

After the call ended, Leanne placed another one.

"Don't tell me you're having car trouble?" a voice on the other end of the call asked Leanne.

"Larry, Rachel is gone," Leanne said, a sniffle in her voice.

"What do you mean, gone?" he asked.

"When she didn't answer the door, I used my key. I found her in bed—she is dead." Leanne began to cry.

THREE

Unlike Lily, Melony Carmichael didn't know Heather and Danielle were mediums, although she believed in the possibility of paranormal activity. She and her fiancé, Adam Nichols, had recently experienced it at the property Ian's parents had purchased.

Chris Johnson, aka Chris Glandon, had been the first of their medium friends to meet Melony on his flight back to Frederickport after a business trip three years earlier. At the time he and Danielle had been dating, and when he showed up at Marlow House with the attractive blonde by his side, Danielle felt a brief mixture of envy and jealousy. She soon learned Melony was an attorney, not an actress or model, despite her looks. And while Chris's interest back then had leaned toward Danielle, it turned out Melony's leaned toward Marie's grandson, Adam Nichols, who had been her high school boyfriend.

They had welcomed Melony and Adam into Danielle's tight-knit group, although the couple didn't know the truth about the mediums or Walt. Both Melony and Adam had become close to Chris and formed a friendship with Heather, who not only worked for Chris, but was a friend, neighbor and fellow medium to Chris, Walt, and Danielle. Many saw Heather as the quirky young woman who dressed in what some described as Goth, who had a penchant for finding dead bodies when jogging along the beach, yet both

Adam and Melony had witnessed another side to Heather, as Chris's competent right-hand person at the Glandon Foundation.

The four friends sat around Melony's kitchen, chatting while waiting for the quiche to come out of the oven.

"I think I needed this girl time," Lily said.

"Too much in-law time these days?" Melony teased.

"I love Ian's family, but..." Instead of finishing her sentence, Lily took a sip of coffee.

"When we drove up, there was a woman pounding on your neighbor's house, calling out for Rachel," Heather said.

Melony glanced toward the kitchen window facing the neighbor's house. "What did this woman look like?"

Heather gave a description.

"That would probably be Leanne Hodge. I call her the Church Lady." Melony grinned sheepishly. "And Rachel is my neighbor. Leanne picks Rachel up for church each Sunday. I'm afraid Rachel's hearing isn't very good, and she doesn't always hear the doorbell."

"Was it strange moving back to your childhood home?" Heather asked.

Lily looked to Heather. "Where did that come from?"

Heather shrugged. "I don't know. Talking about Mel's neighbors, and it got me to wondering how many of them were living here back when Mel lived here with her parents, or if it's basically a new neighborhood."

"All that was going on in your head?" Lily asked.

Heather wrinkled her nose at Lily, and Melony laughed. "Actually," Mel began, "it's about half. Rachel has lived next door since before I was born. But the neighborhood has changed. The house across from Rachel's recently sold. They want to turn it into a bed-and-breakfast, but I'm not sure that's going to happen."

"Why not?" Danielle asked.

"Rachel's opposed to the idea," Melony said. "And from what I understand, the city won't approve the license if neighbors oppose."

"Like with Marlow House," Lily said.

"Fortunately for us, it wasn't a huge deal," Danielle said. "Walt and I had pretty much decided to close anyway. Although, I confess, I do sort of miss it."

"But now you have a baby to focus on," Melony said.

The sound of sirens blaring down the street interrupted the conversation. They all stopped talking and looked to the window.

"That's close," Danielle said.

When the sound got louder, the four women stood up from the table and walked to the window, looking outside.

"They're over at Rachel's house," Melony said.

MELONY and her breakfast guests stood on the property line between Rachel's house and Melony's, watching. They found a police car, ambulance, and fire truck parked out front of the neighbor's. Responders had already gone inside by the time they arrived on the scene.

"It must be Rachel," Melony said. "I hope she's okay, but she's ninety-five, and she's fallen before. A couple of years ago she broke a hip and had to spend two months in a rehab center."

"I think that's Brian and Joe's car," Heather said, pointing to the parked police car.

"How can you tell Brian and Joe's car from all the other police cars?" Danielle asked. "They all look alike."

Heather shrugged. "I just can."

"Oh my gosh, the quiche!" Melony blurted. "I'll be right back." Melony turned and ran back to her house.

"Forgot the quiche was in the oven," Danielle said.

"We don't need to burn down Mel's house," Lily said.

"Perfect time to burn down a house. There is already a fire truck sitting outside," Heather said.

A few minutes later, Melony returned. "I didn't burn the quiche. But I took it out of the oven. Has anyone come outside?" Mel's gaze fixed on her neighbor's house. "I want to know what's going on. Is Rachel going to be okay? Did she fall, or is it something else?"

"Let me see." Heather pulled her cellphone from her pocket. Now holding it in her hands, she looked down and began sending a text. There was no response to her message, but a few minutes later, Brian and Joe walked out of the house with the lady they had seen knocking on Rachel's door and windows. While Joe talked to the woman, Brian silently surveyed the area. When his gaze met Heather, he gave her a brief nod and then glanced at Joe and Leanne.

"I PICK HER UP EVERY SUNDAY," Leanne told the two police officers for the third time. "She gave me a key to her house a long time ago. When she didn't answer the door, I was afraid she might have fallen. So I used the key, and I found her. It looked like she was sleeping peacefully, but then I checked her pulse." Leanne began to cry.

Unable to wait any longer, Melony headed toward Leanne and the two police officers, her friends trailing behind her. When Joe spied her, he said, "Melony?" glancing from her to Heather, Danielle, and Lily. Leanne continued to sniffle while she dabbed her nose with a piece of wadded-up facial tissue.

"Mel lives next door," Brian reminded him.

"Is Rachel alright?" Melony asked. "I've known her since I was a little girl."

"She was like a mother to me!" Leanne blurted.

Melony and her friends looked at Leanne.

"Was?" Melony frowned.

Before anyone could respond, commotion at the front doorway caught their attention.

"I think we need to all move back," Brian said, silently ushering the women away from the front porch.

"Oh no, what happened?" Melony moaned, now watching as the responders carried what appeared to be a body, concealed under a sheet, toward the van parked in front of the house.

"She must have died in her sleep," Leanne explained. "She looked so peaceful. But I'm going to miss her!" Leanne wailed inconsolably.

Joe quickly ushered Leanne away from the others while Brian remained. "Excuse me, will you?" Brian told Heather's friends as he led Heather to the side for a private conversation.

"Seriously, sending me a text when you know I'm in the middle of a situation at work?" Brian asked under his breath.

Unfazed by his scolding, Heather stared up at Brian and assumed an expression of innocence before asking in a soft voice, "Are you going to punish me?"

Brian stared at Heather and grinned, but quickly turned serious. After all, a woman had just died. He leaned closer to Heather and whispered, "I probably should. You are a brat."

Heather's tone shifted from teasing to serious. "I guess I

shouldn't have sent the text. But we were all curious. And I am sorry about Mel's neighbor."

"Did you know her?" Brian asked.

Heather shrugged. "I don't think so. What happened?"

Brian glanced over at Joe, who had finally gotten Leanne to stop sobbing. They stood about six feet away. "It looks like she died in her sleep," Brian said.

Heather let out a sigh and said, "Well, Mel did say she was in her nineties."

"But between you and me," Brian whispered, "there might be more to it."

Heather frowned. "What do you mean?"

"Joe and I arrived first," Brian explained. "We were around the corner when the call came in. After we arrived, I checked for her pulse. I smelled almonds. And she looked flushed."

Heather's eyes widened. Before she could reply, movement by the front door caught her attention. She reached out and grabbed hold of Brian's wrist. "I should ask her if she had a toasted almond before going to bed last night."

Brian glanced in the direction Heather now stared. He saw nothing out of the ordinary. He looked back at Heather and asked, "Do you see Rachel?"

"I assume it's her. Whoever it is just walked through the front door—without opening it. And she looks like she's in her nineties, wearing a nightgown."

RACHEL STOOD on the front porch and glanced around, taking in all the commotion. She saw Leanne had stopped crying and stood with one of the police officers. Then she noticed her neighbor Melony Carmichael. Melony had grown up to be a nice, responsible young woman, yet Rachel remembered how she had been a wild teen, giving her parents fits. She knew Melony was now engaged to Adam Nichols. When she first heard, she wondered what Melony's mother, Jolene, would think about it, considering Jolene's dislike of the young man.

Perhaps now she could ask Jolene what she thought about it. Would she see her again? Rachel wasn't sure how all this worked. Was she supposed to go with her body? Where was that white light everyone talked about? Before coming outside, she had felt compelled to walk through her house one more time. It was something she always did before going on a trip. Was this going to be like taking a trip? Before leaving, she had to make sure Leanne was going to be alright.

The next moment, Rachel stood by Leanne's side. She spoke aloud even though she realized her friend could not hear or see her. What she didn't realize, two mediums stood nearby who could hear her every word.

"I am so sorry you had to find me like this," Rachel told Leanne. The woman continued to sniffle while repeating how much she was going to miss dear Rachel.

"You were so good to me," Rachel told her. "I wish there was some way I could let you know how much I appreciate all you have done for me."

One responder told the police officers, "We're going now." Rachel looked toward the voice. She saw the van where she assumed they had loaded her body.

"Dear, I have to leave now. I want to see where they're taking me."

HEATHER AND DANIELLE silently watched as Rachel scurried from Leanne to the van. A moment later, the two mediums exchanged glances.

"Are you saying Mrs. Moore's ghost is here?" Brian asked in a whisper.

"She was. She just got into that van." Heather nodded toward the vehicle.

"Did she say anything?" Brian asked. "Anything about how she died?"

Heather shrugged. "She was trying to comfort her friend there." Heather nodded to Leanne, who was no longer crying but calmly talking to Joe. "She felt bad her friend found her. Commended her for being such a good friend. I suppose when one goes, there could be something comforting about being found by someone who really cares about you." Heather paused a moment and then added with a shrug, "Or maybe not."

FOUR

Melony and her breakfast guests returned to her house after Brian and Joe drove away with the rest of the responders. The four women sat around Melony's dining room table, each with a plate filled with fresh fruit and a slice of lukewarm quiche. Melony had also prepared mimosas for everyone but Danielle. Danielle had plain juice.

"I feel sorry for her friend, finding her like that," Lily said.

"I imagine Heather knows how she's feeling about now," Melony noted.

"I suspect it's worse for her," Heather suggested. "Because the bodies I find typically are strangers."

"I'm not sure how that would be better or worse," Lily said before taking a bite of quiche.

"Someone will probably contact her family," Danielle said.

"There's no family to contact," Melony said. "Rachel had two daughters. They both died a long time ago."

"She lost both of her children?" Lily asked.

"Yes. One of them died when she was in grade school. And the other one died in a car accident when she was a teenager. This was long before I was even born. So there aren't any grandchildren, and as far as I know, Rachel doesn't have any living siblings. I remember something about an older brother, but I'm sure he's gone now. She was pretty much alone aside from her few friends from church."

"Then what's going to happen to her house?" Heather asked.

"My guess, she left it to her church," Melony said.

An hour later Lily, Heather and Danielle were in Lily's car, heading back to Beach Drive. Danielle had just mentioned seeing Rachel's spirit.

"You actually saw her ghost? Oh, why am I asking that? Of course you saw her ghost. That's what always happens," Lily grumbled.

"She was trying to comfort the friend who found her," Heather explained. "But Brian said something rather interesting when I was talking to him. I don't think I'm supposed to say anything to you two, so whatever I tell you, you didn't hear it from me."

"What did he say?" Lily asked.

"Brian doesn't believe Rachel died in her sleep," Heather explained. "He said something about smelling almonds when he took her pulse after they first arrived. And she was flushed."

"Almonds? You mean like cyanide poisoning almond smell?" Danielle asked.

"I was thinking about asking her ghost if she'd had a toasted almond last night, which might explain the ominous almond smell. Might even explain the flushed complexion. I can't believe anyone murdered her. She was just a harmless little old lady. Why would anyone want to kill her?"

"If you will recall, somebody murdered Marie, and she was a harmless little old lady," Danielle reminded her.

"Marie is not all that harmless," Heather said with a snort.

"Harmless people get killed all the time," Lily said, ignoring Heather's comment. "She has a nice house. Great neighborhood. I bet that house is worth a fortune. According to Mel, she has lived there forever, so I imagine it's paid for. If someone murdered her, just follow the money."

"I don't think so," Heather said. "According to Mel, the woman was ninety-five. Why risk murdering someone who is going to drop dead at any minute? And Mel said she was probably going to leave it to the church. Unless her church is Earthbound Spirits, I doubt they bumped her off."

"That almond smell could be from anything. Like the almond-scented lotion my grandma used to wear," Danielle suggested.

"When you guys saw her ghost, did she say anything about how she died? Did she suspect foul play?" Lily asked.

"No. She seemed more concerned about comforting the friend who found her. She didn't act like somebody who believed they'd been murdered," Danielle explained.

THEY DROPPED Heather off at her house first. Instead of going straight back to Marlow House, Danielle stopped at Lily's. She wanted to give Walt a little more undisturbed writing time. Plus, she knew Marie was at Lily's house, watching Connor so Ian could get his own writing done. Danielle wanted to ask Marie what she knew about the woman who had passed away. According to Melony, Rachel had gone to Marie's church.

Lily and Danielle found Marie in the nursery with Connor, playing blocks on the floor. Lily couldn't actually see Marie, but she knew the woman was there by the way the blocks floated through the air. Before coming into the room, they had stopped briefly in Ian's study to let him know they were home before going into the nursery.

"How are you feeling, my dear?" Marie asked Danielle when the two women walked into the room.

"I'm actually feeling much better," Danielle said. "This morning Walt brought me some dry cereal before I got out of bed."

"I told them about the Cheerios trick," Lily said.

"Ahh, yes. I seem to recall that the worst thing about morning sickness is an empty stomach. Surprising I can recall that after all these years," Marie said.

"Having something bland like that before getting out of bed made all the difference in the world," Danielle said.

"I know some women suffer from morning sickness for months and months during their pregnancy, and other women never have it or maybe just have it for a couple of weeks. Hopefully yours won't last long."

Lily sat quietly, listening to Danielle's side of the conversation.

"How was your breakfast at Melony's?" Marie asked.

"It was more eventful than we had expected. Her next-door neighbor died in her sleep last night. And the ambulance and police showed up when we were there," Danielle explained.

"Are you talking about Rachel Moore?" Marie asked.

"Yes. I assumed you probably knew her. Melony said her name

was Rachel. When we first arrived and pulled up into Mel's driveway, there was a woman knocking on her door, trying to get her attention. She was there to pick her up for church."

"Oh, I bet that was Leanne Hodge," Marie said.

"I don't remember anyone mentioning her last name, but the first name was Leanne," Danielle said.

Danielle recounted what had happened over at Melony's house regarding the next-door neighbor. When she finished, Marie said, "I know Leanne Hodge is a little simple. She's a sweet woman, but her husband, Larry, is a miserable man."

"How so?" Danielle asked.

As Danielle and Marie chatted, Lily picked up Connor to change his diaper.

"They joined my church a few months before…" Marie paused a moment before continuing. Finally, she said, "Before my passing. But I knew them before. They have lived in Frederickport for years."

Danielle recounted for Lily what Marie had said about the Hodges regarding the membership in her church.

"So Pastor Chad charmed them into joining your church," Lily teased.

"Tell Lily no," Marie said. "Those two have joined every Christian church within fifty miles of Frederickport. But it seems they never can get along with the parishioners of the church, and they end up quitting or being driven out, and then they join another church. But I felt sorry for Leanne because I believe she means well. I think she wants to find a church family to belong to, but her husband, he just keeps getting in the way, causing trouble, and then they have no other choice but to leave and try starting over again."

After Danielle repeated Marie's words, Lily asked, "What's wrong with the man?"

"One thing, he has a very peculiar sense of humor. Not appreciated," Marie explained.

"How so?" Danielle asked.

"I remember one incident particularly," Marie began. "This happened before they joined our church. One of my friends attended the funeral of her daughter-in-law's mother. The Hodges were there, and Larry Hodge came up to her and said, 'Well, you're next.'"

"Are you suggesting he told the woman she'd be the next to die?" Danielle asked.

Marie nodded.

"What did she say?" Lily asked, now sitting on the rocking chair with Connor on her lap. Danielle quickly recounted Marie's words.

"He didn't really say that?" Lily gasped.

"He did. The women were the same age, and I guess he thought it was funny to point out she was at the age where death is around the corner. She didn't find it particularly amusing. Nor did her niece, who overheard the comment. The niece told him off. I would have liked to have heard that."

After Danielle repeated Marie's words, Lily said, "He seems like a charming fellow."

"And I remember one church he joined—I can't remember which church it was. Adam told me the story. A friend of his was a member. Apparently, not long after the Hodges joined, one deacon passed away, and Larry Hodge volunteered to replace him, and they accepted. Big mistake. He began causing all sorts of problems for the minister, even attempting to block his annual raise. After a while, the other parishioners recognized he caused more problems than good and was on a power trip, so they forced him out, and the Hodges eventually left the church. I remember Leanne, after she joined our church, telling me how her husband tried so hard to help, and he was such a good man, and the people just didn't appreciate him, and they were jealous of them. Sadly, she believes all that."

"I didn't know you were home," a new voice said from the open doorway. Danielle, Lily, and Marie looked up. They found Ian's mother, June Bartley, standing just inside Connor's room, Sadie by her side, her tail wagging.

"June… um… I didn't hear you come in," Lily stammered.

"I used my key," June said.

Your key? Lily asked silently. *When did Ian give his mother a key?*

"I called earlier, looking for you, and Ian said you had gone to breakfast with some girlfriends," June explained.

Lily frowned. "Oh, what did you need?"

June shrugged. "It isn't important. It's too late now."

"Um… you know, you can always call my cell number if you need to talk to me," Lily reminded her.

"I'm afraid I don't have your cell number saved in my phone, and since Ian works at home and you don't have a job, there really is no reason to keep both your numbers in my phone."

"Mom, what are you doing here?" Ian's voice joined his mother's. The next moment, he stood next to June in Connor's room.

Instead of answering immediately, June walked to Lily and snatched Connor from her arms. He squirmed, but Marie's calming voice convinced him to settle down in his grandmother's arms.

"I came to rescue you, of course," June said, giving her grandson a kiss.

"Rescue me?" Ian frowned.

"When I called earlier, looking for Lily, you told me she was with friends and had left Connor with you."

"I don't think I said she left Connor with me," Ian corrected.

"I asked you if she had taken Connor with her, and you said no."

Ian frowned.

"After spending all your time helping us move yesterday, and knowing you had your own work to do, I thought the least I could do was come over here and watch Connor so you could work," June explained, setting a squirming Connor back on the floor.

"I was watching him," Marie grumbled. But she smiled a moment later when Connor crawled to her and put his arms out, wanting her to pick him up. Instead of treating June to the sight of a flying grandson, Marie sat next to the child on the floor.

June looked at Lily and said sternly, "Lily, you really need to get in the habit of calling me when you leave Connor alone with Ian. There is no reason he needs to disrupt his work with an active toddler. That's why I'm here, dear."

"Mom, I am fully capable of watching my son," Ian said.

"With my help." Marie snickered, knowing only Danielle could hear her.

"Yes, dear, I'm sure you can, but there is really no reason you have to now that I'm here. And if you will excuse me, I need to visit the ladies' room." June smiled and stepped into the hallway.

When Lily heard the bathroom door shut a few moments later, she looked at Ian and asked in a whisper, "When did you give your mother a key to the house?"

Ian frowned. "I didn't give her a key."

Lily arched her brow. "Really?"

FIVE

The question of the house key remained unresolved when June returned to Connor's room several minutes later.

"Ian, you can go back to your work, and if Lily wants to do something with Danielle, I can still watch Connor," June offered.

"I appreciate your offer, Mom," Ian began. "But it's Sunday, and Lily and I had already decided to spend family time—just her and me and Connor—after she got back from breakfast."

June glanced over at Danielle, who now sat on the floor with Connor.

Danielle smiled at June and said, "I just stopped over to say hi to Connor and Ian before going back to Marlow House. Walt and I have plans today too."

June let out a sigh and asked, "Are you sure you don't need me?"

"Like I said, we appreciate your offer, but we already have plans," Ian insisted.

A few minutes later, after walking June out and saying goodbye, Lily watched her mother-in-law pull out of the driveway. She turned to Ian and asked, "What plans do we have today?"

Ian shrugged. "I just said that to get Mom to leave without hurting her feelings."

"You still haven't told me how she has our house key—that she used without bothering to knock," Lily asked.

"I think I know," Danielle said, walking into the entry hall. Marie remained in the nursery with Connor.

Both Lily and Ian turned to Danielle.

"You know what?" Lily asked.

"I know how June has a key," Danielle said.

"Well, I didn't give her one," Ian insisted.

"Umm… you did," Danielle reminded him.

"When? I did not," he argued.

"Remember when you guys got married and your parents stayed here?" Danielle reminded him. "You gave them a key then."

"Yeah, but…" Ian began yet paused. After a moment he groaned and said, "They never gave it back."

"Looks that way," Danielle said. "Well, I need to get home. Thanks for driving today, Lily. And thanks for the Cheerios tip."

"How are you feeling?" Ian asked.

"Much better, thanks." Danielle grinned.

"I'll talk to you later, Dani," Lily said as Danielle headed out the door. On her way out, she could hear Lily starting a rant to Ian about his mother just walking into their house without knocking.

WHEN DANIELLE ARRIVED BACK at Marlow House, she found Walt in the kitchen, making himself a sandwich.

"Did you have an enjoyable time?" Walt asked when Danielle walked into the kitchen.

She closed the door behind her and tossed her purse on the kitchen table while saying, "All except for the neighbor dying." She then told him about their morning.

By the time Danielle finished her telling, Walt sat at the kitchen table with her, eating his sandwich while she nibbled on a cinnamon roll from Old Salts Bakery.

"While death is typically sad, when someone has lived as long as Mel's neighbor, and none of her family remains on this side, I don't see sadness, especially if she went peacefully in her sleep. What is sad is that little girl Evan saw yesterday. Even if she died years ago, she was just a little girl," Walt said.

"True. Oh, and Brian thinks maybe Mrs. Moore didn't die in her sleep. He claims he smelled almonds. And she looked flushed."

"Cyanide almonds?" Walt asked.

"I say it's simply hand lotion."

"I would assume if he suspects something might be off, they'll have an autopsy?" Walt asked.

Danielle shrugged and took a nibble off the cinnamon roll.

Walt looked at the quickly disappearing roll and asked, "Does that agree with you? You say things you normally enjoy, you find unappealing now. Such as the smell of coffee."

Danielle grinned. "No, this tastes pretty good. In fact, I've been craving them."

Walt laughed. "You always crave Old Salts cinnamon rolls."

Danielle giggled. "True. Oh, you know what happened over at Ian and Lily's before I came home?" Danielle told Walt about June, the house key, and Lily's annoyance with her mother-in-law walking into the house without knocking.

Walt laughed.

"What's so funny?"

Walt's laughter subsided, and he grinned at Danielle. "Think about it a minute. Find anything a little ironic in all this?"

Danielle frowned. "I don't get what you're saying?"

Walt pointed to the kitchen door. "What is constantly coming through that door? And the front door?"

She considered his words for a moment and giggled again. "Ahh, I see what you're saying. Marlow House has this open-door policy."

"I'm not sure I would call it our policy. I think of it as their policy. Lily, Chris, Heather, and even Ian have no problem just walking in at any time, day or night. Sometimes using their key. And none of them seem to think twice about knocking."

Danielle stared at Walt a moment and then asked in a quiet voice, "You want me to talk to them about it?"

Walt grinned, reached across the table, and patted one of her hands. "No. I may grumble occasionally, but I'm okay with it."

Danielle leaned back in her chair and said, "To be honest, I sort of find it comforting, knowing they all feel so at home here."

"I suspect that is one reason they feel that way—except for Ian. Marlow House was at one time home for all of them. Lily first and then Chris and even Heather lived here for a short time. And with Ian, we've made it clear Sadie is always welcome, so I figure he assumes that goes for him too."

"True."

"But you have to admit, it is rather ironic, Lily getting upset with Ian's mother," Walt said with a grin.

"I suspect Lily is more at home with us than with June," Danielle pointed out.

NEXT DOOR at Pearl Huckabee's house, Pearl sat alone in her living room, still wearing her church clothes and contemplating her unsettling morning. When first arriving at church earlier that day, she had not worried about Rachel's absence. She and Rachel had become friends in a quilting class, and the two women normally shared a pew with Leanne and Larry Hodge. The Hodges also weren't there when Pearl first arrived at church, which made sense to Pearl, since Leanne typically drove Rachel to church each Sunday.

Pearl tolerated Leanne's annoying husband, Larry, for Leanne's sake. Each Sunday, Leanne drove out of her way to pick up Rachel for church and then would swing back home to pick up Larry. Pearl often thought it would be better if she simply left Larry at home.

When Rachel and the Hodges weren't at church, Pearl assumed they were simply running late. Pearl had talked to Rachel the night before, and the two had made plans to go out to breakfast after church that morning, which meant after Leanne drove Rachel to church, Pearl would take her home.

The church service was under way when Larry Hodge showed up. But Leanne and Rachel weren't with him. Instead of going to the pew and sitting down, he walked up the aisle and interrupted Pastor Chad's service.

"I have an announcement!" Larry shouted from the pulpit, a confused Pastor Chad looking at the man interrupting his sermon.

"Larry, please," Chad said in a quiet voice, attempting to get the man to sit down so he could continue.

"I'm sorry, but I thought everyone would want to know. Rachel Moore is dead."

An audible gasp went over the congregation, and Chad stared at Larry in silent disbelief.

"Leanne went over to pick her up this morning, like she does every Sunday," Larry said, speaking loudly so everyone could hear. "But Rachel wasn't answering the door. Leanne used her key to get in, and she found Rachel in bed, dead. Leanne called the police, and she's still over there with them. She called to let me know what was going on, so I thought I should tell you." Larry smiled proudly after finishing his little speech, making no attempt to go sit down.

"What happened to her?" a voice from one pew called out.

Larry looked at the woman and said, "Rachel was old. She died in her sleep. Didn't I just say that?"

REPLAYING the morning's events over in her mind, Pearl shook her head in disgust. Larry Hodge had been so eager to share the news of Rachel's death with the congregation that he had walked to the church from his house. At least, Pearl assumed that was how he had gotten there, since they only had one car, and according to him, his wife had had it that morning.

WHILE DANIELLE and Walt sat together in the kitchen of Marlow House, discussing the morning's events, and Pearl sat in her living room next door, mourning the loss of a friend, Pearl's neighbor to the south, Heather Donovan, sat down alone in her kitchen, preparing to enjoy a cup of hot tea, when someone knocked on the back door. Leaving her cup of tea on the table, she answered the door.

"Brian? What are you doing here? Why aren't you at work?" Heather asked after opening the door and finding Brian Henderson on her back step.

"We need your help," Brian said, walking into the kitchen and dropping a quick kiss on Heather's cheek.

"Are you on lunch break?" Heather asked, closing the door behind him.

"Technically," Brian said.

"You want me to make you a sandwich?" Heather asked. "I have some sourdough bread. I baked it yesterday."

"Thanks, but I don't have time. I was hoping you would go to the morgue with me," Brian said.

Heather frowned at Brian but did not respond. Instead, she walked to the table, sat down, and took a sip of her tea. "I have heard of some interesting dates before. But the morgue?" Heather wrinkled her nose and took another sip.

Brian sat down at the table with Heather, resting his elbows on the tabletop. He leaned toward her. "When we got back to the station, I told the chief about smelling almonds."

"Are they ordering an autopsy? I remember reading once that cyanide leaves the bloodstream fairly quickly. If you wait too long, they won't detect it."

"I also told the chief about you seeing her spirit," Brian said.

Heather narrowed her eyes and studied Brian for a moment. "You want me to talk to her, don't you? The chief is hoping she's still at the morgue, since she left with her body."

"He would normally ask Danielle for something like this," Brian said. "But…"

"Danielle's pregnant," Heather finished for him.

Brian nodded. "Walt won't let her do something like this."

Heather grinned. "But you'll let me?"

"It's only the ghost of a little old lady," Brian teased.

Heather set her now half-full mug on the table and let out a sigh before asking, "What do you want me to ask her?"

"See if she knows anything about how she died," Brian began.

"From what I overheard at her house, she didn't sound like a murder victim."

"Okay, if she says she simply died in her sleep, ask her if she felt odd before going to bed. And ask her if she used any sort of lotion that gave off an almond scent. I smelled almond on her breath."

Heather arched her brows. "On her breath? She was dead when you checked her out."

"You know what I mean."

Heather rolled her eyes and then asked, "What else?"

"Find out if there was anyone who would want her dead? Did anyone have a reason to kill her?"

"You know, the Frederickport police department is getting awful lazy in their investigations, relying on local mediums to do all their work," Heather teased.

Brian let out a snort. "You have a point."

"And of course, Joe knows about none of this?"

"Joe knows about me smelling the almonds."

"Did he smell it too?" Heather asked.

Brian shook his head. "No. He's been fighting a head cold. Can't smell anything."

"I hate colds." Heather frowned and leaned toward Brian. "You wash your hands around Joe. I don't want a cold." The next moment, Heather kissed Brian.

SIX

Police Chief MacDonald greeted Heather and Brian when they arrived at the morgue on Sunday afternoon.

"No one is here," MacDonald said, quickly ushering them inside. He looked at Heather and asked, "Did Brian explain what we need to know from Rachel?"

"Yes. And if you don't mind, I would rather do this alone," Heather said, looking at the door leading to where they held the bodies.

"I suspected you would," the chief said.

"Why? Because that's what Danielle prefers?" Heather asked.

The chief smiled at Heather. "Danielle says non-mediums can distract when she's trying to communicate with a new spirit."

"It's true," Heather agreed.

A moment later, the chief and Brian watched as Heather walked through the doorway leading to the room holding Rachel Moore's body.

As Heather suspected, she found two Rachels. One a lifeless body, and the second a spirit who sat next to the body. The spirit startled when Heather entered the room and closed the door while asking, "Hello. Mrs. Moore? Or can I call you Rachel?"

Rachel's eyes widened. "You can see me?"

"I can hear you too," Heather said. She pulled up a chair and sat down. "I'm Heather Donovan. I'm a medium."

Rachel frowned. "Did you say Heather Donovan?"

Heather returned Rachel's frown. "Um… yes. Have you heard of me? I work at the Glandon Foundation. It's a philanthropic organization. We give away money. Lots of it."

"Yes. I know what the Glandon Foundation is. Who in Frederickport doesn't? But you, you live next door to Pearl Huckabee, don't you?"

Heather arched her brows. "That sounds more like an accusation than a question."

Rachel shrugged. "Pearl is a friend of mine. She's told me about you."

"Wow, Pearl has a friend? Who knew?" Heather said under her breath.

"What do you want?" Rachel asked.

"I'm here on behalf of Police Chief MacDonald. He has some questions he wants me to ask you."

"Are you telling me Edward MacDonald knows you claim to be a medium?"

Heather chuckled. "You say that as if it's still to be determined. I'm talking to you, aren't I?" Heather paused a moment and asked, "Ahh… you do realize you're dead?"

"Of course," Rachel snapped. "If I'm not dead, who's that?" Rachel pointed to her lifeless body. "A long-lost twin who showed up dead in my bed one night, wearing my nightgown?"

"But you just said—"

"I was just surprised Edward MacDonald buys into all this medium talk, regardless of it being true or not," Rachel explained.

"Well, the chief's youngest son is a medium," Heather explained.

Rachel narrowed her eyes. "Really? Interesting…" After a moment of reflection, she said, "Okay, what do you want to ask?"

"The chief thinks someone might have murdered you," Heather said.

Rachel laughed. "That's ridiculous. No one murdered me. Who would murder me? Why would anyone want me dead?"

"By any chance did you use any lotion or hair product that smells like almonds?" Heather asked.

Rachel cringed. "Heavens no. I don't care for that fragrance."

"Did you eat any almonds last night? Or have something with almonds in it?"

"Why would I eat anything that contained almonds if I don't care for the smell?"

"Do you have a rodent problem?" Heather asked.

"What kind of question is that?"

"I just wondered if maybe you handled rat poison or something like that."

"No, but if I did, I would hire a pest company. I certainly would not start trapping or poisoning rats."

"Who did you see on Saturday?"

"No one. I stayed home all day," Rachel said.

"No one came over and visited you?"

"No. I spoke to a few friends on the phone, but no one came over."

"What did you eat yesterday?" Heather asked.

"Is this really important?"

"Please humor me."

"In the morning, I had a cup of coffee, oatmeal, and banana. For lunch, I had a cup of soup. At dinner I ate the rest of my can of soup."

Heather wrinkled her nose at the menu. "Nothing else to eat or drink? No snacks?"

"I drink water during the day. I wasn't very hungry yesterday."

"Do you take any medicine? Prescriptions?" Heather asked.

"No. I only take a vitamin supplement in the morning and melatonin at night, to help me sleep."

"Then tell me, how did you feel last night. Before you went to bed? Did you feel sick?"

"I had a headache, but I get headaches frequently. I was a little dizzy, but I occasionally experience bouts of vertigo. It's not life threatening, just annoying. I suppose I felt a little worse for wear last night, but I am ninety-five. I have good days and bad days." Rachel paused a moment and then asked, "Or should I say, I was ninety-five?"

"Let's pretend someone murdered you," Heather suggested.

"Why would I do that? Is this normal?" Rachel asked.

"Is what normal?"

"To interrogate a…" Rachel paused a moment and asked, "What am I now?"

"While you are here, on this plane, I would consider you a ghost

—or spirit. But once you move on, you're no longer a ghost, just a spirit," Heather explained.

"Move on where?"

"Some call it the next leg in your journey."

"So there is more than this?" Rachel asked.

"You certainly didn't think you'd be hanging out in the morgue for eternity, did you?"

Rachel scowled at Heather. "You needn't be snotty. I see Pearl was right about you. And of course not. For one thing, I seriously doubt they'll keep my body here for eternity. And you didn't answer my question."

"Question?" Heather asked.

Rachel let out an exasperated sigh. "Yes. My question. Is this normal? Do ghosts typically get interrogated after their deaths by mediums?"

"No. If that were the case, I imagine they'd solve more murders."

"And I said I was not murdered. I would like to learn more about this place you mentioned, after we leave here."

"Some call it Heaven," Heather began. "It's where you'll be reunited with your family, loved ones, those who died before you. At least, that's what I understand."

"If true, why am I still here?" Rachel asked. "I would like to go now."

"You'll get there, but first…"

Rachel let out a gasp, cutting off Heather's sentence. "Is that the light they talk about?"

"Wait, before you go, I need to ask—" Rachel disappeared before Heather could finish her sentence.

Heather stood up and glanced around. "Rachel? Hello? Are you here?" She stood in silence for a moment and then said, "Dang. I had more questions. You could have at least said goodbye."

SINCE BRIAN HAD MISSED LUNCH, the chief suggested he have something to eat with Heather before coming back to work. They decided on Pier Café. When they arrived, they found Walt and Danielle sitting in a booth. Walt asked Brian and Heather to join them, and they did.

"Danielle had a craving for apple pie," Walt told Brian and Heather after the two sat down with them.

Heather looked at Danielle and grinned. "Little Mama is taking full advantage of this."

"Little Mama?" Brian frowned, picking up a menu.

"That's my new name for Danielle," Heather told him.

Danielle rolled her eyes.

"And how is Little Mama feeling?" Brian asked.

"Oh, stop, not you too!" Danielle scolded; Walt laughed.

"Hey, now that you're pregnant, I have to take your place as the Frederickport Police Department's medium, so I should be able to call you Little Mama," Heather said.

"What are you talking about?" Danielle asked.

Heather and Brian then told Walt and Danielle about their visit to the morgue.

"Doesn't sound like someone murdered her," Walt said when they finished their telling.

"No, it doesn't. But I have this gut feeling," Brian said.

"You once had certain gut feelings about me," Danielle reminded him with a grin.

Brian shrugged. "True."

The next moment, Marie appeared. Everyone at the table could see her except for Brian. She took a seat in an imaginary chair at the end of the booth.

"Hello, Marie," the mediums chorused.

"Marie is here," Heather told Brian.

"Yes, I figured that out," Brian said.

Carla showed up the next moment to take their orders, momentarily forcing Marie from her imaginary chair. Although Brian and Heather hadn't had time to look at the menu, they had already decided what they wanted. After Carla left, Marie grumbled a bit before returning to where she had been sitting.

Heather repeated for Marie what they had just told Walt and Danielle.

"I was planning to stop by the morgue and see Rachel," Marie said.

"I doubt you'll find her there," Heather said.

"Perhaps I'll see her at her funeral."

Heather shook her head and said, "I'm sure she moved on already."

"That wouldn't surprise me," Marie said. "Rachel didn't have many close friends. No reason to stick around."

After Heather told Brian what Marie had told them, Danielle said, "I got the impression she was close with Leanne Hodge."

Marie nodded. "True. Leanne was one of the few people Rachel was close to. I suspect she felt a little sorry for her, and Leanne was awful good to Rachel. Leanne lost her mother not long after she joined our church. They needed each other. Rachel was also close to your neighbor Pearl Huckabee."

"Pearl?" Danielle asked. "Seriously?"

After Heather repeated her words to Brian, Marie said, "It's just the impression I got when I'd stop by the church."

"Rachel mentioned something about being friends with Pearl," Heather said.

"After I died, I periodically dropped by the church to see what was going on," Marie explained. "I noticed your neighbor Pearl started sitting in the pew with Rachel and Leanne. Of course, Larry was there, but when Leanne and Larry weren't looking, Rachel and Pearl would exchange that look."

"What look?" Walt asked.

"The look that said they both thought the man was an idiot," Marie explained.

After Heather repeated for Brian Marie's side of the conversation, Brian said, "Ask Marie if she knew Rachel very well."

Heather chuckled. "Remember, Marie can hear you. Ask her yourself."

"Tell Brian I've known her my entire life. We grew up together. She was about a year older than me. Our husbands were friends, but we were never particularly close. Rachel was a private person. Never shared much. She lost a daughter when the child was in grade school. She never talked about it. Kept it all to herself. And then her oldest daughter died in a car accident. She was just in high school."

"Gosh, no wonder she wanted to move on," Heather said before telling Brian what Marie had said.

A few minutes later, Carla showed up with their beverages, once again temporarily forcing Marie from her place at the end of the booth.

"Were you on the call for Rachel Moore this morning?" Carla asked Brian as she set his glass of iced tea in front of him.

"Yes. I see news still travels fast in Frederickport," Brian said.

"What was she, like, ninety-eight?" Carla asked.

"Ninety-five," Danielle said.

After handing out all the beverages, Carla faced Danielle, her balled fists resting on her hips. "You knew Rachel?"

"No. But we were at Melony Carmichael's this morning, and Mel lives next door," Danielle said. "Mel told us how old she was."

"You were friends?" Brian asked.

"I wouldn't say friends, exactly. She was a regular customer. At least she became more regular once she got chummy with Pearl Huckabee. The two would come in here after their quilting class," Carla explained. "Sometimes after church."

"I wonder if Pearl knows yet," Danielle said.

"I'm sure she does if she was in church," Carla said. "Millie Samson told me Larry Hodge came in, right in the middle of Pastor Chad's sermon, and announced to the entire congregation she had died. His wife is the one who found her."

"He announced it to the church?" Heather asked with a frown.

Carla shrugged. "Larry Hodge likes to be the center of attention. Of course, no real surprise she died. After all, she was pushing a hundred. There's going to be a couple of people I know happy to hear she checked out."

"Who's that?" Brian asked.

"Does it really matter? It's not like they actually killed her or anything. She died in her sleep, didn't she?" Carla asked.

Before Brian could reply, a bell rang from the kitchen, and Carla abruptly excused herself and scurried away.

SEVEN

"Aren't you going to ask Carla who was glad Rachel died?" Heather asked Brian as they headed for the exit door after they finished lunch. Walt and Danielle had already left Pier Café for home.

Brian paused at the doorway and glanced back at Carla, who was taking an order on the other side of the café. "I'm going to wait until we get the lab report back. If the report doesn't show something suspicious in her system, no reason to get Carla all worked up. The minute I question her about what she said, she'll jump to the conclusion someone murdered Rachel, and whoever Carla was talking about will become murder suspects in Frederickport, regardless of whether there was an actual murder or not."

"Aw, that's sweet," Heather cooed, taking hold of Brian's left hand and leading him out of the restaurant.

Brian frowned yet followed Heather. "What's sweet?"

"How you're trying to protect someone from being falsely accused and having to deal with all the social stigma attached. I remember hearing how you were constantly accusing our Little Mama of murder. You've evolved."

"I wasn't constantly accusing her of murder," he grumbled.

"And you thought Chris was capable of murder," Heather added.

"As I recall, so did you at one time," Brian reminded her.

Heather rolled her eyes. "What's your point?"

ADAM AND MELONY sat on the sofa in her living room, with two glasses of wine, an open box of pizza, two paper plates, and several napkins sitting on the coffee table. Melony had just helped herself to a slice of pizza when she started to tell Adam about her neighbor's death.

"She just died in her sleep?" Adam asked as he picked up a slice of pizza.

"It looks that way. The Church Lady was picking up Rachel for church—"

Adam's laugh cut Melony off. She gave him a frown.

He shrugged and before taking a bite of pizza said, "It cracks me up how you always call her that."

"It just seems to fit her. But as I was saying before you so rudely interrupted me…"

"I'm sorry." He didn't sound sorry. Melony ignored his comment and then continued recounting the morning's events.

"Any idea what will happen to her house?" Adam asked.

"Why, you want her listing?" Melony teased.

Adam grinned. "I'd like to think I'm not one of those ghoulish agents who pore over the obits each day looking for new listings. But chances are whoever inherits the house will probably list it. And hey, they might as well list it with me."

"I'm a little curious myself. Ever since poor Rachel died, I've been wondering who inherits her estate."

"I guess this means you weren't Rachel's attorney," Adam said.

"My dad used to be her attorney. But she never cared for Clarence, so after Dad died, she took her business to another law office. I have no idea where. Mom once mentioned Rachel was one of the clients who went elsewhere after Clarence took over. Rachel was always a very private person, so she certainly would not share personal information with Mom. And Rachel never approached me for any legal advice."

"Does she have any family?"

Melony shook her head. "As far as I'm aware, there wasn't anybody left. But I suspect she probably left everything to the church. Two things Rachel loved, her church and quilting."

"Well, if that's the case, I imagine Pastor Chad's going to be happy. Rachel's estate will bring significant cash into the coffers. I assume he'll want to sell the house. I should stop over there and talk to him. Although, maybe they'll want to keep it and put it in the rental program. It would bring them a steady income. More than what's put in the collection plate each week."

"Adam, do you ever just turn off business for a while and stop thinking of ways to make money?" Melony asked, only half teasing.

"Then I guess this is probably a bad time to talk about selling this house before we get married, and having me list it," Adam asked with a chuckle.

Melony smiled. "Funny you bring that up. Because I wanted to talk to you about it."

"How so?"

"I've been giving this house a great deal of thought. I can't imagine you'd want to move in here after we get married."

Adam cringed. "Me living in your parents' house?"

"Technically, it's my house now. What, are you afraid Mom's ghost is hanging around, ready to haunt you?" Melony teased, her eyes gleaming mischievously.

"Well, after what we saw over at John Bartley's property, nothing would surprise me anymore," Adam said seriously.

"If it's any consolation, I've never experienced paranormal activity here. I don't imagine there are any ghosts hanging around," Melony assured Adam.

"You never know, dear," Marie Nichols said moments after arriving. She had come over to Rachel's house to see if Rachel's spirit might have returned. But when Marie noticed her grandson's car next door, she popped over to Melony's.

"I never thought that I would stay in this house for as long as I have," Melony told Adam, unaware the spirit of his grandmother hovered nearby, listening. "And I certainly don't see it as a place we'd make our home after we get married, but I also can't see us moving into your house."

Adam glanced around and said reluctantly, "I have to admit, this house is nicer than mine."

"Your place is nice, Adam. But we should sell both of our houses and buy something that's ours. And the bonus for you, you'll have two new listings."

"That's a good idea," Marie said from the sidelines.

Adam studied Melony for a moment and then smiled. "I like your idea. And it's not because I would get two listings out of the deal. But we should start fresh with someplace that belongs to both of us."

Melony grinned. "I'm glad you like the idea."

"I do. But now that you've told me you want to sell, I kinda wish Rachel could have held off a few months before checking out."

"I doubt it was Rachel's idea to go. But she was ninety-five, so it could have happened at any time. Why would it have been better if she'd waited a few months?"

"There's a good chance that whoever inherits Rachel's house will put it on the market. Then there will be two houses for sale on the same street right next door to each other."

"I just thought of something else," Melony said.

"What?"

"Remember when we were talking about the buyers across the street wanting to turn their house into a bed-and-breakfast?"

"Which looks like they'll probably be able to do now. She was the only one on the street who objected, wasn't she?" Adam asked.

"Yes. I'm sure they'll go ahead with their plans. How will potential buyers view a B and B almost across the street from them? I never thought it would impact property values, but now that I'm considering selling, maybe it's something to think about. Should I block it?"

"Personally, I wouldn't object. If the city denies the permit, then no one on this street can open a bed-and-breakfast. Not unless they jump through major hoops to get it overturned. In this current market, your property might go for a little more if a buyer has the option of opening a B and B."

They discussed local zoning laws for a few minutes and then turned their attention to the pizza while Marie said a silent goodbye and left to go check out Rachel's house. After Adam and Melony each ate their fill of pizza, Melony set her plate and napkin on the coffee table and settled back on the sofa, glass of wine in hand.

"Since you've been thinking of selling your place and mine, have you also been thinking where you'd like to move?" Adam asked.

"I would love to have oceanfront property like Chris, and Ian and Lily. Actually, I rather like the Beach Drive area."

"Too bad I didn't know that before. I wouldn't have sold Ian Grandma's house, and we could have moved into that one."

PASTOR CHAD SAT ALONE in a booth in Lucy's Diner on Sunday evening. He was just picking up his burger when a voice said, "Are you eating all alone, Chad?"

He looked up and found Ruby Crabtree standing by his table. "Evening, Ruby," Chad greeted her.

"Are you waiting for someone?" Ruby asked.

"No. Beth is still visiting her mother, and I didn't feel like cooking."

"Would you mind if I sit down with you? I have a to-go order, and I'm waiting on it," Ruby asked.

Chad motioned to the empty seat at his booth. "I'd love the company. And if your order is just for you and you're not taking it to someone, you can eat here."

"Thanks. I think I will." Ruby motioned to the waitress and told her she would sit with Chad and to bring the food to the table instead of takeout.

After she sat down, she looked at Chad and said, "That was some interesting sermon this morning. Larry Hodge sure knows how to make a dramatic entrance."

Chad groaned and set his burger back on the plate. "I was really sorry to hear about Rachel. But I wish Larry wouldn't have announced it the way he did."

"I was sorry about Rachel, too. But she lived a long life. Got to stay in her home."

"And she buried two children and a husband," Chad reminded her solemnly.

"True. But now she can be with them, right?"

Chad smiled at Ruby, picked up his burger, and took a bite.

"And now the church can get the new roof it's been needing," Ruby said.

Chad frowned. "Excuse me?"

"Not right away. I imagine it has to go to probate, and then you'll need to sell Rachel's house."

"Are you suggesting Rachel left her estate to the church?" Chad asked.

"Sure. She didn't have anyone, and over the years she's made comments about leaving her estate to the church. I don't imagine she would leave it to another church," Ruby said with a snort.

"When was the last time she mentioned this?" Chad asked.

Ruby considered the question and shrugged. "A couple of years ago. But I can't imagine she changed her mind."

"She did," Chad said, taking another bite of his burger.

Ruby frowned. "Are you saying Rachel didn't leave everything to the church?"

"That's exactly what I'm saying. Rachel told me over a year ago she'd changed her will and would no longer be leaving her estate to the church. Said she wanted to tell me personally, so when her time came, I wouldn't be shocked."

"Who did she leave it to?" Ruby asked.

Chad shrugged. "I have no idea."

EIGHT

Walt didn't have to bring Danielle a cup of Cheerios on Monday morning. She had remembered to take a cup with her on Sunday evening before going to bed. When Walt woke up, he found Danielle sitting, leaning against her pillows, and quietly nibbling on the dry cereal while her cat, Max, sat next to her, his nose gently nudging her hand holding the cup of Cheerios.

"No, you can't have any," Danielle whispered.

Walt rolled over and looked up at her, propping his elbow against the mattress as he rested the side of his head against his right palm.

"Good morning. Is that helping?" Walt asked in a soft voice. He briefly turned his attention to Max, silently conveying a message. The cat looked at Walt, meowed, and then curled up next to Danielle, no longer begging for cereal.

Danielle smiled down at Walt. Before popping more cereal into her mouth, she said, "Sometimes I think Max is a dog. But yes, it helps. It doesn't take away the queasy feeling totally, but I feel better."

"You look beautiful this morning," Walt told her, his eyes never leaving her face.

Danielle frowned. "I haven't even brushed my hair yet. I'm a mess. I feel like a mess."

Walt chuckled. "You need to learn how to take a compliment."

He sat up, gave Danielle a quick kiss, shoved his pillows against the headboard, and then leaned back on them. Together he and Danielle gazed across the room.

Danielle let out a sigh. "I suppose you're right. And you've been pretty sweet lately."

"Aren't I always sweet?"

Danielle chuckled. She reached over with one hand and patted Walt. "I love you."

"It's a good thing. You're stuck with me."

Danielle gave Walt another pat and then turned her attention back to the dry cereal. The two sat in silence, each lost in his or her private thoughts. After a few minutes, Danielle glanced over to Walt and noticed he was staring at his wrist while running his fingertips over his skin.

"What are you looking at?" Danielle asked.

"My scar." Walt looked from his wrist to Danielle. His scar resembled a horseshoe.

"Pretty deep in thought."

Walt shrugged. "I was thinking of Clint. Of our baby. And wondering…"

Danielle studied Walt, who failed to finish the sentence.

"Are you wondering whose baby this will be—genetically?" Danielle asked softly.

"It's not that, exactly."

"Then what is it?"

"You must admit, we have a—most unusual situation."

Danielle laughed. "You could say that."

"This baby is mine, regardless of how I got into this body. But considering the changes to this body since I moved in, I find it rather curious. At one time, I would assume Clint would be our child's biological father."

"Like having a sperm donor?" Danielle suggested.

"Exactly. But I'm not sure that's the case now. It's like this is my body—not just because I now occupy it. But genetically my body—my spirit's body."

"I know what you mean. A while back, I was going through some photos I saved from Clint's Facebook page. And there was something different about how he looked then and how you look now. It wasn't just the clothes and haircut."

Walt grinned. "I seem to remember you being rather tongue-tied when you first met him, thinking I had somehow come to life."

"It was extraordinary. I wasn't expecting you and Clint to look so much like each other. But now, when I look at his photos, I can actually see the difference between you two. It is very subtle. Like how someone close to a set of twins can tell them apart. Yet now, now I don't see Clint in you anymore."

"At one time I might have suggested it's because I've introduced my mannerisms, which could make you see Clint's body differently." Walt glanced down at his wrist and added, "But after all I've experienced, I suspect there is more to it."

"I've been reminded—over and over again—of one thing during this experience."

"What's that?" Walt asked.

"That there's so much in this universe I don't understand."

Walt nodded. "True."

Danielle reached over and set the now empty cup atop the nightstand. "I want to sit here a few minutes before I try to get up."

"Do you feel alright?"

"Yeah, but… let me just sit here a few minutes."

"Do you still plan to go to the bank this morning?" Walt asked.

"Yes. We need to get some cash."

"Then let me take you."

"If you have to work, I understand," Danielle said. "You don't have to take me. I can go myself."

"I was thinking we could go to the bank and then stop at the hardware store and pick up some paint."

"Paint?" Danielle asked.

"If we're going to be moving to our old bedroom, I think we should give it a fresh coat of paint first."

Danielle giggled. "Cracks me up when you call it our old bedroom."

Walt shrugged. "It was my bedroom before I died, and yours when you moved here. So that qualifies."

"We'll have to hire someone to paint it. I'm a lousy painter. And your spare time is better spent on your writing."

"Even if you were a professional painter, I wouldn't let my pregnant wife paint our bedroom."

"You are so bossy," Danielle teased.

"And it's not too soon to look at paint for the baby's room," Walt reminded her.

"I think we should wait until we find out if it's a boy or girl," Danielle said.

Walt shook his head. "I just can't get used to the idea we'll be able to know what we're having months before the actual birth. And who knows, maybe we'll find out you're having twins."

Danielle glared at Walt. "Twins? That is not funny."

Walt turned an innocent expression to Danielle. "I wasn't being funny. Remember, twins run in my family."

KELLY BARTLEY STEPPED out of the bank and noticed the Packard that had just parked next to her car. She paused a moment and watched as Walt Marlow got out of the vehicle and then walked over to the passenger side of the car to open the door for his wife. With a sigh, she asked herself why more men didn't dress like Walt Marlow. She rarely saw him in blue jeans, never in sweatpants, and she doubted any of his clothing was made of polyester. Today he wore his calf-length overcoat over his shirt and dark slacks. Once, when shopping with her fiancé, Joe Morelli, she had convinced him to try on a similar overcoat. She found something sexy about a man dressed in a well-tailored overcoat. Getting Joe to try on the garment was easier than convincing him to add one to his wardrobe. He made it clear, *not happening*.

"Morning, Kelly," Danielle greeted her when she and Walt came walking up to the bank a few minutes later. Unlike her husband, Danielle dressed far more casually, in dark stretch pants, boots, and a long sweater and jacket.

"Morning, Danielle, Walt. How are you feeling?" By Kelly's gaze now focused on Danielle's belly, they understood she had directed the question to Danielle.

"Much better, thanks."

Kelly's gaze moved upward to Danielle's face. "Can I ask you a question?"

"Sure," Danielle said with a shrug.

Kelly glanced nervously from Danielle to Walt and back to Danielle. "Did you guys know before Connor's party about Brian and Heather?"

"You mean that they're a couple?" Danielle asked.

Kelly nodded.

"Um, yeah. We've known for a while," Danielle said.

"Don't you find it... um... odd?" Kelly asked.

Walt quietly reached over and took Danielle's hand in his, giving it a reassuring squeeze.

Never looking away from Kelly and returning Walt's squeeze, Danielle asked, "You mean like how everyone thought Walt and I were odd?"

Kelly's eyes widened.

Danielle laughed. "Oh, Kelly, I get it. I don't expect people to understand how or why Walt and I got together. And I imagine Heather feels the same way. But like they say, the heart wants what the heart wants."

Kelly stood in silence, unable to utter a response.

"Kelly," Walt began, "we had quite the harrowing experience with the kidnapping and being left in the mountains. I imagine if you would have suggested to either Heather or Brian prior to that experience that one day they would be a couple, they would not just find it odd, but a ridiculous suggestion."

"But—" Kelly stammered, only to be interrupted by Danielle.

"It really doesn't matter what any of us think. The only important thing is that our friends are happy. Right?" Danielle asked.

"I BELIEVE Ian's sister was looking for a different response from us," Walt told Danielle after they said goodbye to Kelly and entered the bank.

"She came to the wrong people," Danielle grumbled.

"It really was pointless to ask the chief not to say anything to the boys about the baby until later. The word is out," Walt said.

"Danielle, Walt, hello," a familiar voice interrupted. They turned and found bank employee Susan Mitchell walking toward them.

"Morning, Susan," Danielle said when Susan reached them.

"I wanted to congratulate you both. I heard the news," Susan said, her gaze darting briefly to Danielle's stomach, as Kelly's had a few minutes earlier.

"Thank you," Danielle returned.

"Told you so," Walt whispered in Danielle's ear.

They exchanged a few more words when Susan abruptly changed the conversation.

"Someone said you were there when they found Rachel Moore's body," Susan said.

"We weren't there exactly," Danielle said. "We were next door at Mel's house when the police car and fire truck showed up."

"Did you know Rachel Moore?" Susan asked.

Danielle shook her head. "No, we didn't."

"Rachel was one of the first people I met when I moved to Frederickport. She was a reserved woman, but always very sweet when she came into the bank. Brought us homemade cookies every Christmas."

"Rachel Moore sounded like a nice woman," Danielle said.

"She lived a long life, but I was sad to hear of her passing," Susan said.

"Rachel Moore is dead?" a man's gruff voice barked from behind Danielle and Walt. They turned abruptly and found Herman Shafer, cane in hand, standing a few feet from them. Well into his eighties, Danielle's encounters with the elderly man had been during her more trying experiences. While she had not actually encountered him during the hijacking, he had owned the Arizona property where the kidnappers had landed the aircraft. He was also one of the historical society members who had tried to bury unflattering information about his ancestors.

"Yes, she passed away yesterday," Susan told Herman.

"I just get back into town and get hit with this news?" Herman grumbled.

"I'm sorry, was she a close friend of yours?" Danielle asked.

"I wouldn't call Rachel a close friend. But I've known her for years," Herman said. He let out a sigh and then said, "I suppose I'm just being selfish. I should think about poor Rachel rather than myself." He looked at Susan and asked, "How did she die?"

Susan told Herman what she knew about Rachel's death, including the fact Danielle had been next door when the police found her body. When she finished the telling, Herman let out a grunt and said, "I suppose this changes my plans for today." He said an abrupt goodbye, turned, and walked away, heading toward the exit.

Susan, Walt, and Danielle watched as Herman left them. When he was out of earshot, Danielle said, "That was an odd reaction."

Susan shrugged. "You know, he used to be the manager of the bank before Steve. He and his wife were good friends with Beverly, from what I understand."

"I wonder how Beverly is doing," Walt mused. "Think he visits her at the prison?"

NINE

Herman Shafer hadn't bothered calling ahead to see if Chad was at the church. When he pulled into its parking lot, he spied Chad's car. It was the only vehicle there. A moment later, he parked next to the pastor's car. It took Herman a few minutes to unbuckle his seatbelt, grab his cane from the passenger side of the vehicle, and then juggle the cane while attempting to open his door before exiting. With determination, the elderly man slowly made his way to the church entry. Herman found the front door to the building unlocked.

"HERMAN?" Chad said in surprise when the man walked into the fellowship hall. The pastor had just poured himself a cup of coffee.

"Morning, Chad, I was hoping you'd be here," Herman said, making his way toward the pastor.

Chad raised his cup briefly and asked, "Would you like some coffee?"

"No, I already had my coffee," Herman said, taking a seat in a nearby chair. He made a grunting sound after sitting down, as if the trip from his car to this spot had been exhausting.

"When did you get back in town?" Chad asked, sitting down at the table with Herman. "Did you have a nice time?"

"This morning. Good trip. But I just stopped at the bank and heard about Rachel. Is it true?"

"If you mean did she pass away? Yes. I'm afraid so."

"Susan Mitchell said Rachel died in her sleep."

Chad nodded. "That's what I heard."

"When I go, that's how I want to do it. In my sleep." Herman gave the floor an abrupt tap with his cane.

"I suppose you're here to arrange Rachel's funeral?" Chad asked.

"I'd like to get it done as soon as possible. Can we do it tomorrow?" Herman asked.

"No. But we could arrange it for Wednesday. Of course, you need to speak to the funeral home."

"Since we're having the service here, that shouldn't be a problem. I want to get this over as soon as possible so we can have the reading of the will. That's how Rachel wanted it. I think she watched too many old movies." Herman let out a snort after his last sentence and leaned back in the chair.

"What do you mean?" Chad asked.

"She was adamant about having the reading of her will following her service. Like one of those old movies."

"Ahh, yes, I see what you mean. As I recall, she made arrangements for use of the church library following her service," Chad said. "I'll have to check and make sure it's free if you want to have it on Wednesday."

"I'd like to have it tomorrow," Herman grumbled.

"Sorry. But we're booked up for tomorrow."

"Fine. Check to see if the library is free for Wednesday, and we'll do it then. I assume she already gave you her selected hymns and verses for her service? She promised she would take care of all that if I'd be her executor," Herman said.

"Yes. I never realized you were that close," Chad said. "When she told me you were her executor, I was surprised."

Herman shrugged. "I agreed after her husband passed away. She didn't seem to know what to do, and I felt a little sorry for her back then."

"She also told me the church was no longer her beneficiary," Chad said.

Herman chuckled. "Rachel liked to change her will periodically. She couldn't decide who she wanted to leave it to."

"We'll also need to check on the fellowship hall if you want to have a gathering after the service. Or are you planning to go back to her house for that?" Chad asked.

"I forgot about that… You think the ladies from the auxiliary would put together a potluck?" Herman groaned and then added, "I really did not want to come back from my trip and have to deal with something like this."

LEANNE WALKED into her family room and found her husband, Larry, sitting at the computer. "What in the world have you been doing on that thing all morning? I swear you haven't budged from that chair since breakfast."

Larry looked up from the computer and grinned. "Checking out real estate prices."

"Real estate prices?" Leanne frowned.

"I want to know what we can get for Rachel's house," he told her.

Leanne froze. She stared at her husband, who continued grinning in her direction.

"Oh, don't look so deer in the headlights," Larry chided. He flipped off his computer monitor and leaned back in the chair, still studying his wife.

"I don't know what you mean," she stammered.

"About what? About how much we can sell Rachel's house for, or why you look like someone just kicked your puppy."

When she didn't answer, Larry's smile vanished. "I know, Leanne. I know Rachel left you her house."

Leanne continued to stare at Larry yet made no response.

"What I want to know, why didn't you tell me?" he asked.

Leanne closed her eyes and groaned. A moment later, she opened them again and walked to the nearby sofa and sat down. She looked at her husband. "How did you find out?"

"I overheard her tell you. You both thought I was taking a nap. But I got up to get some water, found the two of you sitting in the kitchen, while Rachel tells you how she's planning to leave you her house."

Leanne let out a sigh. "Just because she told me I was in her will doesn't mean she really left me anything."

"Why didn't you tell me?"

Leanne stared blankly at her husband a moment before answering. "For one reason, I was afraid how you might act around her if you knew."

"That's not the reason," he snapped.

"What do you mean?" she asked nervously.

"I heard what she said. Not just about leaving you her house. I heard everything," he accused.

"Larry—"

"That old battle-ax didn't like me. I heard what she said about me, and you didn't even defend me. And I also heard how she said inheritances aren't community property. How you wouldn't have to share any of it with me. I got the feeling she wanted you to take the money after she died and leave me."

"Larry, I would never leave you. I love you!" Leanne insisted.

"You bet you aren't leaving me. Remember our vows, until death do us part. And unless you plan to go the way of Rachel, you're still my wife."

"What are you going to do?"

"First thing we're going to do, figure out how much that old battle-ax's house is worth and then put it on the market."

"YOU WANTED TO SEE US?" Brian Henderson asked Chief MacDonald as he and Joe Morelli walked into his office on Monday afternoon.

Sitting at his desk, the chief motioned to the two empty chairs and told Brian to close the door. With a nod, Brian closed the door, and the two officers sat down and faced the chief's desk.

"Your hunch was correct; Rachel Moore died from cyanide poisoning," the chief said.

"You got the lab results back?" Brian asked.

The chief leaned back in his office chair. "Ten minutes ago."

"And to think if I had given Brian my cold, we probably would never know," Joe said.

"Her flushed skin tone was a red flag," Brian reminded him. "Even if I hadn't noticed the almond smell, they might have run the tests."

"So are we looking at murder?" Joe asked.

"I'd like you to go through her house again. See if you can find anything that might show an accidental poisoning. I find it difficult to believe anyone had a motive to kill Rachel Moore." The chief looked at Brian when he said it. Both men remembered how Rachel's spirit had told Heather she hadn't been murdered.

"Someone will inherit her property," Joe reminded him. "She has lived in that house for years; I imagine it's paid for. That's one of the nicest neighborhoods in Frederickport. It might not be right on the water, but I've seen what some of those houses go for in that area. Kelly and I have been pricing houses lately."

"You guys thinking of buying a new house?" Brian asked.

"Kelly keeps saying where we're living now is my house. She'd like to start our marriage in a house that's both of ours," Joe said. "I guess I understand. But anyway, that house across the street from Moore's sold recently, and they got a fortune for it. I heard the new owners want to turn it into a bed-and-breakfast. So I imagine whoever inherits Moore's house will get a fortune for it. And who knows what other property she owns."

"While money is always an excellent motive, Rachel Moore was ninety-five," the chief reminded him. "Why risk a murder charge when the intended victim could go at any time?"

"Unless the killer needed the money now," Joe reminded him.

"Rumor has it she left everything to the church," the chief said.

"While Pastor Chad has been known to show a lapse of judgment on occasion, I don't see him bumping off a parishioner to get a new roof for the church," Brian said.

THE NEXT MORNING, over at the Seahorse Motel, Sam had just taken over for the night clerk and was busy making a fresh pot of coffee when his boss, Ruby Crabtree, walked in.

Sam looked up from what he was doing. "What are you doing here so early?"

"You didn't get my message?" Ruby asked, now standing at the front counter.

Sam shook his head.

"You need to check your emails more often," she scolded.

"What's going on?"

"I thought it would be a good idea if we had a little meeting before Rachel's funeral. I've called Andy. He's on his way over," Ruby explained.

"Do we know when her funeral is?" Sam asked.

"I spoke to Herman last night. He's made arrangements with Chad to hold the service tomorrow, and we know what that means," Ruby said.

"The reading of the will, and then we can get on with our project," Sam said.

Ruby let out a sigh. "Depending on who Rachel left the property to."

The next moment, Andy Delarosa walked into the motel registration office. "Hey, it's a great day? Isn't it?" Andy greeted them. He gave a sniff and said, "Is that fresh coffee I smell?"

"Help yourself," Sam said, pointing to the empty coffee mugs.

A few minutes later, the three sat on the small sofa in the lobby, each with a cup of hot coffee in hand.

"Can you believe our good luck?" Andy said after he took his first sip of coffee. "Of course, it was not such good luck for ol' Rachel."

Ruby narrowed her eyes at Andy. "You might want to check that enthusiasm unless you want to find yourself behind bars." Ruby looked like a Strawberry Shortcake doll, in appearance and stature, yet she could intimidate, and while Andy might have laughed had Sam made the same comment, hearing Ruby say it gave Andy chills.

"What's going on?" Sam asked.

"When I spoke to Herman last night, he told me the police hadn't released Rachel's body to the mortuary yet."

"Didn't they take it directly to the mortuary after they found her?" Sam asked. "That's what they did when my grandma died at home."

"I guess they don't do that in Frederickport if they suspect murder," Ruby retorted.

TEN

Walt and Danielle had only been up for about an hour on Wednesday morning when Heather came knocking on their kitchen door. She would have simply walked in, but they hadn't unlocked the door that morning.

"What are you guys doing today?" Heather asked while she filled a mug with water before putting it in the microwave.

"Tea bags are in the pantry," Danielle said. She sat at the table with Walt. He drank coffee while she sipped on mango juice.

"Thanks. But I brought my own." Heather pulled a tea bag from her pocket and dangled it in the air to show Danielle. When the microwave turned off a minute later, she removed the cup of hot water and took it to the table.

"Aren't you working today?" Danielle asked.

"Remember, the offices are closed for the rest of the week. So, what are you two planning for today?" Heather said as she took a seat next to Walt.

"We need to find someone to paint my old bedroom," Danielle said. "Walt and I looked at paint yesterday but couldn't decide on a color."

"Ahh, you're still switching bedrooms?" Heather asked while dunking her tea bag in the hot water.

"Yes. We're turning Lily's old room into a nursery, and the attic will be Walt's office," Danielle explained.

"If all you have to do is look for painters, how about you guys go to a funeral with me?" Heather asked.

"Funeral? You talking about Rachel Moore's funeral? That's today," Danielle said.

"Yeah. Please," Heather begged.

Walt frowned at Danielle. "I thought you never met Rachel Moore?"

"I didn't," Danielle said.

Walt looked at Heather. "Why would Danielle want to go to a funeral for someone she never met? Did you know her?"

"Not when she was alive," Heather explained. "But I met her at the morgue."

"Is that why you want to go?" Danielle asked.

"Sort of. Kinda. Um… did you know she was murdered?" Heather asked.

"Murdered?" Danielle frowned. "I know you told me Brian suspected foul play."

"So you didn't know they got the results back?" Heather asked.

Danielle shook her head and looked at Walt. He gave her a shrug. He hadn't known either.

"Well, she was murdered. The chief got the results Monday afternoon, but he's tried to keep it hush-hush. I suppose he didn't say anything to you because he doesn't want to upset you."

"Upset me? I never met the woman," Danielle said. "I'm sorry she died. And if she was really murdered, then that's awful, and I hope they find out who did it. But I'm not sure what the chief is worried about."

"It's because you're pregnant," Heather explained. "He doesn't want to upset you. Brian said the chief told him that while you're pregnant, he doesn't want to ask you for paranormal help."

Danielle wrinkled her nose. "That is just silly."

"Of course, that doesn't mean I won't ask you for help," Heather said. "Little Mama is tougher than that."

Walt chuckled and then asked Heather, "What do you expect to accomplish there? I don't imagine you're going just to pay your respects."

"No. I told Marie I was sure Rachel had already moved on. And maybe she has. But if she hasn't and shows up at her funeral, I'd like to ask her a few more questions now that we know she really was murdered. You're so much better than me at getting spirits to open up. And I suppose it's possible she wasn't murdered, and she can tell us how she came in contact with cyanide. It's worth a shot."

"Well, that is rather civic minded of you," Danielle teased.

"I suspect this is more about Heather helping Brian," Walt said.

Heather flashed Walt a grin.

ONE OF THE first people Walt, Danielle, and Heather saw when they walked into the church for Rachel's service was Pearl Huckabee. Their neighbor stopped abruptly and looked the three up and down critically.

"What are you doing here?" Pearl demanded.

"Um, paying our respects?" Danielle said.

"You didn't even know Rachel," Pearl snapped. "I know you didn't. Ghoulish going to a stranger's funeral."

"What are you, the funeral bouncer?" Heather snarked.

Danielle reached over and grabbed Heather's hand, silently asking her to refrain from commenting.

"Mrs. Huckabee," Danielle said with measured calm, "I'm so sorry for your loss. I understand you were friends. You probably don't know, but Heather and I were next door to your friend's house when the police found her body. Our friend, Melony Carmichael, has known Mrs. Moore her entire life, and we've come today to give her moral support during this loss."

Pearl frowned and then reluctantly said, "Yes, Rachel was fond of Melony Carmichael."

"IS MEL GOING TO BE HERE?" Heather asked, glancing around as they walked toward an empty pew. "I didn't even consider that."

"I assume she'll be here," Danielle said with a shrug.

"I certainly didn't think she would be here," Walt said, coming to an abrupt stop.

Heather and Danielle stopped walking and turned to Walt. They looked to see what had gotten his attention. On the other side of the church stood a little girl with a yellow Labrador retriever.

"I love animals, but do they let dogs in here during a funeral?" Heather asked in a whisper. "Where are her parents?"

Danielle looked at Walt and asked, "You think that's who Evan saw?"

"It looks like the same dog," Walt said. "And she's dressed just as Evan described."

Heather looked from Danielle to Walt and frowned. "Who is she?"

Instead of answering, they continued to stare at the little girl and her dog. Heather looked back at the girl, and the next moment, the girl and dog vanished.

Heather gasped and said, "That's the little girl you told us about, the one Evan saw."

AS DANIELLE PREDICTED, Melony showed up at the funeral, accompanied by Adam. Melony and Adam were both surprised to see their three friends in attendance, since they had not known Rachel, yet they accepted Danielle's explanation about feeling the need to go after being at Mel's on Sunday morning when they found Rachel's body.

Melony and Adam sat on the pew with Walt, Danielle, and Heather. The three mediums kept an eye out for Rachel, hoping to talk to her, yet she never showed up. The only ghosts they saw were the little girl and dog.

After the service, the three mediums followed Mel and Adam into the fellowship hall. It did not surprise Danielle to see Ruby Crabtree and Sam at the service, since both attended Pastor Chad's church. What surprised Danielle was seeing Andy Delarosa, a cousin of Pearl's who had been one of the previous owners of Pearl's house. Ruby was a distant cousin to both Pearl and Andy, and from what Danielle understood, Ruby barely knew either cousin. Yet today, Andy stood with Ruby and Sam, and the three looked rather chummy.

Walt and Adam discussed local house painters while Mel wandered off to chat with someone. Heather stood with Danielle by one of the banquet tables, and Danielle found herself preoccupied with watching Pearl, who stood on the other side of the fellowship hall, giving her cousins the evil eye.

"I'm surprised to see Andy Delarosa here," Heather whispered, interrupting Danielle's train of thought.

"I was just thinking the same thing. I remember Ruby telling me once she had met Andy. Looks like they've become friends," Danielle said.

"They are related," Heather reminded her.

"I know. But that family seems like such a mismatch of personalities, Ruby, Andy, and Pearl," Danielle mused.

"And here comes Pearl now," Heather whispered as she reached down and picked up a cupcake and napkin. She handed it to Danielle before picking up one for herself.

Danielle absently accepted the offering and watched as Pearl marched by, heading straight for her cousins. By Pearl's expression, Danielle did not expect a joyous family reunion.

"I know why you're here," Pearl snapped.

Ruby, Sam, and Andy looked up at Pearl, startled at her abrupt words.

"We're here to pay our respects," Ruby said.

"You weren't even friends with Rachel!" Pearl accused.

"I knew her for longer than you," Ruby snapped back. "We attended the same church long before you ever moved to Frederickport."

Pearl pointed to Andy. "He wasn't friends with Rachel. He tormented her!"

"Don't be so dramatic," Ruby chided. "Andy didn't torment anyone."

"If you think you're going to push your bed-and-breakfast through now that Rachel is gone, you're wrong. She loved her home and didn't want to turn her lovely neighborhood into some sort of strip mall!"

"Strip mall?" Sam frowned.

"We might be related, but you're nutty," Andy told Pearl.

"I mean it. You won't get approval for the B and B. I'll make sure the new owner does what Rachel wanted!" Pearl hissed.

"Pearl dear," a calming voice called out. Danielle and Heather turned to see Leanne Hodge walking to Pearl. Leanne wrapped an arm around Pearl's shoulder and said, "You are just upset. We all are."

"But they can't do this to Rachel. Dance on her grave!" Pearl cried.

"They won't, dear," Leanne said in a soothing voice, leading Pearl away to the church library.

MELONY GLANCED AT HER WATCH. She had returned to her friends, who now sat at a round table in the fellowship hall, crumb-filled paper plates before them. "I have to go to the church library in about ten minutes."

"Why?" Heather asked.

"It seems there's going to be a reading of a will, and it looks like Mel is in it. Herman asked her to be there," Adam told them.

"Really?" Danielle arched her brows.

"You think she left you her house?" Heather asked.

"I seriously doubt it." Mel chuckled. "But I am curious."

WHEN MELONY WALKED into the church library, she found Herman Shafer sitting at the front of the room at a desk, shuffling through papers. He looked up at Melony, gave her a nod, and suggested she sit down. Someone had set up four folding chairs in the front of the room, all facing the desk. Melony flashed Herman a smile and sat down in one of the chairs.

Also in the room were Pearl and Leanne, who huddled together in a corner by the window, whispering. Herman called out their names, suggesting they too take a seat. Reluctantly, the two women left their corner and sat down in the chairs near Melony. A moment later, Pastor Chad walked into the room.

"Good, everyone is here. Chad, please shut the door and come sit down so we can get on with this," Herman said.

Melony greeted the pastor when he took a seat next to her.

"Rachel prepared a letter she instructed me to read," Herman began. He cleared his throat, looked up to make sure everyone was paying attention, and then proceeded to read.

"*If Herman is reading this, that means I'm dead. I was not afraid to die. I lived a long life, and frankly, I was tired. But before I say goodbye, I would like to make my final bequest of my worldly possessions.*"

Herman paused a moment, took a sip of water, and continued reading.

"*I leave the quilts I made for my daughters to Melony Carmichael. She will find them stored in the cedar chest at the end of my bed. I am also leaving the cedar chest to Melony so she will have a place to store the quilts until she has her own children and can put the quilts to use.*"

I guess they'll stay in the cedar chest forever, Melony thought to herself.

"*To Pearl Huckabee, who has been a dear friend*," Herman continued, "*I leave the contents of my sewing room.*"

Pearl began to cry.

"*To my church, I leave the contents of my savings account at the local bank. To make it easier on Pastor Chad, I have already added the church as my beneficiary.*"

"Really?" Chad perked up. "Rachel told me she changed her will."

"She did," Herman said. "In her previous will, she left the church the house and her bank account."

"Oh," Chad said, glancing over to Leanne, who sat quietly, listening.

"*And to Leanne Hodge, who has been like a daughter to me*," Herman continued, "*I leave my house and my remaining assets.*"

ELEVEN

Aside from the cupcakes Heather had snagged for Danielle and herself, Danielle had nothing to eat at the church. When it was time to head home, Walt, Danielle, Mel, and Adam stopped at Pearl Cove for a late lunch. They asked Heather to join them, but she declined. Danielle suspected she was on her way to meet Brian.

An hour later, Walt and Danielle sat with Mel and Adam in a booth at Pearl Cove, waiting for their lunch to be served. Outside, it had started to rain.

"I wonder if the Hodges are going to be your new neighbors," Adam said.

Melony groaned. "I hope not. From what I've heard about the man, he's not someone I want to live next door to."

"It seems like a lot of house for just two people. Didn't you say it had five bedrooms?" Danielle asked.

Melony nodded. "Rachel rambled around in that big old house alone for years after losing her daughters and husband. I always wondered why she just didn't sell it and move into something smaller."

"You think they knew they were inheriting the house?" Danielle asked, thinking of what Heather had told her about Rachel being murdered.

"I had no idea she was leaving me anything, and I don't think Pearl knew she was in Rachel's will. But by Leanne's reaction, she probably did. She didn't act surprised. And from what Pastor Chad said, he knew she once intended to leave the church her entire estate, but that she had changed her will," Mel explained.

"But she left the church her money," Danielle said.

"I wonder how much that is," Adam mused.

Melony shrugged. "I overheard Herman and Pastor Chad discussing it when I was getting ready to leave after the reading of the will. Pastor Chad asked how much was in the account. I guess the church needs a new roof. Herman said he didn't have the current balance. He obviously saw no reason to check with the bank before the reading. Frankly, he didn't seem thrilled being her executor."

"So no clue what the church inherits?" Adam asked.

"Herman said the last time he discussed it with Rachel, she had a little over two hundred thousand in the savings account at the local bank—and she listed the church as the beneficiary. And considering she lived off her social security, her house was paid for, she didn't have a car, and she was frugal, Herman figures it should be about the same amount," Melony explained.

"Leanne got the grand prize. That house is worth far more than two hundred thousand. But it looks like the church will get its new roof," Adam said.

"I suppose. But Leanne didn't seem all that excited about inheriting the house. Which is why I suspect she knew about the inheritance. Unlike Pearl, who broke into tears when she learned Rachel left her all her quilting supplies."

"Why? Because she was disappointed all she got was some lame quilting crap?" Adam snarked.

Melony shook her head and said, "No, Pearl was genuinely touched. I think the gesture meant a great deal to her, whereas Leanne seemed unmoved."

"I wonder if she feels uncomfortable with the inheritance," Danielle asked. "After all, it was initially going to the church."

"I just feel her lack of reaction was due to the fact she already knew about the inheritance. If she was uncomfortable with it, she could always donate it to the church," Melony said.

"Oh, I don't think you were there when Pearl confronted Ruby, Sam, and Andy about being at Rachel's funeral. Did you know they were the ones who wanted to open a B and B in your neighborhood?" Danielle asked.

"I didn't know Ruby was involved until Adam told me this morning," Melony said. "I knew Andy Delarosa had purchased the property with some investors, but I didn't know it was Ruby and Sam."

"Really?" Danielle looked at Adam.

"I found out yesterday," Adam told Danielle. "I ran into Ruby, and she told me she was one of the partners with Delarosa. I had forgotten they were related."

"They are also related to Pearl," Walt reminded them.

"I forgot that!" Melony said.

"So Ruby wants to branch out and get into the B and B business?" Danielle said.

"After you closed down, she began realizing this town could use both a good B and B and a motel," Adam explained. "I can understand how Ruby and Sam became business partners, not sure how Delarosa got involved. Ruby didn't say. But I imagine they didn't expect their other cousin would toss a wrench into the works."

"Pearl?" Walt asked.

Adam nodded. "I don't think Rachel would have opposed the permit if Pearl hadn't gotten her all worked up about it."

"I agree with Adam," Melony said. "In all the years I've known Rachel, she kept to herself and didn't get involved in local politics of any kind."

"Now that Rachel is gone, do Ruby and her partners have a chance of getting the B and B license approved?" Walt asked.

"Yes. I guess Andy Delarosa had been on Rachel's case to change her vote," Adam said.

"Pearl accused Andy of tormenting Rachel. I wonder if that's what she meant," Danielle asked.

"I wouldn't be surprised," Adam said.

Danielle looked at Melony and said, "I'm assuming you had to vote on the petition too, since it's in your neighborhood."

"I did, but I wasn't opposed," Melony said.

The next moment, the sound of thunder interrupted the conversation. They all stopped talking and looked outside. Dark rain clouds filled the sky overhead, blocking out the afternoon sun as rain poured down.

"Wow, that's not a typical rain," Danielle said, looking outside.

RACHEL DIDN'T HAVE to die. It was her own fault. Did she have to be so stubborn? With a sigh, the killer looked outside and watched as lightning streaked across the sky. Overhead, the sound of rain battered the shingle roof. The killer had no desire to go out in this weather, but this couldn't be put off. With Rachel gone, only one obstacle remained—Pearl.

Why did Pearl have to be such a busybody? Couldn't she just keep her nose out of other people's business? Didn't she realize there was a lot of money at stake? There was no other choice. Pearl had to die, just as Rachel had to die.

WHEN THE ELECTRICITY went out on Wednesday evening, Pearl Huckabee peeked out her bedroom window to see if her neighbors had also lost power. Marlow House was dark, as was the Bartleys' across the street. From where she stood, it looked as if everyone along this stretch of Beach Drive was without electricity.

Pearl commended herself for having the foresight to install a new woodstove in her living room before winter's arrival. As an older woman living alone, she wanted to remain self-sufficient, even if it meant hauling in firewood from the shed to feed her new woodstove so she wouldn't freeze to death.

Flashlight in hand, she headed downstairs. Once there, she took her jacket off the coat rack, slipped it on over her nightgown, and went outside to bring in more wood before going back to her bedroom. The salesman had told her the catalytic woodstove would keep her home toasty through the night if she filled its firebox before going to bed. Knowing heat rises, she felt confident her bedroom—above the living room with the stove—would stay warm while she slept. Pearl assumed the electricity would be back on by morning.

Thirty minutes later, wearing her flannel nightgown and fuzzy pink socks, Pearl snuggled down under the blankets and closed her eyes to sleep. Rain pelted the roof overhead while tree limbs beat persistently against the house. Pearl opened her eyes and looked up at the dark ceiling, momentarily thankful the wind hadn't been blowing like that when she'd gone out to the woodshed. Even the rain had momentarily stopped when she went outside, but it had started up again, along with the wind.

She closed her eyes, and just as she drifted off to sleep, the sound of a door slamming shut woke her. Abruptly sitting up in bed, she listened. She heard it again, a door opening and shutting with the wind.

"Drat," Pearl grumbled, reluctantly climbing out of her warm bed. The back door she'd gone through to get the wood didn't always latch securely. If not locked with the deadbolt, wind could push it open. She had been meaning to get it fixed, but she had procrastinated, knowing the deadbolt kept the door shut. Of course, if she forgot to latch the deadbolt, as she must have done tonight, and just locked the doorknob, wind could send it crashing open, which had obviously happened.

Cursing under her breath, Pearl fumbled around to find the flashlight she had left sitting on the nightstand next to the bed. In her haste, she knocked it to the floor. As it fell, the flashlight landed on her stocking-covered big right toe before rolling under the bed. She let out a yelp and jumped around on the uninjured foot while reaching down with her left hand, trying to grab her throbbing toe to comfort it. She jumped to the bed, sat on the edge of the mattress, and grabbed hold of the toe. She sat in the dark and rubbed it for several moments. When the throbbing stopped, she let out a sigh and reluctantly got down on her hands and knees to retrieve the flashlight. Once on the floor, she let out a groan and prayed she could get back up again.

Leaning under the bed, she reached out and groped around in the darkness. When she found the flashlight, she clutched it with one hand while using the other hand to pull herself up by grabbing hold of the side of the mattress. After she struggled a moment, she got back on her feet. Once standing, she turned on the flashlight. Pearl stood silently for a moment, flashlight in hand, and listened. She no longer heard the door slamming open and shut. She assumed it had finally slammed closed again, but that didn't mean she shouldn't lock the deadbolt.

Not taking the time to find her slippers, Pearl headed toward the bedroom door leading to the hallway. Downstairs a few minutes later, she used the flashlight to guide her way. Overhead, rain continued to pound the roof, and she heard thunder.

When Pearl finally reached the back door, she found it shut, but the deadbolt unlatched.

"I really thought I had locked it," Pearl muttered under her breath as she secured the deadbolt. Turning from the now locked door, she headed back toward the stairs.

With one hand on the handrail and the other holding the flashlight, Pearl plodded up the staircase. The hand holding the flashlight swung absently at her side, sending a ray of light zigzagging along the wall. Amused at the play of light, Pearl swung the flashlight in a wide arc, sending light to the second-floor landing. What she saw the next moment she did not find amusing. A dark shadow ran down her upstairs hallway. Someone was in her house.

Pearl turned abruptly and started back down to the first floor. She heard footsteps behind her, coming closer. She picked up her pace, and in her haste, her stocking feet slipped on the edge of one step. Still clinging to the handrail, Pearl avoided tumbling down the stairs. Yet only for a moment. Whoever was in her house was now right behind her. She could hear them as they closed the space between them. A hand slammed against her back. The flashlight flew from Pearl's grasp as she tumbled headfirst downward. Pearl's scream of terror momentarily filled the room.

Everything went silent.

TWELVE

Pearl's assailant paused for a moment on the staircase and looked down into the darkness. The intruder glanced to the right and spied the flashlight Pearl had been holding, now abandoned in the downstairs hallway, its light illuminating the baseboard along an inside wall.

From a coat pocket, the intruder pulled another flashlight, turned it on, and pointed it at Pearl, who now lay sprawled at the base of the staircase.

THE EXCRUCIATING PAIN Pearl experienced when her head hit the hardwood floor lasted only a moment. Pearl opened her eyes and blinked, surprised her head no longer hurt. The attacker hadn't followed her downstairs. Pearl watched the ominous dark shadow standing on the stairs, a lit flashlight in one hand, pointing in her direction. It was the only light in the darkened house aside from the flashlight Pearl had dropped after falling down the stairs.

Pearl wasn't about to wait around for the homicidal maniac to finish her off. She jumped to her feet, pivoted toward the front door, and started running as fast as she could, ignoring the fact she wore just a nightgown and socks. If she had survived a tumble down the stairs, she wasn't about to let some wind and rain keep her from putting space between her and the intruder.

It did not surprise Pearl when her attacker followed her outside into the night. Running next door to Marlow House or one of her other neighbors for help did not seem like an option. They were probably all in bed, and by the time they might answer the door, the attacker would have already gotten to her. And, for all she knew, the intruder carried a gun, and he would simply kill her and any neighbors who might answer their door. Without thinking, Pearl ran into the darkness, determined to hide herself until she could call the police.

A WET NOSE woke Chris Johnson on Thursday morning. Reluctantly, he opened his eyes and stared into the face of his pit bull, Hunny. The dog sat beside the bed, her big head resting along the edge of the mattress as she stared into Chris's face.

"Didn't you get the memo? We don't have to go into the office today. We get to sleep in," Chris groaned. Hunny responded by swiping a wet tongue over Chris's mouth before backing up away from the bed, her stump of a tail wagging, as she waited for her human to get up and take her outside.

After wiping dog spit from his mouth with the back of his hand, Chris glared down at Hunny and noted she showed no remorse at waking him, her expression goofy as she panted anxiously, her tongue hanging out the side of her mouth. Chris groaned again and reluctantly threw off the covers and stumbled from the bed. Clad in just boxers, Chris reached for the robe hanging on the hook on the back of his bedroom door.

"I'm not going outside with you," Chris grumbled as he pulled on the robe. "You're on your own."

Hunny followed Chris from the bedroom, down the hallway and to the front door. Before opening the door, Chris peeked outside. "Hey, at least it's not raining. There's even some blue in that sky."

MORNING SUNSHINE WASHED OVER PEARL, who sat huddled under a massive rhododendron bush in front of Chris

Johnson's house. Pearl opened her eyes and glanced around. Last night she had become disoriented, and until she opened her eyes moments earlier, she wasn't sure where she had landed.

By the position of the sun, Pearl guessed it was around 7:30 a.m. Still sitting on the ground, she looked down, surprised her nightgown and socks weren't soaking wet. They should be, considering last night's rain. Pearl stretched her legs out and wiggled her toes in her socks, delighted to discover nothing seemed to be broken—and nothing hurt—not even her head, which had hit the floor. After the tumble down the stairs and spending last night sleeping on the street, she expected her body to ache.

Pearl thought about last night's intruder. Who was it? Before disappearing into the darkness the night before, Pearl hadn't gotten a good look at the person; he or she was simply a shadowy figure.

Still sitting under the massive bush, she heard a nearby door open. She looked toward Chris's front porch. He had just let Hunny outside. Instead of waiting for the dog, Chris headed back inside his house, but left his front door propped open so the dog could reenter.

Hunny quickly did her business, but instead of going right back inside the house, she spied Pearl sitting under the rhododendron bush. The pit bull rushed to her side.

"Oh, Hunny." Pearl laughed when the curious dog shoved her snout in Pearl's face. "I bet you're wondering why I'm sitting in your yard." Pearl reached out to pet the dog, but her hand passed through the dog's head. Pearl swayed as if drunk and closed her eyes.

"Oh my," Pearl muttered, her eyes still closed. "I think that knock to my head did more damage than I thought. Is this what a concussion feels like?"

The next moment, Pearl's eyes flew open. She looked at Hunny. The two stared into each other's eyes. Pearl closed her eyes again and shook her head. "Fiddle, this is more than a hallucination," Pearl muttered. "I could swear I heard you ask what a concussion was."

In response, Hunny let out a bark, turned abruptly, and rushed back to her house, disappearing through the doorway.

"Hunny!" Pearl called after the dog before stumbling to her feet. Again shaking her head, Pearl muttered, "I could swear that dog just said she was going to get help."

EYES CLOSED; Danielle's left hand reached over to her husband's side of the bed. It was empty. Leaving her fingertips resting on a portion of the sheet where Walt had been sleeping, Danielle yawned, opened her eyes, and turned to face Walt's side of the bed. Disappointed to find herself alone, she let out a sigh and looked up to the ceiling, thinking of the comforting sound of rain that had serenaded them through the night.

Without sitting up, she reached for the cup of dry cereal she had left on the nightstand the night before. She took a few nibbles and then sat up, leaning against the headboard.

A meow interrupted the silence. The next moment, her cat, Max, jumped onto the mattress and sauntered toward her. If it weren't for his white-tipped ears, he would look like a miniature black panther.

"Good morning, Max," Danielle greeted him, sitting up straighter in the bed, and propping the pillows behind her back, adding Walt's to the pile before leaning back on them. Max gave another meow and climbed onto her lap atop the blankets. He curled up and purred.

"I hope you stayed in the house last night," Danielle whispered as she stroked the cat's back. "That was quite some storm. We almost moved downstairs to sleep by the fire, but Walt kept me warm." She smiled at the memory and then dropped a kiss on Max's head before leaning back on the pillows.

Absently stroking the cat, Danielle closed her eyes, reluctant to get out of bed for fear she would get nauseous again and throw up.

"Good morning," Walt's voice called out as he walked into the bedroom. "How are you feeling?"

"Not bad." Danielle glanced toward the window. "What do you think the weather's going to be like today? More rain?"

"It was clear when I looked out earlier."

Danielle reached over and set her cup of cereal back on the nightstand. She climbed out of bed and stretched. "Wow, I do feel good today."

She walked to the window, opened the blinds, and looked outside. With a sigh, she rested her elbows on the windowsill and took a deep breath. "This is what October should look like. Please, no more rain for a while."

Walt walked to Danielle. Her back was to him as he wrapped his arms around her and pulled her close. Together, they gazed out the window.

"We still need to pick out the paint," Danielle said. "And then find someone to paint."

Walt chuckled. "I wrap my arms around you and that makes you think of painting?"

Danielle leaned back, resting the back of her head against Walt's shoulder. "No."

"Is that Pearl?" Walt blurted.

Danielle turned in Walt's arms and looked up at him. "What are you talking about?"

Walt nodded to the window. Danielle turned back around and looked outside. Walt reached for the nearby spotting scope and took a closer look.

"It is. What is she doing walking down the street in her nightgown?" Walt asked.

Danielle frowned at the sight of the elderly woman, who now crossed the street in front of her house, making her way from the sidewalk in front of Lily and Ian's house to the sidewalk in front of Marlow House.

"If she looks up here, she's going to see you looking at her through that thing," Danielle said, her eyes still on their cranky neighbor.

"So? You worry she'll stop liking us?" Walt teased.

Danielle giggled. "I wonder where she's coming from."

"I don't think she has shoes on. Those look like socks," Walt said.

"I wonder why she's traipsing around in her nightgown and socks."

"It looks like we're about to get company." Walt nodded back out the window. Danielle spied Lily crossing the street, clad in pajamas.

Danielle looked down at Lily and said with a frown, "Maybe the neighborhood is having a pajama party, and we weren't invited. Why weren't we invited?"

LILY LOOKED surprised to find Walt and Danielle standing in the kitchen when she walked in the back door. Had she entered a minute earlier, they would just be walking into the kitchen from the hallway.

"Dang, you scared me!" Lily gasped. She paused a moment before closing the door behind her. "I thought you would both still be in bed."

"Morning, Lily," Walt greeted her.

"What are you pilfering from our kitchen this morning?" Danielle teased as she took a seat at the kitchen table.

"Coffee. I forgot to pick some up at the grocery store." Lily sat at the table with Danielle.

"Want me to pour you a cup?" Walt asked Lily. He stood by the coffeemaker.

"Sure, but I'll need to steal some to take back over to Ian. He's still sleeping. I think the poor guy is exhausted. Having his parents living so close is wearing him out."

"I have to admit, it's rather quiet over here now that all our guests have gone home," Danielle said.

"So how's the morning sickness?" Lily asked.

"The Cheerios are still helping, thanks," Danielle said. "And for that, I won't call the chief and report you breaking and entering."

Lily giggled and then took the cup of coffee Walt offered her. Before taking a sip, she said, "Thanks, I'm super relieved."

"We saw you walking over," Walt said, sitting down with the two women.

"I wondered if the neighborhood was having a pajama party with you and Pearl. Any idea what she was doing out in her nightgown?" Danielle asked.

Lily frowned at Danielle. "What are you talking about?"

"Pearl, you had to have seen her. She walked right by your house when you came outside," Danielle said.

Lily frowned. "Pearl? I didn't see her."

"She was crossing the street from your side to ours when you first came outside. She was wearing a nightgown and socks. No shoes," Walt explained.

Lily shook her head. "No, I didn't see her."

THIRTEEN

Pearl approached her front gate with hesitancy. When she reached it, she paused and looked up at her house, now backlit by the morning sun. She assumed her attacker was long gone by now. About to take another step, Pearl paused and cocked her head slightly, her gaze still fixed on her house. She wondered, *Why am I not afraid anymore?* Perhaps she was wrong, and the attacker might be inside, waiting for her. Maybe they had watched the house, and when the police never showed up, they returned.

Still going over in her head what had happened the night before, she remembered the moment of terror on the staircase when her flashlight's beam caught the fleeting shadow of an intruder upstairs. Fortunately, she had survived the fall and escaped her attacker, but everything after that—up until finding herself in Chris Johnson's yard—was a muddle. Terror had morphed into anger. Pearl took a deep breath and walked by the front door, reluctant to go into her house. When she reached the back door she lost track of what she was doing and suddenly found herself standing in the middle of her kitchen. She paused and looked back at the closed door. With a frown, she thought, *I don't remember opening that door, much less closing it.*

Deciding the attack had left her more rattled than she realized, Pearl took a deep breath and told herself, *Just call the police, report the break-in.*

She walked toward her cellphone; it sat on the kitchen counter.

En route, she remembered she wore only a nightgown, hardly a suitable outfit for meeting with the police. "I can change my clothes after I call them," she said aloud, thinking for a moment about what outfit she would put on.

Now standing by her kitchen counter, Pearl reached for her phone, yet picking it up to make the call proved a challenge. Each time her hand reached for the cellphone, it appeared to pass through it, as if the phone itself were some hologram illusion.

Hesitantly, Pearl backed up from the counter, no longer reaching for the phone. When doing so, she glanced down and glimpsed her clothes. To her surprise, she no longer wore the nightgown, but instead wore the outfit she had been thinking about changing into a few minutes earlier. She froze and continued to stare down at her clothes.

"I already changed?" Pearl muttered. *What is going on with me? I can barely remember much of what happened after the attack. I don't remember opening the door to get back inside, and I can't even get my hand to pick up the telephone. Now this? I must have hit my head worse than I initially thought.*

Pearl stood for a moment in her kitchen, considering everything. Finally, she said aloud, "I must not have been wearing my nightgown last night when I fell down the stairs."

Pearl pivoted from the counter and headed for the hallway leading to the staircase. Confident she hadn't been back to her bedroom since returning home this morning, Pearl needed to see her nightgown, still in her bedroom, to prove to herself that the knock to her head had left her confused, and that she had not been wearing her nightgown during the attack.

Pearl didn't make it to her bedroom. She came to an abrupt stop after almost tripping over the lifeless body of a woman lying sprawled out on the floor at the foot of her staircase. Who she was, Pearl didn't know, because she couldn't see the woman's face; it looked away from her. What she knew, the woman wore Pearl's nightgown.

"Is she dead?" Pearl asked aloud, stepping closer, her gaze remaining fixed on the lifeless form. "Why is she wearing my nightgown? Who is she?"

A series of thoughts raced through Pearl's mind. Was this woman someone Pearl knew? Why would a stranger be in her house, wearing her nightgown? Perhaps the woman showed up after the attacker had chased Pearl from the house. Maybe she got soaked from the rain and had found Pearl's nightgown upstairs and put it on. Perhaps the woman was not someone Pearl knew, but just some poor woman seeking shelter from the storm, and after she put on Pearl's nightgown, the intruder had returned and found her in the house, mistaking her for Pearl, and then finished her off.

But why would the intruder want Pearl dead? Was it some burglar, whom Pearl interrupted, and then later, when he or she had returned to finish pilfering Pearl's property, stumbled upon a poor woman seeking shelter from the storm?

Pearl knew she needed to get to the police. And she didn't want to stay in a house with a dead woman. Without another thought, Pearl rushed out of the house and headed for the street. She was already on the sidewalk in front of her house when she realized she couldn't even remember opening her front door to get outside. Shaking her head at her jumbled thoughts, she headed down the sidewalk, but stopped when she reached the sidewalk in front of Heather Donovan's house.

HEATHER STEPPED OUTSIDE WEARING a green jogging suit and rain jacket. She wore her straight black hair pulled up into a high ponytail, and her straight-cut bangs almost touched her eyebrows. This morning she wore no makeup. As she closed her front door, she spied her neighbor Pearl Huckabee standing on the sidewalk, staring in her direction. Tempted to go back inside to avoid some nasty confrontation with the woman, Heather took a deep breath and continued on her way. If she walked slowly, perhaps Pearl would be down the street by the time she reached the sidewalk.

Nope. That didn't work, Heather thought when she finally reached the sidewalk. Pearl hadn't taken a step since Heather first noticed her. The older woman continued to stare in Heather's direction.

Forcing a cheerful smile, Heather said, "Good morning, Mrs. Huckabee."

Heather intended to continue on her way without another word but stopped when Pearl blurted, "Is your boyfriend here?"

Heather, who had already turned toward Marlow House, paused a moment and looked at Pearl. "Excuse me?"

"Your boyfriend," Pearl snapped. "It's certainly not a secret, especially along Beach Drive. He parks his car in your driveway at all hours of the night."

"If you are inquiring about my love life, it is certainly none of your business," Heather countered.

"Oh poo, I could not care less about your love life and how you want to carry on. I just want to know if he's here. I need to talk to him."

"You want to talk to Brian?" Heather asked.

"Isn't that what I just said?" Pearl snapped.

"Brian isn't here. He's at work," Heather told her.

"Fine." Pearl sighed. "I'll just have to go to the police station to see him. That's where he is, right?"

Heather shrugged. "I don't know. Maybe he's riding around in a squad car, or out arresting dangerous criminals, or somewhere eating donuts."

Pearl frowned at Heather and gave a little huffing sound before turning away and starting down the street toward town. She was about ten feet away when Heather called out, "You aren't walking down there?"

Pearl stopped and looked back at Heather. "What does it look like?"

"Why don't you drive?" Heather asked.

"If I can't use a phone, I don't imagine I'll have much better luck with a car," Pearl said before turning her back to Heather and starting on her way.

Heather remained standing on the sidewalk, watching Pearl. After a moment, she dug her cellphone from her back pocket and made a call.

"Morning, Heather, you're up early. Thought you said you were sleeping in today," Brian said when he answered the call.

Still watching Pearl while holding a phone to her ear, Heather said, "It's almost nine. I'm not a teenager anymore."

"What does being a teenager have to do with anything?" Brian asked.

"When I was in high school, I could sleep in until noon on Saturdays. I don't do that anymore."

"It's because you're old," Brian teased.

"You're one to talk, old man," Heather countered.

Brian laughed and then asked, "So what's going on?"

"I just wanted to warn you, if you're at the station, expect a visit from Pearl." Heather then told him about her encounter with the surly neighbor.

After Heather finished her telling, Brian grumbled, "I should never have given her that business card. So, what are you up to?"

Still holding the phone to her ear, Heather turned around and started for Marlow House. "I'm going over to Walt and Danielle's. I'm curious to find out what Mel told them about the reading of the will."

When Heather got off the phone a few moments later, she tucked it into her pocket just as it started to rain. She picked up her pace and pulled the hood of her jacket over her head.

"HI, LITTLE MAMA," Heather greeted Danielle when she walked into the back door at Marlow House and slipped off her rain jacket. Danielle sat at the kitchen table with Walt.

"Morning, Heather," Walt greeted her, while Danielle scoffed at her new nickname.

Heather flashed Walt a smile and poured herself a cup of coffee.

"If you'd rather have tea, I have tea bags in the pantry," Danielle told her.

"Thanks. But coffee sounds good this morning." As Heather walked to the table, she added, "That Pearl was sure acting odd this morning."

"Still running around the neighborhood in her nightgown?" Danielle asked.

Heather frowned at Danielle as she took a seat at the table. "What are you talking about?"

Danielle recounted what they had seen that morning. When she finished, Heather said, "Pearl wasn't wearing a nightgown when I saw her. And I'm fairly certain she had shoes on. But now that I think about it, she wasn't wearing a rain jacket." Heather then told Walt and Danielle about her encounter with Pearl.

"Do you really think she intends to walk all the way to the police station, in the rain, without a jacket?" Danielle asked.

"Well, it wasn't raining when she left," Heather said with a shrug.

"I was hoping it would not rain today." Danielle let out a sigh.

"I assume you talked to Brian after you left Rachel's service," Walt began. "Any news on the murder investigation?"

"No. Nothing really. They looked through her house again, looking for any signs of accidental poisoning, but they couldn't find anything on the premises that contained cyanide," Heather explained.

"I imagine they're now looking for motives," Danielle said.

"Yeah. Which is one reason I stopped over. I was curious what Mel told you about the reading of the will," Heather said.

Danielle told Heather what she knew. When she finished, Heather said, "I wonder if Leanne is going to vote against the B and B or let it go through."

"Sounded like Pearl intends to pressure Leanne to honor Rachel's wishes," Walt said.

"But will she?" Heather asked. "What, I wonder, is Pearl's problem with B and Bs? I understand why she didn't want to live next door to one. But why does she care what happens in another neighborhood?"

"From what I've learned about Pearl," Danielle began, "she's against any commercial venture in a residential neighborhood. And perhaps she's afraid if more and more neighborhoods approve B and Bs, then maybe the city zoning will change the rules and simply allow them everywhere without an approval process. After all, it seems a little unfair that one neighbor can prevent you from using your property in a way that's allowed in practically every other neighborhood."

FOURTEEN

I *must be running on adrenaline*, Pearl thought as she stood in front of the Frederickport Police Station. It seemed as if one minute she had turned and walked away from Heather Donovan and the next she had arrived at the police station. The walk hadn't tired her, and the rain hadn't bothered her. But she understood that being attacked in her home and then seeking refuge for the night in a neighbor's yard would get anyone frazzled. Not to mention the dead body in her house. Once she talked to the police, reported the attack, and they removed the dead body, she could go home, Pearl told herself.

She was about to open the door to enter the police station when a police officer, one she had never seen before, barreled into the station, practically pushing her aside. Before the door closed on her, she rushed in after him and called out, "Officer!"

He ignored her call and kept walking, exiting through a door in the back wall of the front waiting area. Adjacent to the doorway, a window looked into the receptionist's office. Pearl approached the window, noting the circular aluminum speak-thru for visitors in the waiting area to talk to the receptionist. As Pearl got closer, she spied the receptionist sitting at a desk on the other side of the window. The woman wore a headset and a name tag. The name tag said Betty Cook.

Pearl walked closer to the window, and Betty smiled her way.

"I need to speak to Officer Brian Henderson," Pearl demanded.

"I'm sorry, he's not in," Betty said.

"Then I want to see Chief MacDonald," Pearl said.

Betty sat there a moment, not answering her. Finally, she said, "I'm afraid he's off today."

"There must be someone I can talk to. Who's in charge?" Pearl demanded. Once again, Betty did not immediately respond. Finally, she said, "I'll tell him you want to talk to him."

"Thank you. And please hurry," Pearl said.

Betty muttered something under her breath, stood up, removed her headset, set it on her desk, and turned from Pearl.

"You are getting someone?" Pearl asked.

Betty walked away, her back to Pearl.

"Can't you answer my question?" Pearl shouted. Without answering Pearl, Betty exited a door at the rear of her office, closing it behind her.

"Someone needs to teach these people communication skills," Pearl muttered as she glanced up at the wall clock. With a sigh, she waited for Betty to return with an officer. Fifteen minutes later—according to the wall clock—Betty had not returned. Frustrated, Pearl knocked on the glass pane, hoping to get someone's attention. But instead of making a knocking sound, Pearl's right hand moved through the window. She screamed at the sight and jumped back, withdrawing her hand. Pearl looked down, relieved to find she had not cut herself. She then looked at the glass; it did not seem to be broken. For a moment, she had believed her hand had smashed through the glass. Pearl took a deep breath and told herself her mind was still playing tricks on her. Annoyed it was taking so long to see an officer, Pearl sat down on a chair in the waiting room. Certainly, Betty would return shortly.

PEARL WASN'T certain how she had gotten home. The last thing she remembered was sitting in the police station, waiting for someone to help her. That woman at the front had been no help at all; she had simply left and never returned. And so Pearl waited and waited, and when no one came, Pearl started thinking about how she wanted to go home. She wanted to put all this behind her. And then the next thing she knew, she stood in her bedroom. Instead of dwelling on how she had gotten home, she wondered if she should try calling the police again. But her cellphone was still sitting on the kitchen counter downstairs.

She was reluctant to go downstairs because she was fairly certain there was still that matter of the dead body lying at the foot of her staircase, wearing her nightgown. Who was the woman?

Pearl knew she couldn't stay in this house with a dead body on her floor and a killer on the loose. Perhaps the killer might return. She didn't dwell on the fact that she had somehow been at the police station one minute and then her home the next, nor on the fact she hadn't been able to pick up the phone the last time she had tried. Instead, Pearl assumed most of her confusion had to be associated with the fact she had severely hit her head when the maniac shoved her down the stairs.

Once again Pearl thought about her cellphone, asking herself how she could get from her bedroom to the kitchen without having to go by that sad dead woman downstairs. And then, the next minute, Pearl stood in her kitchen just like she wanted to be a few moments earlier. Pearl was both confused and somewhat relieved.

Glancing at the cellphone, she took a deep breath and said aloud, "You can do this, Pearl; you can pick up your cellphone and call the police." Unfortunately, Pearl found herself unable to pick up the phone.

"I have to do something," Pearl said aloud. Standing alone in her kitchen, she looked at the doorway leading to the hall and staircase. "I have to find out who she is. I might know her."

Reluctantly, Pearl walked from the kitchen, heading to the staircase. Once there, she looked at the lifeless body sprawled on the floor. The blood in the woman's gray hair was now matted and dry. Pearl knelt and looked at the woman's face.

HOW LONG WOULD it take for someone to find Pearl's body? Loose ends were always so annoying. And with Pearl Huckabee, it might be days before somebody found her decaying corpse. She had few friends. Who would miss her?

The killer looked out the window at the night sky and yawned. Time to go to bed and stop obsessing over all the loose ends. Everything was going to work out.

LARRY HODGE SLEPT in on Friday morning. The last few days had been stressful, but things were looking up. Sleepily, he opened his eyes and smiled up at the ceiling, remembering the ideal piece of real estate they had inherited. Technically, his wife had inherited the house, but what she owned was his.

Larry attended church every Sunday with Leanne. For him, church was not about God or religion. It supported the lifestyle that promoted the husband as head of the household, an idea Leanne embraced. Unlike other women these days, she knew her place. Unfortunately, not all the Christian churches he attended over the years shared his perspective.

One minister had told him that being the head of the family didn't mean he could rule his wife as a dictator, as if she had no say in such things. Larry thought that minister was a moron. He didn't know what he was talking about. That was why he voted to deny the minister's raise. Unfortunately, that blew up, and he and Leanne ended up leaving that church. Yet it all worked out for the best. Larry rather liked the church in Frederickport. It also kept his wife occupied. Which helped to keep her nose out of his business.

PEARL HUCKABEE SAT on the bottom step of her staircase, mesmerized by the dead woman just inches away. She wasn't certain how long she had been sitting there, but considering night had fallen and the sun had again risen—judging by the light coming in the nearby window—she assumed she had been there since yesterday.

"Is this what it means to be dead?" she asked herself. "Now what?"

Knocking on her front door broke the silence. She stood up and walked to the window and looked outside. Standing on her front porch stood Leanne Hodge.

"Pearl, oh Pearl! It's Leanne!"

Without thinking, Pearl stepped through the wall and stood next to Leanne, who continued to shout and call out her name.

"I'm here," Pearl said, yet wasn't surprised when Leanne couldn't hear her and continued to knock and call out her name.

Pearl shoved her face in front of Leanne and shouted, "Boo!"

When Leanne did not react, Pearl let out a sigh and moved back inside the house. Finding Leanne's persistent knocking annoying, Pearl made her way to her bedroom upstairs, carefully stepping over her dead body as she did.

HEATHER STEPPED OUTSIDE to get her mail on Friday afternoon and for a moment experienced a sense of déjà vu. She heard a familiar voice shouting out a name while accompanied by a loud knocking. It was not the same name Heather had heard the voice call out before. That time it had been Rachel. Now the woman called for Pearl. Curious to see if it was the same woman, Heather walked out onto the sidewalk toward Pearl's house. As she suspected, Leanne Hodge was the persistent knocker.

"I don't think she's home," Heather said, now standing at Pearl's front gate.

Leanne turned around and faced Heather. With a frown, she asked, "Who are you?"

"Heather Donovan. I live next door. I don't think she's home." Truth was, Heather didn't know if Pearl was home or not, she just found Leanne's shouting annoying.

"Her car is in her driveway," Leanne retorted.

"She might have walked down to Pier Café. She does that," Heather said.

"I've been trying to call Pearl since last night, and I haven't been able to get ahold of her," Leanne told her. "Pearl and I recently lost a close friend. I know she's been upset. I'm worried about her."

As Heather listened to Leanne, she glanced upstairs. There, standing at the upstairs window, stood Pearl, looking down at Leanne. Heather glanced back at Leanne, who started pounding on Pearl's door again. Heather looked back at the upstairs window. Pearl continued to stare down at Leanne.

After standing there a moment, Heather realized Pearl didn't want to see this woman.

"Please stop knocking!" Heather blurted.

Leanne turned to Heather with a frown and said, "I told you—"

"Yes, I know. You are worried about her. I tell you what, when I see Pearl, I'll let her know you were here. I'm sure she is probably down at Pier Café. If you want to see her, go down there. But please, enough with the shouting and knocking. It's annoying." Heather glanced back at the upstairs window. Pearl was no longer there.

Leanne stared at Heather a moment and then let out a sigh before saying, "Fine. When you see her, please tell her Leanne Hodge stopped by, and have her call me. I want to make sure she's alright."

"Why wouldn't she be alright?" Heather asked.

"I told you, we lost a close friend," Leanne snapped.

FIFTEEN

Chris Johnson, aka Chris Glandon, intended to lounge around his house all weekend and do nothing. He planned to spend most of Saturday in front of his television set, wearing flannel pajama bottoms, a sweatshirt, and flip-flops, while eating junk food and drinking beer.

Hunny refused to go along with Chris's agenda. She had been antsy the last few days, beginning Thursday morning, when Chris had let her outside to do her business. Ever since then Hunny had been going to the front door as if she wanted to go outside. Chris would let her out, but she just sniffed around in the rhododendron bush, looked down the street, and whined. So when Saturday afternoon rolled around, and Danielle called and invited him over for pizza, he accepted her offer. He knew Ian and Lily would be there with their dog, Sadie. Chris figured Hunny needed some playtime with her friends.

When Chris arrived at Marlow House on Saturday afternoon, he found everyone in the living room. Lily and Ian sat on the floor with Connor, playing an indoor version of fetch with their golden retriever, Sadie. Hunny joined the game, and the two dogs began taking turns bringing Connor a tennis ball. In turn, Connor rolled the ball for the dogs.

Heather sat on the sofa with her boyfriend, Brian Henderson. Chris had almost gotten used to seeing the two of them together. If someone had told him six months ago that Heather and Brian would hook up, he would suspect the person had been visiting local head shops too often. Once he'd disliked the cop. But now, he had to give Brian credit for how he had accepted the knowledge about Walt and the mediums.

Walt and Danielle sat on the chairs facing the sofa. She seemed especially happy. Perhaps there was some truth to the notion a pregnant woman possessed a special glow. More animated than normal, she chatted away with her friends, talking about how they planned to move their bedroom to the second floor and ideas about the nursery. There was a time Chris had imagined a future with Danielle. But he now realized she belonged with Walt.

The conversation shifted from Danielle and the nursery to their neighbor next door, Pearl Huckabee.

"Chris, do you know why Pearl was running around the neighborhood in her pajamas Thursday morning?" Danielle asked Chris after Heather brought up the topic.

"I have no idea what you're talking about," Chris said. They recounted what had happened that morning.

"I'm wondering if that's what had Hunny so anxious the other day," Chris suggested.

"What are you talking about?" Lily asked.

"I let Hunny out front Thursday morning, and when she came back inside, she was antsy and kept wanting to go back outside again."

"What time was that?" Danielle asked. After Chris told her, she said, "That was about the time we saw Pearl outside."

"Well, Hunny and Pearl certainly seem to be chummy these days," Heather said.

As if Hunny knew she was the topic of the conversation, she abandoned the game with Connor and Sadie and walked to Walt, resting her chin on his knee.

The friends continued to chat about Pearl's strange behavior, sharing a story or two while Walt and Hunny looked each other in the eyes, having their own private conversation.

After a few moments, Walt said, "I think we have a problem here."

Everyone stopped talking and look to Walt. "What's wrong?" Danielle asked.

"I'm afraid something may have happened to Pearl," Walt suggested.

Heather frowned. "Why do you say that?"

"According to Hunny, when she went out the other morning, Pearl was sitting under Chris's rhododendron bush," Walt began.

"What do you mean she was sitting under my bush?" Chris asked.

"Just that. She was in her nightgown—well, I assume it was a nightgown considering how Hunny described her. Dogs aren't good with fashion. According to Hunny, Pearl was just sitting in your rhododendron bush."

"She was running around the neighborhood in her nightgown," Danielle said with a shrug. "But I didn't know she was also sitting in shrubbery."

"It's not just where she found her. It's that they had a brief chat," Walt said.

"That's nothing unusual. At least, not since Hunny became Pearl's hero instead of a monster who was about to rip out her throat at any minute," Heather said. "I've overheard all sorts of conversations between those two. Well, at least her side of the conversation."

"This was a two-sided conversation," Walt said.

They all grew silent. "What do you mean, a two-sided conversation?" Danielle asked.

"Just what I said. According to Hunny, she understood what Pearl was saying—and she was fairly certain Pearl understood what she was trying to say. And for that to be possible, you know what it means," Walt said.

"Are you suggesting Pearl's dead?" Brian asked.

"I saw her yesterday afternoon," Heather said. "That was when that Leanne Hodge was pounding on her door, calling Pearl's name when she wouldn't answer. I saw Pearl standing at her bedroom window, and I just figured she didn't want to talk to Leanne. But she was dead all the time?"

"It would explain why she was running around the neighborhood in her nightgown," Danielle said.

"You're just speculating because…" Brian began yet finished his sentence with a groan.

"Say it," Heather told Brian. "Because of what a dog told Walt. I'm wondering, why did she want to see you? That was later

Thursday morning, and if Walt is right, then that was Pearl's ghost who wanted to see you."

"Wonderful," Brian said dryly. "This means if Pearl is really dead, she'll continue to bother me in the afterlife."

Heather shrugged. "Luckily for you, you won't be able to see or hear her."

"Where's Pearl's car?" Chris asked.

"It's parked in her driveway, behind her house," Brian said. "I suppose I need to go over there, check on her."

Lily groaned. "Oh please, don't tell me she's dead over there."

Brian stood. "This could all be a misunderstanding, and I'll find her alive. I'll go over there and tell her Heather mentioned she wanted to talk to me."

"If she is alive, that would be better than telling her you were just checking to see if she was dead," Ian said with a snort.

Walt stood up. "I'll go over there with you in case there's a problem."

"You don't need to go. I'm sure I can handle things," Brian said.

"Walt does have special gifts," Heather reminded him.

"Fine, Walt can go with me. And if his hunch is right, I'll need someone to communicate with her spirit if it's over there and not in her body," Brian said.

"I'm going too," Heather said.

Brian looked at her. "Why?"

"For one thing, if she is dead and her ghost is hanging around, I'd rather deal with her now. I don't want to stumble over her ghost when I'm not expecting it."

"If she is dead, then there is probably more than her ghost that you'll stumble over," Brian reminded her.

"True, but like I said, I'd like to do it on my terms," Heather insisted.

Danielle stood up. "I'll go with you guys."

"No!" her friends chorused all at once.

Danielle glanced around. "What?"

"If Pearl is dead, and she's over there, we have no idea what they're walking into. You don't need to be traumatized in your condition," Lily scolded.

Danielle rolled her eyes but sat back down. Fact was, she wasn't particularly eager to find Pearl's dead body, and if Hunny was right, that was what they might walk in on. If being pregnant gave her an excuse to sit this one out, she would take it. With both Walt and Heather going with Brian, they really didn't need her.

After discussing how they should proceed, they decided Walt, Brian, and Heather would walk next door to check on Pearl Huckabee. Brian suggested it was probably best if Chris stayed behind, just in case she was alive. It would be difficult enough to explain to Pearl why he had Walt and Heather with him.

A few minutes later, Walt, Heather, and Brian approached Pearl's side yard. They looked around and didn't see anyone. When they arrived at the back door, Brian knocked loudly and called out.

"Mrs. Huckabee, hello? This is Brian Henderson; are you home?"

There was no answer. Hesitantly, Brian reached down and tested the doorknob; it turned. A moment later, he pushed open the door and glanced back at Walt and Heather. "It's unlocked."

They watched as Brian pushed the door all the way in and stepped inside the quiet house. "Mrs. Huckabee, hello?"

Walt and Heather followed Brian as he walked all the way into the kitchen. Still calling out Pearl's name, Brian headed for the doorway leading into the hallway. A few moments later, Brian stopped abruptly when he saw her, at the foot of the stairs, lifeless and sprawled out in her nightgown. The three stared at the body.

"That's what she was wearing when we saw her," Walt said.

Brian approached Pearl's body while Walt and Heather stayed behind, silently watching. He knelt beside her and felt for a pulse. After a moment he looked up and said, "She's dead."

"No surprise, really," Heather said with a sigh. She looked at Pearl's stocking-clad feet and said, "She must have slipped on the stairs and then fell, hit her head, by the look of all that dry blood. Stupid of her going up and down those stairs in stockinged feet at her age. Accident waiting to happen." Heather wrinkled her nose and added, "Pretty stinky. Must mean she's been here a while."

"That's rather rude," Pearl Huckabee's voice said from the top of the staircase. Both Walt and Heather looked upward and spied Pearl, no longer wearing her pajamas.

Brian, who had not heard Pearl, continued to kneel beside her body. Heather reached over and tapped his shoulder. "She's here. Pearl's here."

"Yes, I can obviously see that," Brian said, now coming to his feet and taking the cellphone out of his back pocket to call in the report.

"No, I mean she's here." Heather tapped Brian's shoulder again. He looked up, and she pointed to the top of the staircase. He glanced to where Heather pointed and saw nothing but the staircase.

Walt shook his head and said, "Heather, you can point all you want, but he's not going to see her."

"Are you telling me Pearl's ghost is in this room?" Brian asked.

"Is that what I am, a ghost?" Pearl wondered aloud, now walking down the stairs toward them.

Heather looked at Pearl. "You understand you're dead?"

"Of course. I'm not stupid," Pearl snapped.

"And you're not surprised I can see you?"

Pearl paused a moment on the stairs and looked at the three. She cocked her head slightly, as if considering what Heather had just asked. Finally, she spoke. "Well, I'm not particularly surprised you can see me because I knew you could. You saw me the other day. Of course, at the time, I didn't realize I was dead. But I don't think you knew then either. What made you come over now?"

"Hunny told Walt she thought you were dead," Heather explained.

"I don't quite understand that, but the way Walt Marlow is looking at me, he can see me too, can't he?" Pearl asked.

"He can," Heather said.

Brian quietly listened to the one-sided conversation.

Pearl frowned. "This death thing is confusing."

Brian held his cellphone in his hand and said, "I'm going to call this in, but before I do, can you ask Pearl why she wanted to talk to me yesterday?"

"Brian Henderson can't see me, right?" Pearl asked.

"No. He's not a medium," Heather explained.

"And you and Walt Marlow are mediums?" Pearl asked.

"Yes."

"What is she saying?" Brian asked.

"Pearl," Walt began, "Brian needs to know. Why did you want to talk to him yesterday?"

"Because I was murdered, of course."

SIXTEEN

Before calling in the report, Brian leaned back down to Pearl's body. With a furrowed brow, he looked from the body to the staircase, back to the body, scrutinizing the scene.

"Why do you think you were murdered?" Walt asked Pearl.

"She wasn't murdered," Brian announced, standing back up.

"I was too!" Pearl snapped.

Not being able to hear Pearl, Brian said, "Looks like Heather was right. How she fell, the position on the floor, appears she lost her footing, which is easy to do wearing socks on stairs, and she tumbled down. I'm sure that's the conclusion the coroner will come to."

"That's not what happened! I have to wonder how many murders go undetected because of shoddy police work like that!" Pearl said.

"You didn't understand," Heather told Brian, looking from him to Pearl and back to Brian. "Pearl claims someone killed her. Walt was asking her why she thinks that."

"What did she say?" Brian asked.

"So far, nothing. She's been too busy ranting over your accidental-fall theory," Heather told him. She and Walt turned to Pearl, waiting for an explanation.

"Someone pushed me," Pearl blurted.

"She says someone pushed her," Heather told Brian.

"Mrs. Huckabee," Walt began.

"Oh, call me Pearl," Pearl said begrudgingly. "Now that I'm dead, it seems silly to insist people still call me by my last name. Especially since I don't imagine there are many people I can talk to now, anyway."

"Pearl." Walt started over. "Please tell us what happened the night you died."

With a sigh, Pearl told them all that she remembered. When she finished her telling, Heather repeated the story to Brian.

"Does she have any idea who pushed her?" Brian asked.

"No." Heather shook her head. "But that's why she wanted to talk to you. At the time she didn't realize she was dead, only that someone had broken into her house and attacked her."

"Does she have any idea who would want her dead?" Brian asked.

"No one wanted me dead," Pearl insisted. "Some hooligan obviously broke into my house to rob me, panicked when I interrupted him. After he pushed me down the stairs and realized he'd killed me, he ran off. You should look into past offenders with a history of break-ins. And I'm fairly certain the person worked alone. After he pushed me, he never spoke to anyone."

Heather repeated Pearl's words to Brian.

"It was a man who attacked you?" Brian asked.

"I said I didn't see my attacker," Pearl said. "I don't know if it was a man or a woman."

Heather looked at Brian. "She doesn't know. When she explained what happened, she just referred to her attacker as a he. But she never saw him—or her."

"It was just a dark shadow," Pearl said.

"She said it was a dark shadow. But I'm not sure I buy the theory it was some random thief. I find that a little too much of a coincidence, two murders within a week. Friends of each other," Heather said.

"Are you suggesting Rachel Moore's killer is responsible for Pearl's death?" Brian asked.

"What are you talking about? No one killed Rachel. She simply died in her sleep," Pearl insisted.

"You didn't know?" Heather said.

"She didn't know what?" Brian asked.

"That someone killed Rachel Moore," Walt told him. He looked at Pearl and said, "I'm afraid to have to tell you, someone killed your friend. Cyanide poisoning."

Pearl gasped. "Are you suggesting my own cousin murdered me?"

Walt frowned. "What are you talking about?"

"Andy Delarosa. He obviously murdered Rachel because she planned to stop his proposed bed-and-breakfast. And he was furious with me. Called me all sorts of ugly names. You can ask Carla; she was there."

Again, Heather repeated Pearl's words to Brian while Walt said, "You did tell your cousin at Rachel's funeral you would make sure whoever inherited her house would stop his project, and that was the night of your murder."

"I need to call this in," Brian said.

KELLY PEERED in the side window at her brother's house but didn't see anyone. Her fiancé, Joe Morelli, stood on the doorstep next to her.

"I told you we should have called first," Joe said.

"Both of their cars are in the garage," Kelly said. "And I don't need to call first."

"To find out if they are even home?" Joe asked.

Kelly knocked again and said, "Sadie's not here either. Or she would be at the door, barking."

"Not necessarily," Joe reminded her. "Not sure how Ian did it, but he's taught Sadie not to bark when Connor is sleeping."

With a shrug Kelly said, "I guess I'll use my key."

She reached into her purse when Joe grabbed her hand and yelled, "No!"

Kelly frowned at Joe. "What is the problem?"

"If they are here and not answering the door, and Connor is sleeping, they might be…"

Kelly's eyes widen. "Ohhh, I didn't consider that." With a sigh, she turned from the door and was about to start back to the car when she glanced across the street. She froze and said, "They're at Marlow House."

"How do you know?" Joe asked.

"I just saw Sadie in the window. Come on, let's go over there."

"Do we really want to barge in on them?"

"We're not barging in. I just want to talk to my brother."

"Call him."

"Oh, come on," Kelly said, taking Joe's hand.

CHRIS ANSWERED the door at Marlow House and found Kelly and Joe standing on the front porch.

Instead of a hello, Kelly asked, "Is my brother here?" The next moment, Sadie and Hunny raced out to the entry and greeted Kelly and Joe.

"Sure, he's in the living room," Chris told them, opening the door wider.

A few moments later, Chris led the pair into the living room. Ian and Lily sat on the sofa, with Connor standing between them. The boy bounced up and down and waved at his aunt when he saw her.

"Where's Walt and Danielle?" Joe asked as Kelly walked to her nephew. She started to pick him up but changed her mind when she realized how heavy he had become. Kelly settled him back on the sofa between his parents as she held his hands and gave him several quick kisses.

"Danielle's in the bathroom. I imagine she'll be spending a lot of time in there for the next few months," Lily said. "And Walt is next door with Brian and Heather."

Still holding Connor's hands, Kelly looked up and said, "Brian and Heather are here too?"

"Next door at Pearl Huckabee's?" Joe asked.

"Yeah, the other day she told Heather she wanted to talk to Brian about something. Walt went with them," Lily explained.

"Wow," Kelly said with a sigh as she let go of Connor's hands. "Those two really are a couple." Connor sat back on the sofa with a plop.

"What are you guys up to?" Ian asked.

"We stopped over at your house," Kelly began. "When you weren't there, I looked over here and saw Sadie. I wanted to talk to you about something—"

"Hi, you two," Danielle greeted them when she walked into the room.

As Joe and Kelly turned toward Danielle, they all heard sirens. Chris moved quickly to the front window and looked outside.

"Looks like they're going to Pearl's house," Chris said.

While the others rushed to the window, Danielle picked her phone up from the coffee table. She looked at it. As she suspected, Walt had sent her a text. "She's dead. And she's here." Danielle quickly closed the message and put her phone in her pocket.

JOE INSISTED Kelly and the rest stay behind at Marlow House while he went next door. When he arrived, he found Brian talking to one responder while someone from the coroner's office was busy inspecting the body.

"Hey, Joe," Brian greeted him with a nod when his fellow officer approached him.

"What happened?" Joe asked once he was alone with Brian. He glanced from Pearl's body to Walt and Heather, who stood silently on the sidelines, observing.

"We came over here to see why Pearl wanted to talk to me, and found her like this," Brian explained.

"How did you happen to come into the house?" Joe asked.

Brian didn't answer immediately. Finally, he said, "Heather told me Pearl seemed upset the other day when she wanted to talk to me, and Leanne Hodge was over here yesterday, wanting to see Pearl. Pearl didn't answer the door, but her car was here. When we came over today and she still didn't answer, I got concerned. Tried the side door; it was unlocked. And we found her."

One of the people from the coroner's office walked up to Brian and said, "I suspect it was an accident. She probably slipped on those stairs and fell. It looks like she's been dead for a couple of days."

Brian groaned inwardly. It wasn't an accident, but having the coroner's office declare it one would make it more difficult to bring Pearl's killer to justice. While he couldn't see or hear Pearl, he suspected she was probably ranting about now. He glanced at Walt and Heather, and by their expressions, he guessed he was right.

"That's probably what it was," Joe said when he and Brian were alone again. "I can't imagine anyone would want to kill Mrs. Huckabee. Perhaps she wasn't the most pleasant woman, but push her down the stairs? And by the way she's dressed, I'd say it happened at night or early morning."

Brian momentarily cringed, wondering if Pearl had overheard Joe. "I'm a little troubled by the fact Pearl's good friend, Rachel Moore, was recently murdered. And the last time anyone saw Pearl alive was probably at Rachel's funeral."

"Didn't you say Heather talked to her? That Pearl wanted to see you? When was that?" Joe asked.

Brian groaned inwardly. It had been on Thursday, yet he couldn't say that because Pearl had told them she had been murdered Wednesday night. Since learning about the mediums on Beach Drive, Brian had been privy to the complications that could arise when a medium unknowingly gave inaccurate information, such as when they might have seen a victim alive, when, in fact, it had been a ghost they had seen.

"I think it was at the funeral," Brian lied.

"TOTALLY INCOMPETENT," Pearl grumbled to Walt and Heather.

Heather flashed a smile at Walt and turned her attention to Pearl, who hadn't taken her eyes off Joe and Brian.

"If it makes you feel any better, Brian knows you were murdered," Heather told her.

"None of this makes me feel any better. I'm dead, remember?" Pearl snapped.

Motion from the staircase caught Walt's attention. Startled, he reached for Heather; grabbing hold of her hand, he said, "There she is again." He nodded toward the staircase.

Both Heather and Pearl looked toward the front door. Standing next to Pearl's body stood the same little girl Evan had met a week earlier. The golden Labrador retriever sat next to her. The little girl walked around the dead body while her dog watched. Periodically, she would stop and lean down close to the body, studying it curiously.

"Who is that, and what is she doing in my house? And with a dog!" Pearl asked. "Why are they letting her so close to my body? Why isn't someone doing something; this is no place for a child!"

"She's not a child—well—not exactly," Heather said.

"What do you mean, she's not a child?" Pearl asked. "She can't be more than ten or eleven."

The little girl ghost looked Pearl's way. They locked gazes. The girl ghost studied Pearl for a moment and glanced back at the body before her. A moment later, she looked back up at Pearl, her eyes now wide. Both the girl and her dog vanished.

SEVENTEEN

Kelly stood by Marlow House's living room window with her brother, looking outside. Over on the sofa, Lily sat with Danielle while Connor played on the floor with Chris, pushing around toy trucks. Both the dogs had gone out to the side yard right after Joe had left for Pearl's.

"Joe wanted me to call you," Kelly whispered. "But I wanted to talk to you in person."

Ian glanced over at his sister with a frown. "Is there a problem?"

"No, not really. When I noticed Sadie over here, I figured you'd be here too. I thought we would come over, say hi, and we could talk for a minute alone. If I waited until tomorrow or tonight, it might be too late, you'd already have plans."

"What's going on?"

"It's about Mom. Now that they live here, she wants to have us over for regular Sunday dinners. It's important to her since we've all lived so far from her for all these years. She hoped to start tomorrow night."

Ian let out a sigh. "Every Sunday night?"

"It would be family night," Kelly said.

"I don't see it happening every Sunday," Ian said, briefly glancing over to his wife.

"Mom thought you would say that. Especially after last Sunday."

"Last Sunday?" Ian frowned.

"She came over to your house to help you with Connor when Lily was off with her friends. And you didn't seem too happy about it. And you told her Sunday was family time for you and Lily, and she asked me, aren't we family anymore?"

Ian resisted the temptation to roll his eyes. Instead, he asked, "What about Joe's family? Are you planning to spend every Sunday with our parents? How does Joe feel about that?"

"Of course, we talked about it. And Mom understands if we can't come sometimes because of Joe's family. But Lily's family doesn't live in Frederickport. And you do have their only grandchild," Kelly said.

"PEARL IS REALLY DEAD?" Lily whispered to Danielle. She glanced over to Ian and Kelly, noticing her husband looked annoyed. She looked back to Danielle.

"That's what Walt's text message said," Danielle told her.

"How come you didn't go next door with Joe?" Lily asked Chris.

"He told us to stay here," Chris reminded her while handing Connor a toy car.

Danielle scoffed. "Like that would stop you if you wanted to go see what was going on."

Chris chuckled. "True. I really didn't want to go over there to see, what—Pearl's ghost? She wasn't that neighborly when alive, and I would rather not deal with her ghostly version."

"Did Walt say what happened to her?" Lily asked.

Danielle shook her head. "No. Just that she was dead, and her ghost was there. At least, that's what I assume he meant."

Lily glanced in the direction of Pearl's house. "I wonder what is taking them so long. I'm dying of curiosity to find out what happened over there."

"WHERE DID SHE GO?" Pearl asked after the girl and dog vanished.

Heather shrugged. "Your guess is as good as mine."

Pearl looked at Heather and Walt, her brow drawn into a frown. "She was like me, wasn't she?"

"I suppose," Heather said.

"Officer Henderson, he called me a ghost. Is that what I am now? Is that what happens when you die, you become a ghost?" Pearl asked.

"As Danielle says, this is your first leg in your journey. When you're here, on this plane, you are technically considered a ghost," Heather explained.

"Or a spirit," Walt interrupted.

"What does Danielle have to do with any of this?" Pearl asked.

"Danielle is a medium. We all are. Me, Walt, Chris," Heather explained. "We can see spirits like you."

"Why don't you both go back to Marlow House," Brian said, interrupting their discussion. He had just walked up to them, with Joe trailing next to him.

Heather looked up at Brian. "What now?"

"When they're done, they're going to take Pearl's body," Brian said.

"It looks like it was an accident. She slipped and fell down the stairs," Joe said.

"I did not! Someone pushed me!" Pearl insisted.

"Is that what the coroner thinks happened?" Walt asked.

"That's what they think it looks like," Brian said uneasily, knowing Pearl was probably nearby listening. "But as I reminded Joe, initially Rachel Moore looked like a natural death. What are the chances Rachel's close friend dies the night of her funeral?"

"That's assuming that's when she fell," Joe reminded him. He looked at Heather and asked, "Brian mentioned Pearl wanted to talk to him. When did she tell you that?"

"I told you, it was at Rachel's funeral," Brian blurted.

Frowning, Joe glanced briefly from Heather to Brian.

"Yes, it was at the funeral," Heather lied.

"It was not," Pearl said. She paused a moment and giggled. "I suppose you can't tell him it was the next morning, since I was obviously dead at the time."

Ignoring Pearl, Heather asked Brian, "If Walt and I go back to his house, do you know how long you'll be?"

"I shouldn't be too long. Maybe thirty more minutes, tops," Brian said.

Heather gave a nod and then leaned over and kissed him. "Okay. I'll see you over at Walt and Danielle's."

"Please tell Kelly I'll come back over with Brian," Joe said.

Heather frowned, as if she didn't quite understand.

"Kelly and I stopped over at Marlow House, and Chris explained you had come over here to check on Pearl. When we heard the sirens, I decided to come over and see if Brian needed any help," Joe explained.

"He was just being nosey, not trying to help," Heather told Walt after they started back to Marlow House, and Joe was out of earshot.

"You know, now that I think about it, she looked familiar," Pearl's voice said.

Heather stopped walking and turned abruptly, coming face-to-face with Pearl Huckabee.

"Who looks familiar?" Walt asked.

"The little girl. The other ghost. Now that I think about it, I've seen her before. But I can't remember where. There is something familiar about her," Pearl said.

"Someone you used to know?" Walt asked.

Pearl shook her head. "No. But I've seen her somewhere before."

"It must have been a long time ago, considering her clothes; she's not someone who is recently deceased," Heather said.

"Perhaps it's someone you saw when you used to visit your grandmother," Walt suggested. "Someone who used to live in this area."

"Wasn't Pearl just a little girl back then?" Heather asked. "Is that how little girls dressed back in those days?"

Walt shrugged.

"Well, I don't imagine finding the little girl's identity is going to solve your murder," Heather said. "But I wish you well on your journey." Heather turned abruptly and started back to Marlow House.

Walt flashed Pearl a parting smile and followed Heather.

"You're not going to just leave me here, are you?" Pearl shouted. The next moment, she was again by Walt and Heather's side.

Heather stopped walking and turned to Pearl. "You can't come with us."

"Where am I supposed to go?"

"Follow the light?" Heather suggested.

"Are you always so rude to the ghosts you encounter?" Pearl asked.

Heather shrugged. "Sometimes."

"Pearl, newly departed spirits often follow their bodies," Walt suggested.

"You mean go to the morgue?" Pearl gasped.

"Your friend Rachel did," Heather said.

"How do you know that?" Pearl asked.

"We saw her. Well, Walt didn't see her. Danielle and I did. We were at her neighbor's house when they found her body. We saw her spirit come out of the house and then climb in the van with her body. I went down there later and talked to her," Heather explained.

"Why did you do that?" Pearl asked.

"We wanted to find out if she knew who killed her," Heather said.

"I assume she couldn't tell you?" Pearl asked.

Heather shook her head. "No. She didn't even believe she'd been murdered.

"Where is Rachel now? I want to talk to her."

"I'm pretty sure she moved over to the other side," Heather said.

Pearl frowned. "The other side?"

"Yeah. Remember I told you, follow the light. You do that, you'll probably find her, and you two can talk. If you really were murdered—"

"I was," Pearl snapped.

"Then chances are whoever murdered her probably killed you. I find it a little farfetched to think there are two different killers in Frederickport bumping off old ladies," Heather said.

Pearl glared at Heather. "Old ladies?"

Heather shrugged. "What was your friend, ninety-five?"

"I am not in my nineties," Pearl said primly.

"It should be—you weren't in your nineties. Past tense," Heather corrected.

"Heather, be nice," Walt chided. "Poor Pearl is just getting used to her new reality."

"Well, I'm tired," Heather grumbled. She started walking again.

Walt followed alongside Heather, who refused to look back to Pearl. When they finally reached the back door of Marlow House,

Heather paused a moment and asked Walt, "She's behind us, isn't she?"

"Yes, she is," Walt told her.

"I'm not going anywhere yet," Pearl called out.

PEARL SAT on the fireplace hearth in Marlow House's living room, Hunny sitting to her right, and Sadie to her left. She pointed to Kelly and asked, "And that one can't see or hear me either?"

Hunny conveyed an answer Pearl understood, and then Pearl looked to Lily and Ian and asked the same question about them.

"Interesting," Pearl murmured. "But the baby, you say he can?"

"YOU'RE TELLING me Pearl's ghost is sitting on the fireplace hearth, talking with Hunny and Sadie?" Lily asked. She had just followed Danielle into the kitchen to get some cookies and beverages to bring back to the living room.

"Not talking exactly, but doing that thing Walt does with animals," Danielle corrected.

"Why did she come over here?" Lily asked.

Danielle shrugged. "I couldn't get much from Walt or Heather, not with your sister-in-law here."

Lily groaned. "From what Ian told me a minute ago, we're going to his parents' house for dinner tomorrow night."

"That could be nice, couldn't it?" Danielle asked, now placing cookies on a platter.

"He also said his mother wants us to come to their house for dinner every Sunday."

Danielle paused a moment and looked at Lily. "You know, I wish my parents or Walt's were alive, and we could have a family dinner with them every week."

"Oh, stop, Dani! Gee, I hate when you do that!"

Danielle arched her brows. "Do what?"

"You always make me feel so guilty."

Danielle shrugged. "Sorry. That wasn't my intent. I was just being honest."

Lily snatched a cookie from the platter and sat down at the

table. She took a bite and chewed. After a moment, she let out a sigh and looked over to Danielle, who had finished filling the tray with cookies.

"I know you're right. Family is important, and Ian loves his. And frankly, if my parents lived in town, I'd rather like regular family meals."

"Kinda like *Blue Bloods*," Danielle said with a grin as she took a seat at the table with Lily.

Lily returned Danielle's grin. "Yeah, like in *Blue Bloods*. I suppose it might be good for Connor."

Danielle let out a sigh. "Probably."

"I imagine the state of our family dinners aren't top on your list at the moment," Lily added with a chuckle.

"True, I am a little preoccupied with something else right now."

"Could it be that ghost currently sitting in your living room, chatting with the dogs?" Lily asked.

"Exactly. I'm wondering, how long is she going to stick around?"

EIGHTEEN

As soon as Joe and Kelly said their goodbyes and left Marlow House on Saturday evening, those who remained stopped talking and turned to where Pearl sat on the fireplace hearth with the dogs. Even Brian, Lily, and Ian, who couldn't see ghosts, looked her way.

Noticing the abrupt silence, Pearl looked up, surprised to find all eyes on her. After a moment of no one saying anything, Pearl finally asked, "I thought they couldn't see me?" She nodded to Ian and Lily and then to Brian.

"They can't," Heather said. "But they know you're sitting there."

"Those other two, Officer Morelli and his girlfriend, they don't know about any of this, do they?" Pearl asked.

Lily stood up. "We're going back home. You know how I hate one-sided conversations." She looked at Danielle and said, "Fill me in later."

"Come on, Sadie," Ian said while picking up Connor. The dog jumped up, gave Pearl a last look, and then left with her human family.

"No, Joe and Kelly don't know about any of this. Mrs. Huckabee, I'm sorry about your death," Danielle said politely after Lily left with her family.

Pearl looked at Danielle and gave her a nod. "Thank you for

that. No one has expressed any condolences for my death until you." She flashed Heather a scowl and then turned her attention back to Danielle. "And please call me Pearl. You can all just call me Pearl. It seems a little silly to be so formal now. Now that I am… dead."

Pearl turned to Hunny, who remained by her side. She smiled at the dog. "Thank you, Hunny, you are a dear."

The room looked at Walt, curious about what the dog had just said to Pearl. Walt only smiled.

"Mrs. Huck… I mean, Pearl, do you have questions for us before you move on?" Danielle asked.

"Before I move on?" Pearl frowned. "Where am I going to move on to?"

"I explained all that. Follow the light," Heather reminded her.

"You didn't exactly explain it all," Walt said.

Heather shrugged. "I'm sure she can figure it out. They all do."

Pearl looked at Heather. "You don't want me here, do you?"

"You weren't exactly very nice to us when you were alive. So why does that surprise you?" Heather asked.

"Pearl," Chris interrupted, "why are you here?"

Pearl frowned at Chris. "Because I am dead. Isn't that obvious?"

Chris couldn't help it; he smiled. "No, I mean, why are you here at Marlow House? Why did you follow Walt and Heather after they found you? When someone dies, they often go with their body. And then later, they sometimes attend their funeral so they can see family and friends one more time, until those friends and family members eventually join them."

"I have no desire to go to a morgue. And I have more important things to do than attend my funeral."

"Such as?" Chris asked.

"Find out who killed me, of course."

Danielle let out a sigh and muttered, "I knew that was coming."

"But you said you know who killed you," Heather said.

"I said I think I know who did it." Pearl pointed to Brian and said, "And he needs to prove it."

Before Heather conveyed Pearl's words to Brian, the ghost of Marie Nichols materialized. She stood in the middle of the living room, her back to the fireplace and Pearl.

"Good, you're all here," Marie said. "Heather, please tell Brian

I'm here. And you need to tell him what I have to say. I believe it may be important."

"Marie just got here," Heather whispered to Brian.

Heather glanced over to Pearl and noted how her eyes widened as she stared at the apparition of an elderly woman standing in the middle of the room, wearing a floral house dress, straw garden hat, and a pair of sneakers with fuzzy pink socks.

When no one responded, Marie turned around, as if she could feel someone staring at her.

"Oh!" Marie said with a laugh. "I guess you can't answer me with her here." Marie frowned and then added, "What in the world is Pearl Huckabee doing here?"

Hunny made a whimpering sound while everyone silently watched. Marie looked to Hunny and frowned. "Oh, don't be silly, Hunny. I don't even know why you like that horrid woman."

Pearl gasped and stood abruptly. "You don't even know me!"

"What's going on?" Brian asked Heather in a whisper.

"Shhh, just a minute. Dang, I wish I had some popcorn," Heather whispered, never taking her eyes off the ghosts.

Popcorn? Brian silently asked.

"Oh my, she's dead! And her ghost landed here!" Marie blurted.

"Who are you?" Pearl demanded.

"Um, I suppose introductions are in order," Danielle said calmly.

"I know who she is," Marie snapped. "What is she doing here? I suppose she's the one I heard rumblings about."

"What do you mean?" Danielle asked.

"I heard there might be a suspicious death in the neighborhood." She looked at Pearl and arched a brow before asking, "Did someone murder her?"

"Yes, pushed down the stairs, but she didn't see who did it," Heather said.

"She's another ghost!" Pearl gasped.

"Duh. Live people don't suddenly materialize in the middle of your living room," Heather drawled.

"But I don't even know her. Why is she saying such mean things about me?" Pearl demanded.

Hands on hips, Marie marched over to Pearl, glaring at her. "Oh, I know you. Like when Walt and Danielle were on their honeymoon, and you tried to coax Max out of the kitchen so you could put him in a cage and get rid of him. I gave you a few good smacks with the pet door. Now do you remember me?"

Pearl cringed and sat back down on the hearth, looking embarrassed as she stared at Marie.

"That's all behind us now," Danielle said, walking over to the two ghosts. "Pearl has become much nicer to the pets on Beach Drive. In fact, Hunny is quite fond of her."

"Hunny is a pushover," Marie grumbled, her hands no longer on her hips as she stepped back from Pearl.

"What did you mean, you smacked me with the pet door?" Pearl asked.

Marie glanced at a magazine sitting on the coffee table. She then turned to Pearl and said, "Let's pretend that magazine is the pet door in the kitchen." The next moment, the magazine flew across the room, heading straight for Pearl's head. Pearl ducked, and the magazine paused in midair, floating above Pearl.

"Are you doing that?" Pearl asked in awe.

Marie shrugged. "Maybe."

With a sigh, Danielle marched over to the magazine and snatched it from the air, returning it to the coffee table.

"Will I be able to do that?" Pearl asked, now sitting up again. "How can I do it?"

Marie shrugged again. "Probably not."

Danielle turned back to Pearl and Marie. "Some spirits can, some can't. But as I was trying to say, Pearl, this is Marie Nichols. She is a friend of ours, and she died before you moved to Frederickport. Spirits normally move on, as I imagine you will. But Marie stayed, for her own reasons."

"Why do you assume I'll move on?" Pearl asked. "This is getting interesting."

"I still don't understand why you're here, sitting in Walt and Danielle's living room," Marie said.

Ignoring Marie's comment, Pearl studied Marie for a moment, cocking her head from side to side. Finally, she blurted, "The baby! That was no magic trick! You're the one who made the baby look like it was flying. It wasn't an illusion created by one of Walt Marlow's magic tricks, was it?"

"Not really sure. Which time? It might have been Walt or me. I can't remember." Marie took a seat on an imaginary chair. She appeared to be floating above the floor.

Pearl frowned. "I don't understand."

"That's not important," Danielle said. "Let's discuss your murder and see if we can figure out for sure who did it, and then you can be on your way."

"On my way where?" Pearl asked. "I told you, this is getting interesting. Why would I want to leave?"

LATER THAT EVENING, Danielle snuggled up under the quilts with Walt in their attic bedroom. Wrapping his arm around her, Walt pulled Danielle closer and kissed the top of her head as they lay in bed. Together they stared across the dark room, enjoying the soothing sound of rain pattering against their rooftop.

"I thought they would never leave," Danielle said, snuggling closer to Walt, the warm quilts covering both of their bodies.

"It was a long day."

"While I'm grateful Marie offered to take Pearl down to the cemetery to meet some of the others, I'm not sure that was a terrific idea, considering she seems reluctant to move on," Danielle said.

"I just didn't want her to take up residence in our living room," Walt said. "I was getting ready to suggest she go with Hunny when she and Chris headed home, since those two seem like such pals."

Danielle chuckled. "Oh, Chris would have loved that."

"Better him than us."

"True." Danielle snuggled closer to Walt.

"You know what this means?" Walt asked.

"What?"

"We're getting a new neighbor. We really should have asked Pearl who she left her house to."

"I actually thought of that," Danielle said. "But I figured it might be an insensitive question so soon after her death."

"She seems to have adjusted. Perhaps too well," Walt said.

"I just hope she doesn't decide to stick around. I can deal with Marie and Eva popping in unannounced—"

"In fairness to Eva, there is the glitter. So she technically announces her entrance," Walt reminded her.

Danielle chuckled. "True."

"I just hope Pearl's first theory is not correct."

"What first theory?" Danielle asked.

"Pearl initially thought her death resulted from a botched break-in. I hate to think there's a violent burglar on the loose."

"If it was intentional, is Pearl right about her cousin? Would he really do it because of the bed-and-breakfast?"

"We didn't consider killing her after she closed Marlow House. Of course, we'd already decided to close," Walt said.

"Is that the only reason we didn't consider killing her?" Danielle teased.

"That, and the fact we understand killing someone doesn't make them go away," Walt said.

Danielle laughed. "Gee, I hope that's not what keeps us from offing people we don't like."

IF PEARL COULD PINCH HERSELF, she would. It all seemed so bizarre; one moment she believed it had to be a dream, and then the next moment, she knew it wasn't. Meeting Eva Thorndike had been a thrill. Celebrities had not impressed Pearl, but meeting the spirit of someone like Eva Thorndike, a legend in Frederickport, had been overwhelming. Even for someone dead.

Pearl finally told Eva and Marie goodbye for the evening. She intended to go back to her own house and think about what she wanted to do. But on her way home, she decided to first stop at Rachel's house. Perhaps Heather was wrong, and Rachel hadn't moved on, and she was at her house, adjusting to her new reality before going.

When Pearl arrived at Rachel's, she could see one light on in the living room. It didn't mean anyone was there. Rachel had several of her lights on timers, and Pearl suspected those timers remained set.

When Pearl entered Rachel's house, she discovered there was someone in the living room. But it wasn't Rachel. It was the little girl and dog she had seen at her own house earlier that day. The girl and the dog stood in the middle of the room.

NINETEEN

"Who are you? And what are you doing in Rachel's house?" Pearl demanded.

The little girl ghost turned to face Pearl. By her side, the dog remained standing, tail wagging. He barked once but did not approach Pearl.

Pearl looked at the dog and frowned. "Really? Your name is Charger? Nice to meet you, Charger, but why are you in this house?"

The dog refused to answer, and the girl only stared.

"And why were you in my house earlier?" Pearl asked.

"That was you on the floor, wasn't it?" the girl asked.

"Yes. Why were you there?" Pearl asked.

"I was looking for you," the girl said.

Pearl frowned. "Why? I don't know you."

"But I know who you are. What happened? Did you trip on the stairs? My grandma always told us to be careful on the stairs. When she was just a little girl, she fell down a flight of stairs and broke her leg."

"I did more than break my leg."

The little girl let out a sigh. "You should have been more careful. I would think someone your age would be more careful on the stairs."

"Someone pushed me!" Pearl said.

"Someone pushed you down those stairs?"

"Yes. I was murdered. And so was my friend who lived in this house. Rachel. Someone murdered her, and we believe whoever killed her also killed me."

The little girl and dog vanished.

HEATHER CURLED up on her side at the edge of the mattress, her back to Brian, who had slept over. She opened her eyes to the morning sunlight streaming into the bedroom. With a sigh, she rolled over to face Brian, but instead, found an elderly woman sitting on her bed, between her and Brian. Pearl Huckabee. Heather screamed.

Jerked from sleep, Brian leapt from the bed and made a clumsy attempt to locate his gun while jumping from one foot to the other. Suspecting what he was trying to do, Heather shouted, "Your gun's not there, but even if you could shoot her, I'm afraid it wouldn't do anything but put a hole in the mattress."

Now awake, Brian stood at the side of the bed, slightly dazed, looking down at Heather. "Did you have a nightmare?"

"Not until I woke up," Heather said dryly, flashing Pearl the evil eye.

"He shouldn't be here, anyway. Or did you two get married since I died?" Pearl asked, making no attempt to leave the middle of the bed where she perched.

With a grumble, Heather rolled out of bed, her long black hair tangled and partially secured by a hair tie. She wore an oversized red T-shirt; it fell mid-thigh.

"Pearl is here." Heather nodded to the ghost.

Wearing just boxers, Brian looked to the bed while rubbing sleep from his eyes. "Are you saying Pearl is in the bed?"

"Unfortunately," Heather said, grabbing a robe from a nearby chair and tossing it to Brian. "Here, you might want to put this on."

Brian quickly slipped on the robe, ignoring the fact the oriental satin garment—clearly designed for a woman—belonged to Heather.

"What are you doing here?" Heather demanded. "You can't just pop in people's bedrooms whenever you feel like it."

"I'm going to make coffee," Brian announced before leaving the room.

"Clearly I can," Pearl said.

Heather narrowed her eyes at Pearl. "I repeat. Why are you here?"

Pearl let out a sigh and floated from the bed, landing on her feet where Brian had stood a few minutes earlier. "I'm sorry. I guess it was wrong of me. I admit that. But… well, I was afraid."

"Afraid of what? You're dead. The worse that can happen to you already has," Heather said. She walked over to her dresser and pulled a pair of yoga pants from a drawer.

"I saw her again. The little girl and dog," Pearl told Heather.

Sitting on her bed, Heather pulled on the stretch pants. "You went back to your house?"

"I was going to. I had a very interesting time with Marie and Eva. Eva was very nice to me, and I have to say, Marie wasn't rude like she was at Marlow House."

"Rude?" Heather rolled her eyes at Pearl's comment and stood up, pulling her pants waistband up under her T-shirt.

Ignoring Heather's reaction, Pearl continued, "But then I stopped by Rachel's. I thought maybe she might be there."

"I told you, she moved on."

"You said you thought she had moved on. But you weren't sure."

"Was she there?" Heather asked.

"No. But the little girl was. With her dog."

HEATHER AND PEARL found Brian down in the kitchen, sitting at the table, sipping a cup of coffee. He still wore the satin robe.

Motioning to the stove with his full cup, he said, "I put water on for you. It should be ready in a minute."

"Thank you." Heather leaned down and quickly kissed Brian. "But I think I'll have coffee this morning instead of tea." She turned off the burner under the teapot and said, "Pearl has recognized she was out of line, showing up in my room like that. She promises it won't happen again."

"Did she leave?" Brian asked, sipping his drink.

Filling her cup with coffee, Heather paused and looked at the kitchen table. "No. She's sitting next to you, on your right. She needs to talk to you."

LILY SAT in the rocking chair in Connor's room, talking on the phone while he played on the floor with wooden blocks.

"Any news on Pearl?" Lily asked.

"Not really. Aside from the fact she popped up in the bed with Heather and Brian this morning," Danielle told her.

"What?"

Danielle laughed and repeated what Heather had told her about the morning's events.

"Who do you think this little girl is?"

"My guess, she's connected to Pearl in some way, but Pearl can't remember. It's a child; perhaps Pearl knew her from when she visited her grandmother; that was a long time ago. Look at Walt. He couldn't remember Daisy until he had a dream about her."

"I just wish they would find the killers," Lily grumbled. "Why do things like that keep happening in our neighborhood?"

"WHY DO things like that keep happening in your neighborhood?" June Bartley asked that evening during Sunday dinner at her house. Lily and Ian sat around the dining room table with Ian's parents, Kelly, Joe, and Connor, who sat in a highchair.

Lily giggled.

June arched her brow at her daughter-in-law. "You find murders in your neighborhood amusing?"

"It's just that I asked Dani practically the exact same question today," Lily explained.

"It probably has something to do with Marlow House," Kelly said.

Lily frowned at her sister-in-law. "What is that supposed to mean?"

"Think about it, Marlow House is like a death magnet. It's the site of… how many murders? And then there are those bodies they found next door. And the dead guy in the tunnel, and now Pearl. Am I missing anyone?" Kelly glanced around the table.

"Yeah, well, I never thought of it as a death magnet before," Lily grumbled, spearing salad lettuce with a fork.

"Perhaps there's a curse on Beach Drive. You should consider moving. There is a lovely house down the street from our lot that just went on the market. You should have Adam show it to you," June suggested.

"Mother, we are not moving," Ian said.

"Yeah, Mom. I don't think Ian is going to give up his beachfront property. At least, not before our wedding," Kelly said. "Anyway, I like Beach Drive."

"Even though it's a death magnet?" Ian asked his sister with a chuckle.

Kelly gave her brother a shrug and flashed him a smile.

"Does this mean you and Joe have accepted our offer to have your wedding at our place?" Ian asked.

"If it's really okay with you both. It is asking a lot," Joe said.

"If we didn't mean it, we wouldn't have offered," Lily said.

Joe smiled at Ian and Lily.

"But I do wonder, are you sure you want Brian Henderson as your best man?" June asked.

"Mother," Kelly said under her breath, "don't."

With an expression of wide-eyed innocence, June looked at her daughter. "What? I just wonder why Joe doesn't want his brother-in-law, Craig, to be his best man. They are family, and he seems like such a nice young man, and Joe's sister is throwing you that lovely bridal shower."

Kelly let out a groan and looked at Joe apologetically.

"Yes, Craig is a great guy," Joe agreed. "But Brian and I have been through a lot."

"Yes, of course. You two work together," June said dismissively. "But it's not really necessary to invite all your co-workers—"

Before June could finish the sentence, her husband, John, cut her off, "Enough, June. It is *their* wedding."

June looked at John a moment and then let out a sigh. "I understand. But that woman, does she really have to come to your wedding?"

"Mom, I told you. Even if Brian weren't Joe's best man, Brian would bring her to the wedding."

"Why? She's not even a friend of yours," June argued.

"That's how it works," Kelly reminded her.

June looked to Ian for support.

Ian's gaze met his mother's. "Maybe Heather is not a close friend of Kelly's; she is a good friend of ours. She can be a little quirky, but Heather has a good heart. And Connor adores her. Frankly, even if Brian stopped dating Heather, I would hope Kelly and Joe would invite her to the wedding. In fact, I hope they send Heather her own invitation. Not just because she's our friend and we're hosting the wedding, but both Joe and Kelly have done things socially with Heather, and it would be awkward, rude, and hurtful to exclude her, especially when she lives practically across the street from where the wedding's being held."

AFTER DINNER, everyone sat in the living room of John and June's rental house, chatting, while Connor sat on the floor, playing with some toys his grandmother had bought to keep at her house.

Overwhelmed by the toys surrounding him, Connor picked each one up before dropping it and then picking up another. He didn't enjoy playing alone, even with all the new toys. Connor looked at his mother, intending to convince her to come play with him. But he momentarily froze when an apparition appeared before him—a little girl and dog.

Connor grinned at the dog, who held a tennis ball in its mouth. He loved throwing the ball for his dog, Sadie, but she had stayed home tonight. Connor reached out to the dog and laughed, wanting it to bring him the ball.

"You can see us, can't you?" the little girl asked.

Connor laughed, picked up a toy, and handed it to the girl.

She moved closer to Connor. "I'm afraid I can't take it. It would just fall to the floor." She sat down next to Connor. He dropped the toy on her lap. It fell through her and to the floor. They both looked down at the toy, and Connor laughed.

"CONNOR CERTAINLY KNOWS how to entertain himself," Joe observed.

Lily narrowed her eyes and studied her son, noting the way he played.

Has Marie tagged along? Lily wondered.

Connor pointed to the spot where he had dropped the toy and said, "Gurl." He then pointed in another direction and said, "Dog."

TWENTY

On Monday morning, Joe and Brian sat in the chief's office, discussing Pearl's death. The two officers faced the chief, who sat behind his desk, the office door closed.

"If it weren't for Rachel's murder, the coroner's office might consider signing off on Pearl as an accidental death," the chief began. "How she landed, it looked like she slipped on the steps and fell. But with Rachel's recent murder, the fact they were close friends, and it looks like Pearl died Wednesday night, the same day as the funeral, along with what Danielle saw, the coroner is not convinced it was an accidental death."

"What do you mean, what Danielle saw?" Joe asked.

The chief looked to Joe. "Danielle couldn't sleep Wednesday night—the storm. She was on the second floor, and when she looked out one of the bedroom windows to the south, she saw someone going out Pearl's front door. Initially, Danielle assumed it was Pearl, but after they found her body, Danielle started wondering. She called me this morning, asked if the coroner's office had determined Pearl's time of death. Then she told me what she saw and when, and that falls within the range for her time of death. It's possible it wasn't Pearl Danielle saw leaving the house, but the killer. Unfortunately, Danielle only saw someone come outside. After that, Danielle headed back to her bedroom. So if the person drove off in a car, she wasn't looking out the window to see it."

"You say killer like you believe Pearl was murdered. She could have been going out to get wood for her woodstove. The power went out that night," Joe reminded him.

"The firewood was out the back door, not the front door. And I'm not comfortable with the coincidence of Pearl dying so soon after her friend's murder. Danielle told me Pearl got into an altercation with Andy Delarosa, Sam, and Ruby at the funeral," the chief said.

"You can't believe Sam or Ruby had anything to do with Pearl's or Rachel's deaths, do you?" Joe asked.

"Rachel stood in the way of their bed-and-breakfast," Brian said.

Joe looked at Brian and frowned.

"Heather told me about it," Brian explained. "She also witnessed the altercation at the funeral."

"Why do things like this always happen on Beach Drive?" Joe grumbled.

"Aren't you getting married on Beach Drive?" Brian teased.

Joe flashed Brian a reluctant smile. "Yeah, Kelly has her heart set on a beach wedding. Laura talked her into it."

"Lily's sister?" Brian asked.

Joe nodded. "They've gotten pretty close. In fact, Laura's flying back to attend the bridal shower, and Kelly asked her to be in the wedding."

Brian arched his brows. "Really? You didn't tell me."

"You guys can discuss that later. We have two murders to solve," the chief said.

"We need to talk to Carla. When she first learned about Rachel, she said something about certain people being happy about Rachel's death. I didn't pursue it because we didn't have the lab results back, and she could have simply died in her sleep," Brian explained.

"You want to go now?" Joe asked.

Brian nodded. "Might as well unless the chief wants us to do something else first."

The chief stood up and waved toward the door. "No. Go talk to Carla."

Joe and Brian stood. Brian looked at Joe and said, "I'll meet you at the car. I need to talk to the chief about another matter first."

Joe nodded and then left the office without closing the door.

Brian stood there a moment, listening to Joe's footsteps walk down the hall. When convinced he was out of earshot, Brian turned to the chief and asked, "So Danielle saw someone running out of Pearl's house, did she?"

The chief chuckled and then whispered, "No. But she helped me come up with that story this morning. That was about the time Pearl said her attacker ran out the door. I needed something else to justify pursuing this as a homicide."

"What, the word of a ghost isn't enough?" Brian snarked.

IT WASN'T necessary to ask Carla to come talk to them. The moment Joe and Brian took a booth at Pier Café, Carla rushed over, coffeepot in hand.

"I heard about poor Pearl," Carla said while she poured them each a cup of coffee without asking them if they wanted one. "First Rachel, and now Pearl. Is it true someone murdered Rachel? That's what they're saying around town." Carla set the pot of coffee on the table and joined the two officers at the booth—again, without first asking if she could.

"We wanted to talk to you about Rachel," Brian began.

Still clutching the handle of the coffeepot, Carla leaned over the table toward Brian and whispered, "No one said how they killed Rachel. But I figure it must be poison, right? After all, when they found her body, no one said anything about her being shot or stabbed or anything. What kind of poison?"

"We can't really discuss that right now," Joe said. "But we have several questions we need to ask you."

Carla released hold of the coffeepot and leaned back in the booth. "Someone said Pearl fell down the stairs. She wasn't murdered too, was she? Did someone push her? You know, she was good friends with Rachel. The two used to come in here together." Carla let out a sigh and said, "I'll miss them. They weren't terrific tippers, but they always ordered the same thing. Pretty easy customers. I always knew, when it got busy in here, if Rachel and Pearl were at one of the tables, that was one less table that would have me running in circles."

"When I was in here the other day, after Rachel's death, you mentioned someone who would be happy she was gone," Brian said.

"I really shouldn't have said that. At the time, I had no idea she had been murdered. They would never do something like that," Carla said.

"Who is 'they'?" Joe asked.

Carla stared at Joe a minute before answering. Finally, she said, "It's really no secret; Ruby, Sam, and Andy bought the house across the street from Rachel's. They planned to open a bed-and-breakfast. I guess Ruby's branching out. Not everyone who comes to town wants to stay in a motel. At least, that's what Andy said when he told me about it."

"And Rachel planned to stop them?" Brian asked.

"Yeah, looked that way. Andy was pretty pissed, but he's not the type to actually kill anyone. He doesn't have the cojones for it." Carla gave a shrug and added, "Actually, he was more upset with Pearl over it. Did you know they're cousins? Not first cousins. But related. Ruby's related to them, too."

"What did Andy have to be upset with Pearl about?" Joe asked.

"Because Pearl's the one who convinced Rachel a bed-and-breakfast on the street was a bad idea. Would ruin property values. Not sure Rachel would have objected if Pearl hadn't gotten involved. At least, that's what Andy told me. He came in here one night ranting about Pearl. He practically hates his cousin. But I don't think he was really that angry with Rachel. Just Pearl," Carla explained.

"How upset were Ruby and Sam?" Brian asked.

"They weren't happy. I could tell. But Ruby said something about just putting the house in one of the rental programs if they denied the license."

MILLIE SAMSON FOUND Pastor Chad in his office on Monday morning. She greeted him with, "Did you hear about Pearl Huckabee?"

Chad looked up at Millie, set his pen on the desktop, and said, "Yes. I was just going over the calendar, trying to decide when to schedule her services."

Millie sat down on an empty chair and plunked her purse on Chad's desk. "The poor thing tripped and fell down her stairs. They figure she lay there three days before they found her. I keep thinking, what if she was lying there suffering for days before she died?"

"I was told the fall broke her neck. She died instantaneously," Chad said.

Millie leaned back in the chair and sighed. "Even so, to die all alone. I worry about that, living alone. I could be in my house for days, dead, before anyone would find me."

Chad reached across the desk and patted Millie's right hand. "I seriously doubt that. You're so involved with everything from the museum to the church, you wouldn't be missing thirty minutes before someone would go looking for you."

Millie smiled. "Thank you. That is some comfort." She glanced at his desk calendar. "Did Pearl have an executor like Rachel who'll be handling the funeral?"

"She may have an executor to manage her estate, but I'm handling the funeral. She came to me not long after she joined the church and made her final arrangements. Just a simple service, and she wants to be buried next to her grandmother. But no gravesite service."

Millie frowned. "I assume you're talking about the grandmother who used to own her house. But I don't imagine there are any empty plots next to her. That would be one of the older sections of the cemetery."

"Pearl told me the grandmother purchased two cemetery plots, side by side. One for her and one for her husband," Chad explained.

"You mean the bigamist?" Millie asked.

Chad nodded. "Pearl ended up with that plot. I'm not sure how. It might have gone to her mother, or maybe she purchased it from the estate. She never said. But Pearl told me she made arrangements with the mortuary for her burial and gave me instructions for her service here."

"I can't fathom how we've lost two of our congregation in such a short time." Millie paused a moment and asked, "Did Pearl leave any of her estate to the church? I don't think she has much family. Although she's related to Ruby and Andy, but they aren't on the best terms."

"I don't know if she left anything to the church," Chad said.

"Speaking of that, have you gone to the bank yet? I understand Rachel made the church the beneficiary, so no reason to wait for probate. And we really need to get working on that new roof," Millie said.

"I'm waiting on the death certificate. I had to order one."

Millie frowned. "Didn't Herman give you one?"

Chad shook his head. "No. He told me I'd have to do that myself."

"The bank knows she's dead. Everyone does. Can't you just go over there and transfer the money into the church's account?"

"No. I've been through this before. We need a death certificate."

"WHAT DO you mean we have to go through probate?" Larry asked Leanne on Monday afternoon. The two sat in their kitchen, having lunch.

"That's how it works. You know that." Leanne took a bite of her sandwich.

"Didn't she have a trust? Everyone has a trust these days. Makes everything so much easier. Ah… does this mean we'll have to pay inheritance tax?"

Leanne nodded. "If you'll recall, Herman referred to himself as the executor of the will, not the trustee."

"Damn," Larry grumbled as he leaned back in his chair. "The ol' battleax was too cheap to set up a trust."

Leanne silently finished her sandwich while Larry left his sitting on his plate. After a moment, he asked, "Hey, what about Pearl?"

Leanne picked up her napkin and dabbed the corners of her mouth before asking, "What about Pearl?"

"Well, you two were getting pretty chummy there. And the only family she ever mentioned, she couldn't stand. You think she left you anything?" Larry considered his question for a moment, chuckled, and then muttered, "Damn. I didn't even consider that perk."

Leanne stared expressionlessly at her husband. "You can be cold. A woman just died and all you can think about is her estate?"

Larry shrugged and said, "Well, it's not like she's going to use it where she's going."

TWENTY-ONE

Danielle held the paint sample to the wall in her old bedroom while Walt sat on the edge of the bed, watching. "What do you think of this color?" she asked him.

Walt looked at the paint sample and shrugged.

Danielle dropped the paint chart to her side, let out a sigh, and turned to Walt. "You are no help."

"How's this?" Walt asked in a teasing voice. The next moment, the paint sample flew from Danielle's hand and landed against the wall, in the same place Danielle had been holding it.

Arching her brows, Danielle looked at the floating paint sample and chuckled. "Yep, you holding the sample where I just had it is most helpful."

"Good morning!" Marie chirped, appearing in the open doorway. Seeing what floated on the wall, Marie willed the paint sample to her. It flew across the room.

"Morning, Marie," Walt said.

"You're going to paint this room?" Marie asked, now holding the paint sample.

Danielle walked to Walt and sat next to him on the bed. "When we find someone to do it. Walt and I went to buy paint the other day and just ended up bringing home paint samples. We'd like to brighten this room before we move into it, and then tackle the baby's room."

"The baby," Marie said with a grin, flashing a smile at the couple. "So exciting." Marie released the paint sample, and it floated to Danielle. "But let me do it," Marie insisted.

"Do what?" Danielle asked, snatching the paint sample from the air.

"Paint. I used to love to paint. I find it soothing. No reason to hire someone. I painted Connor's room."

"Yes, I remember." Danielle grinned. "And you did such a wonderful job Bill wanted to hire you."

Marie laughed. "I always found him such an annoying boy, but at least he can recognize good work. So, what do you say? Consider it a baby gift."

Danielle looked at Walt. He looked at her, considering Marie's offer. With a shrug, he said, "Sounds like a great idea to me."

"Wonderful!" Marie said. "I'll go with you to the hardware store and show you everything you'll need to buy, and we can pick up the paint then."

"Thank you, Marie." Danielle grinned. "You want to go tomorrow? Walt and I have to go to the bank in the morning, and we could meet you at the hardware store after that."

"I'll check my appointment calendar," Marie teased.

Danielle's cellphone rang. She stood and picked the phone up from the nearby dresser. Before answering, she said, "It's the chief."

Marie and Walt silently listened to Danielle's side of the conversation. When she hung up, she said, "I guess you heard. The chief wanted to know if Pearl remembered anything else."

"Where is Pearl?" Marie asked. "Has she moved on yet?"

"I don't think so. She woke Heather up this morning. Heather was not too thrilled." Danielle told Marie about the little girl and dog.

"Do you have any idea who it might be?" Walt asked Marie.

Marie shook her head. "I don't. Eva doesn't either."

"The chief told me Joe and Brian are going over to Pier Café to talk to Carla. I guess she made a comment about someone she knew who would be happy to see Rachel dead," Danielle said.

"Who said that?" an angry voice demanded, vibrating the room, tipping over the desk lamp, and shattering its bulb.

Walt, Danielle, and Marie abruptly turned to the voice and found Pearl standing by the closet door.

"Did you do that?" Danielle asked Pearl, eyeing the fallen lamp and broken bulb.

Pearl glanced at the desk and shrugged. "I suppose I did. I'm sorry, but the thought of someone wanting Rachel dead is…" She didn't finish the sentence but stared blankly at the broken lamp.

"You haven't moved on," Marie said.

"Neither have you," Pearl countered. "I need to find out who killed Rachel and me."

"The chief is working on it," Danielle promised.

"I'm going down to the diner to keep an eye on things," Pearl said before disappearing.

"Oh dear," Danielle groaned. "It looks like Pearl is harnessing some energy. Not sure if going down to eavesdrop on her case is such a good idea."

Walt stood. "We didn't have much of a breakfast. Perhaps we need to go down to Pier Café and have something to eat."

Danielle stood. "You mean to monitor Pearl."

"That too," Walt said.

"Meet you there," Marie said. "I'll get there before you. I should probably warn Pearl."

"Warn Pearl about what?" Marie had vanished before Danielle voiced her question.

"I suspect she means about the Universe's consequences regarding a spirit's misuse of energy on the living world," Walt suggested.

Danielle turned to Walt and frowned. "Is there such a thing?"

Walt only shrugged in reply.

HEATHER STEPPED out of her house just as Walt and Danielle walked by.

"Hey, wait up!" Heather shouted as she ran to catch up with them.

"Why aren't you at work?" Walt asked when Heather reached them. They all continued walking toward the pier.

"I'm working from home today. They were supposed to be done today, but I guess they had some electrical problem with my office," Heather explained. "Not that I can actually get any work done at home, with Pearl hanging around all the time. She left my house a few minutes ago, and I need to talk to you both... Hey, where're we going?"

"To Pier Café. After Pearl left your place, she showed up at ours. And when she overheard Brian and Joe planned to interview Carla, she wanted to listen," Danielle explained.

Heather groaned. "I think Pearl's learned to harness energy."

"That's why we're going to Pier Café," Danielle said. "I don't think she's figured out how to control it. In fact, I don't think she knows how she's doing it."

"What happened at your house?" Walt asked as they continued toward the pier.

"She's been hanging out all morning, giving me all her theories, telling me to pass them on to Brian. I thought she was annoying before," Heather grumbled.

"What happened with her energy?" Walt asked.

"Every time she'd get worked up, a light flickered or something would fall off the shelf. I told her to stop doing it or she was going to break something. She said she didn't know what I was talking about. And then she left."

"She came to our house," Danielle said.

"And this is why I'll never murder someone," Heather blurted. "Brian is safe with me. He doesn't have to worry about me going homicidal if he cheats on me."

Danielle chuckled. "I assume you mean because then your victim's ghost could hang around and annoy you?"

Heather nodded. "Exactly."

When the three reached Pier Café a few minutes later, they found Marie and Pearl sitting alone in a booth across from Joe and Brian. They said hello to the two officers, but then sat down in the booth with the two ghosts.

"When we got here, they'd already spoken to Carla," Marie explained.

"From what we overheard, they're going to talk to Andy Delarosa," Pearl told them as she stared over at Brian and Joe. "I know Andy has to be the one who killed us. This is not the time to be eating. They need to get over to his house before he escapes." Pearl continued to stare over at the officers, now focusing her energy on Joe's plate of food.

Noticing Pearl's intense focus on the next table, Heather started to say something, but before she could utter a word, Joe's plate flew out from under him, landing on the floor and shattering into pieces.

Joe stared down at his food now on the floor. Speechless and confused at what had just happened, Joe muttered, "What the hell?"

Brian looked over to Heather, who nodded to the space next to her.

"You can't be throwing dishes on the floor," Marie scolded.

"I did nothing," Pearl insisted.

"WHAT HAPPENED BACK THERE?" Joe asked for the third time. He sat in the passenger seat of the police car while Brian drove. Unbeknownst to him, Marie and Pearl sat in the back seat. Heather had given Brian the heads-up before leaving the diner, so he knew they had passengers.

"You are Italian," Brian suggested.

Joe turned to Brian and frowned. "What is that supposed to mean?"

"You people tend to talk with your hands."

Joe arched a brow at Brian. "'You people'?"

"You know what I mean. I've heard you say it yourself."

"What does talking with my hands have to do with my plate flying off the table?"

"You weren't paying attention, and you ended up knocking the plate off the table. I saw it," Brian lied.

"I did not," Joe snapped.

"Then why did your plate fly off the table?"

Silence.

"Poor Joe, gaslighted again," Marie mumbled. She looked over to Pearl and said, "You need to stop doing that."

"I honestly don't know how I did it," Pearl said.

"I think you do. The Universe frowns on such behavior. When you move on, you don't want additional marks against you, do you?"

"Additional?" Pearl frowned.

"Are you telling me you've done nothing in your life that you are a little ashamed of? That someone upstairs would not approve of? I can think of one thing…"

"I told you, I'm sorry about what I tried to do to the Marlows' cat. That was wrong of me. But I honestly don't know how I'm doing this other thing."

"Just try to control your temper, would you?" Marie asked.

When they arrived at Andy Delarosa's house, they found him in his driveway, bringing in his trash bins. He stopped and watched as the police car stopped in front of his house, and the two officers got out.

"Andy Delarosa?" Brian called out as they approached.

"How can I help you?" Andy asked.

"We wanted to ask you about Rachel Moore and Pearl Huckabee," Brian explained. They now stood in the driveway with him. Andy released hold of his trash bin and placed his hands on his hips as he looked at the officers.

"What about them? Is it true someone murdered Rachel?" Andy asked.

"What was your relationship with Rachel Moore?" Joe asked.

"She was a pain in the butt. I guess I'd feel bad about her death if she weren't so old. Her time was about to come, even if someone hadn't prematurely pulled the plug. But I didn't kill her. I'm sure you're aware of her attempt to block our B and B."

"Attempt?" Brian asked.

"She didn't stop us yet. We have a good chance of getting it approved now."

"You're making yourself sound awful guilty," Brian observed.

Andy grinned. "Well, I heard Leanne Hodge found her body that Sunday morning on the way to church. Hell, everyone heard. That jackass husband of Leanne's couldn't wait to announce it to the entire congregation. But I was out of town that weekend." Andy pulled his cellphone from his pocket. He opened his photos app and handed it to Brian. "I spent a few days in Vegas with some friends. Left Friday night, got back late Sunday. I was with people all weekend, and I have the pictures to prove it. You're welcome to check with the airline and hotel. And of course, talk to my friends. I'll give you their contact information."

Brian handed the phone back to Andy and said, "Where were you the night of Rachel's funeral?"

Andy frowned at the question. "That was the night the power went off on the north side?"

Brian nodded.

Andy chuckled and said, "You might want to check with your

guys. I confess, I got a little drunk after the funeral. Maybe I was celebrating a little too much."

"Celebrating after a funeral?" Joe asked.

"I said I didn't kill her, but it doesn't mean I wasn't a little happy she was dead."

"That horrid man," Pearl gasped from the sidelines.

"Calm down," Marie warned.

"I wasn't stupid enough to drive home, so I started walking home in the rain; sun was still up. But I guess public intoxication is still illegal in Frederickport. One of your guys hauled me in, and I spent the night in jail. Did me a favor, really. That storm was getting nasty."

"Even if he didn't kill us, I don't like his attitude," Pearl snapped.

The next moment, Andy's feet flew out from under him, landing his butt in a pothole filled with muddy water.

TWENTY-TWO

"Can we stop by Lily and Ian's before we head to town?" Danielle asked Walt on Tuesday morning. Danielle stood by the kitchen counter, organizing her purse while Walt poured himself a second cup of coffee.

"Sure, why?" Walt asked.

"She wants to make some changes to the back patio for Kelly's wedding."

"Ahh, so they are going to have it there?" Walt said.

"Outside. Although I imagine people will go inside too. But the ceremony is going to be on the beach behind their house."

TWENTY MINUTES LATER, Walt and Danielle stood with Lily and Ian on their back porch, while Connor, dressed in several layers of clothing and a knit cap, sat nearby on a beach blanket, playing in the sand with several of his trucks. Sadie, who had stayed inside, sat by a window, looking outside, watching the humans.

"Have they set a date?" Walt asked.

"It's going to be a July wedding," Ian said. "When exactly? I don't know."

"Wow, that's nine months away. Surprised. I thought they were getting married sooner," Danielle said.

"Kelly wanted a spring wedding," Lily explained. "But Ian's mom felt if it was going to be an outside wedding, they needed to push it to summer to avoid spring showers." Lily shrugged and added, "She's probably right about the weather."

"So, what did you want to see us about?" Danielle asked.

"Since we're going to have nine months before the wedding, we have time to redo the back patio," Lily began.

"We've been wanting to do it anyway," Ian said.

"We were wondering what you thought if we—"

Lily didn't finish her sentence because Danielle shouted, "Walt, over there!" She pointed toward the ocean. Both Ian and Lily looked to where Danielle pointed, but neither one saw anything unusual. Walt looked too. He saw a little girl and golden Labrador retriever.

"It's her again," Walt said, watching the girl.

"Her who? What are you guys seeing?" Lily asked.

Connor looked up from his toys and pointed toward the girl. "Gurl! Dog!"

Girl and dog vanished.

"ARE you telling me a little girl ghost and dog ghost just walked by our house?" Lily asked Walt and Danielle. They now sat in Lily and Ian's living room.

"The one I told you about," Danielle said.

Connor, who sat on the living room floor, tossed the ball for Sadie, which captured the adults' attention and triggered a memory for Lily.

"Oh, my gawd!" Lily gasped. "They were at Ian's parents'. Connor said the same thing over there that he said outside a minute ago."

WHEN WALT PULLED the Flex in front of the bank later Tuesday morning, they found Marie standing on the sidewalk, waiting for them. Walt parked the car, but before he or Danielle exited the vehicle, Marie joined them, sitting in the back seat. She leaned forward, her head between them.

"You're late," Marie said.

"Hmm, and I'm always saying ghosts don't have a concept of time," Danielle muttered.

"I still know how to read a clock," Marie reminded her.

"Sorry, we got a little delayed at Ian and Lily's," Danielle said before telling Marie about the morning's events.

"I wonder who that little girl was," Marie said. "And Lily thinks she was at Ian's parents?"

"Yes. When they had dinner over there Sunday night," Danielle explained.

"What was she doing on the beach?" Marie asked. "Playing with her dog like when Evan saw her?"

"No. It looked like she was calling for someone," Walt said. "But she was too far away, so I couldn't hear who she was calling for. She seemed rather upset, actually."

PASTOR CHAD STOOD in the bank, patiently waiting for Susan Mitchell. She motioned him over to her desk just as Walt and Danielle entered the bank. He didn't see the pair, yet they saw him, as did the ghost who trailed behind them.

"I wonder if he's here about that money Rachel left the church," Marie said.

"I'm still surprised you didn't go to her funeral," Danielle said before she and Walt took a place in line at one teller.

"What was the point? I knew she had already moved on. Funerals are only fun if the guest of honor is in attendance," Marie said.

"Fun and funeral just seem like odd words to use together," Danielle muttered while Marie wandered off to eavesdrop on the pastor.

"I HAVE Rachel Moore's death certificate," Pastor Chad explained, handing it to Susan as he took a seat at her desk. "I understand the church is the beneficiary on her savings account here."

"I think she had two accounts," Susan said, turning her attention to her keyboard and monitor. "A savings and checking, let me see… yes, the church is the beneficiary of her savings account."

"What do we need to do to transfer the funds over to the church account? I'd really like to get working on that new roof the church needs."

Susan cringed as she removed her fingers from the keyboard. "I'm sorry, Pastor Chad, I don't know what you thought Mrs. Moore had in her accounts here, but I don't think two hundred dollars will help much with a roof."

"Are you saying Rachel only had two hundred dollars in her savings account?"

"Yeah, you can see for yourself." As she turned the monitor to face Chad, she added, "It looks like there is a little more than a thousand in her savings, but that's for the social security deposit that just went in, and it's going to be coming back out. They won't let you keep it."

"I don't understand; according to Herman Shafer, her executor, she had over two hundred thousand dollars in the bank."

Susan turned the monitor back so she could see it. After examining the account for a minute, she said, "She did. But last week, she wired most of her money to another bank account."

"Whose bank account? Where?" Chad asked.

Susan shrugged. "I'm not sure I can give you that information. This was all before Mrs. Moore died, and I don't know what the legalities are for giving out private information on someone's account to the beneficiary, even if the person is dead. You will need to talk to the bank manager. But I'm afraid he's not here. You can come back this afternoon and talk to him."

Pastor Chad stood up. "I'm not sure how that would help. From what Herman told me, Rachel only left the church what was in her savings account here. And it seems that is about two hundred dollars."

"DO YOU HAVE A MINUTE, CHIEF?" Danielle asked Police Chief MacDonald. She stood alone in the open doorway of his office. He looked up from his desk, smiled, and waved her in.

"To what do I owe the honor of this visit? You look terrific, by the way. How are you feeling?" he asked.

Danielle took a seat facing his desk. "Walt says I need to learn to take a compliment. But seriously, why do people always tell pregnant women they look radiant?"

"I didn't say radiant," the chief reminded her, leaning back in his chair with a smile.

"I know. Same thing. My point being, I can look in the mirror. I have dark circles, and I'm kind of pale. I don't think I look so terrific, but lately, people are always telling me how great I look. Which makes me wonder, am I really looking as crappy as I sometimes feel? And everyone is trying to cheer me up?"

The chief laughed and said, "Walt is right. You do need to learn to take a compliment. Where is he?"

"I just dropped him and Marie off back at the house. We bought a bunch of paint and painting supplies. He and Marie were going to take it all upstairs. She's planning to paint our bedroom and nursery for us." Danielle grinned.

The chief shook his head and muttered, "I really have stepped into the twilight zone."

"I thought I should stop by and tell you what Marie overheard at the bank." Danielle then recounted what Marie had told her and Walt.

"I wonder who she transferred the money to, and why," the chief said.

"I figured you would want to check it out. Any leads on her case?" she asked.

"Andy Delarosa has an alibi," he began. "Sort of."

"Sort of?"

"We're not sure how Rachel got poisoned. The killer didn't have to be there when she ingested the cyanide. But for now, Andy assumes he's off the suspect list."

"Do you think he might have done it?" Danielle asked.

"Honestly, no. Because if he was the killer, he would know a trip to Vegas a couple of days before her death wouldn't clear him. But he also has a solid alibi for the night of Pearl's murder, so if the same killer is responsible for both deaths, it wasn't Delarosa."

"That will surprise Pearl," Danielle muttered.

"From what Heather told Brian, our newest ghost has already harnessed energy. I didn't think that was possible," the chief said.

"Nothing is impossible. Just some things are rare. And it's not like she's out hurting innocents."

"She knocked Joe's food to the floor," the chief said.

"Oh, you seriously think Joe is an innocent?" Danielle teased. She flashed him a grin and then shrugged and said, "But she didn't actually hurt him. Might have helped him out a little, avoiding all that saturated fat that ended up on the floor."

The chief chuckled and then asked, "How long do you think Pearl is going to stick around? She's making a nuisance of herself."

"She did that when she was alive too, so no big change."

The chief let out a sigh. "I just wish she had gotten a good look at her attacker."

"Yeah, me too. Oh, another thing, that little girl ghost and dog ghost Evan saw. She and her pet have been making the rounds. I'm wondering if she is somehow connected to all this."

"How?" The chief frowned.

"One thing I've learned the last few years, coincidences are rare, if not nonexistent. She showed up at Pearl's and Rachel's. And she claimed to know Pearl, but Pearl didn't recognize her." Danielle told the chief of the other sightings.

The chief let out a sigh and said, "Interesting. And thanks for letting me know what Marie overheard at the bank. At this point, we don't have any solid leads. Pearl insisted Andy was her killer, but he has an alibi for both murders. We need to look closer at anyone who benefited from Rachel's death. And if the two murders are connected, how?"

"Does that mean you're looking at Sam and Ruby?"

"They'll be questioned. Yet I suspect it won't lead to anything. But I'm more interested in finding out why Rachel moved a considerable amount of money from her bank here, just days before her murder."

"And then you have the woman who inherited Rachel's house. That's a pricy neighborhood," Danielle said. "But I doubt that's going to lead anywhere, either."

"Why do you say that?" the chief asked.

"I know that when Leanne found Rachel's body, Rachel's ghost was still hanging around. She was alone with the body before the police arrived."

The chief frowned. "So?"

"Think about it. Even if Leanne thought Rachel's spirit was lingering and could hear everything she said, she's not going to know that spirit can then repeat whatever she said. I have to assume, from what Rachel told Heather at the mortuary, Leanne acted like a woman who had just found her friend dead, not like someone who was responsible."

"You have a good point."

"But I would look at her husband a little closer. I haven't talked to anyone who likes the guy."

TWENTY-THREE

Kelly Bartley pulled her car into her brother's driveway on Wednesday morning and parked. Ian and Lily had invited her over for breakfast to discuss the changes they planned to implement to their back patio before the wedding. On her way to the front door, she paused a moment and glanced up the street to Pearl's house. She wondered briefly who would move in once they settled Pearl's estate.

"Maybe Joe and I should try to buy the house," Kelly said aloud. Once the words left her mouth, she froze. *Where did that come from?* she asked herself. Shaking her head at the absurd idea, she started to turn away when motion from Danielle's old bedroom caught Kelly's eye.

What is going on up there? Kelly wondered. She glanced to see if anyone was walking down the street before opening her purse and quickly pulling out a pair of small binoculars. Holding the binoculars up to her eyes, she couldn't believe what she saw. *What did I see?* It looked like Halloween ghosts floating around the room.

"ARE Danielle and Walt turning their house into a haunted house again this year?" Kelly asked Lily and Ian when she walked into their kitchen a few minutes later.

"I don't think so," Ian said.

Lily, who stood at her kitchen counter making a fresh pot of coffee, looked up and shook her head. "No. With Danielle's bouts of morning sickness, she doesn't want to commit to anything. Why?"

Kelly set her purse on the breakfast bar and said, "I think they changed their minds. I just saw sheet ghosts floating around in the master on the second floor. Probably trying out new decorations."

Lily frowned at her sister-in-law. "What are you talking about?"

"When I was coming up the front walk, I noticed some motion over there. So I got out my binoculars—"

"You were peeping in Dani's bedroom with binoculars?" Lily blurted.

"HEATHER REFUSES TO TALK TO ME," Pearl grumbled to Marie. She sat in Danielle's old bedroom, watching Marie cover the furniture with old bedsheets. Marie didn't place them using her hands; instead they floated around the room like Halloween ghosts.

"It's because you keep pestering her. Leave the poor girl alone," Marie said.

"But I need her to tell Brian Henderson who he needs to investigate."

Marie stopped what she was doing and glanced over at Pearl. "If you have something that might solve yours or Rachel's murder, you can tell me. You need to stop hovering around Heather. And certainly, stay out of her bedroom!"

"You heard about that?" Pearl asked with a sigh.

"We all heard about that," Danielle said as she walked into the room. Pearl looked over at Danielle but did not comment.

"One good thing has come of this," Marie said, now arranging her painting tools.

"What's that?" Pearl asked.

"Heather appreciates me more." Marie snickered.

Danielle smiled at Marie's comment. She stood inside the doorway, looking around the room and the covered furniture.

Pearl shrugged. "She never liked me, anyway. Of course, I was not particularly fond of her. I assume all my neighbors are glad I'm gone."

"You aren't exactly gone," Marie reminded her.

"It's only because I need to help find the killer," Pearl insisted.

"You are doing us a discredit," Danielle said. "No one was happy about your murder."

"But now you can reopen your bed-and-breakfast," Pearl reminded her.

"Walt and I were considering closing it when we came back from our honeymoon," Danielle said with a shrug.

"Considering doing something is not the same thing as actually doing it," Pearl argued.

"Pearl, this is Danielle's home. If you must be rude, perhaps you should go. She does not need the stress, especially in her condition," Marie chided.

"What do you mean by her condition?" Pearl asked.

Danielle groaned and flashed a *why did you have to say anything* look at Marie.

Pearl's eyes widened. She stared at Danielle. "You're pregnant?"

"Yes, I am," Danielle said primly.

Pearl continued to stare at Danielle as if trying to puzzle things out. Finally, she blurted, "Does this mean you're having Clint Marlow's baby?"

"He doesn't go by that name any—" Danielle began, only to be cut off by Marie.

"She knows," Marie told Danielle.

Danielle frowned at Marie. "Knows what?"

"When she asked if you were having Clint's baby, it isn't because she thinks your husband is the man originally known as Clint. She knows about the swap."

Danielle's eyes widened. "How?"

"Eva," Marie said with a shrug. "You know Eva, she believes all new spirits are entitled to truths."

"It's not really Pearl's business," Danielle countered.

"Hello, I am still here," Pearl reminded them. "And frankly, I'm glad Eva told me. I have to say, it improved my opinion of you."

Danielle looked at Pearl and arched her brows. "Um… thank you? I think…"

"But what's important now is finding the killer. If he isn't that useless cousin of mine, it must be Larry Hodge," Pearl said.

"For the house Rachel left to his wife?" Marie asked.

"Of course. That has to be it. He wanted the house, so he got rid of Rachel," Pearl said.

"So why kill you?" Marie asked. "You didn't leave anything to Leanne, did you?"

Pearl laughed. "Of course not, don't be silly. I suppose Leanne is a sweet girl. She was good to Rachel, always doing things for her, going out of her way. But how she puts up with that husband of hers, I lost all respect for her. She should have kicked him out of the house years ago. No, I wouldn't leave her a penny that loser could get his hands on." Pearl turned to Danielle and said, "Which is why I said I had a better opinion of you after Eva told me."

Danielle frowned. "What do you mean?"

"I had heard about Clint Marlow; this is a small town. He had just lost his fiancée, and you took him in. I assumed he was simply conning you. A wealthy young woman opens her home and bank account to some good-looking man. No, I can't respect that."

"But why kill you?" Marie asked, ignoring Pearl's comment about Danielle and Walt.

Pearl turned to Marie. "I've been thinking about that, too. I know Rachel urged Leanne not to tell her husband she'd been put in the will. Of course, she knew there was always a chance Leanne would tell him. After all, he is her husband."

"If she disliked Leanne's husband, why leave her the house?" Danielle asked.

"Leanne doesn't have to share the inheritance with her husband. I suspect Rachel secretly hoped it might actually give Leanne the incentive to leave the loser. She'd have a little nest egg. But Rachel had to know that would never happen. And it wasn't her reason for leaving her the house."

"I still don't see a motive for killing you," Danielle said.

"Because for Leanne to do what she wanted to do with the house, what's right, she would need to stand up to her husband. I could have helped her, given her strength. Larry understood that. Which is why he killed me. He wanted me out of the way so he could continue pushing his poor wife around."

Still not understanding, Danielle looked at Marie. The two exchanged glances, and Marie gave Danielle a shrug.

Pearl stood. "I'll go home now. I have some things I need to mull over, and I'd rather do it there. Please tell Chief MacDonald to arrest Larry Hodge; then I can move on." Pearl vanished.

DANIELLE LOUNGED on her bed in the attic bedroom, talking on the phone, while Walt sat at his computer, writing. Downstairs on the second floor, Marie painted the original master bedroom.

"She's now convinced Larry Hodge killed Rachel and her," Danielle told the chief. She then repeated her conversation with Pearl on the subject.

"Joe and Brian are going over to interview the Hodges as we speak. We're taking a close look at anyone who would financially gain by Rachel's death."

"Any news on what happened to Rachel's money?" Danielle asked.

"Hopefully we'll have something on that by this afternoon. I wish our victims could have been of more help."

Danielle chuckled. "Yeah, well, sometimes having a victim's ghost hanging around causes more of a distraction than it actually helps."

PEARL INTENDED to go home but, instead, stopped at the police station to check on the progress of the investigation. She arrived in time to learn Brian and Joe planned to interview the Hodges. She had no intention of missing the interview.

Leanne Hodge opened the door for Brian and Joe. She let them into her house and led them to the living room, where her husband sat on his recliner, drinking a beer and watching television. When he saw the two officers walk in, he made no attempt to get up, yet he picked up the remote from his side table and turned off the television.

"These officers want to talk to us about Rachel," Leanne said. She motioned to the empty sofa and asked Brian and Joe to sit down. She then asked if they would like a beverage. When they sat down and declined a beverage, she took a seat in the nearby rocking chair.

"I understand Rachel Moore left you her house, Mrs. Hodge," Joe asked.

"Yes. It was so sweet of her. She didn't have to do that, but she didn't have family," Leanne said. "And she was like a mother to me. My own mother died not long after I met Rachel. She was so supportive during that time. She'd lost her own daughters, and I suppose we just naturally developed a bond. I'd take her to church each Sunday. We attended the women's retreat together last year, and she gave me the key to her house so I could check on her. We were very close. You have no idea how much I'm going to miss her." Leanne sniffled and then pulled a handkerchief from her sweater's pocket and dabbed the corners of her eyes.

"Did you know you were in her will?" Brian asked.

Leanne nodded. "Yes. She told me she wanted to leave me the house. She said I had been like a daughter to her. I was touched. But I would much rather have Rachel than her house."

Brian looked at Larry and asked the same question.

"I overheard them talking about it," Larry said. "I never said anything, and Leanne never said anything to me."

"Why?" Joe asked.

Larry shrugged. "Old people say crap like that all the time. About putting you in their will, normally because they want you to do something for them. I didn't take it all that seriously."

"Do you know anyone who would want to hurt Mrs. Moore?" Brian asked.

"No. No one would want to hurt Rachel," Leanne insisted.

"What about the people who wanted to turn the house across the street into a B and B? They were pissed," Larry reminded her.

"Yes, they were pretty upset with her. But they would never physically hurt Rachel because of it." Leanne turned to Joe and Brian and added, "I understand the police are investigating Rachel's death, but I don't believe for a minute there was foul play."

"When was the last time you saw Rachel alive?" Brian asked.

"The previous Sunday. We normally saw each other more frequently, but I had been feeling under the weather and felt it best if I stayed away. I didn't want her to catch anything. But we talked on the phone each day," Leanne explained.

"What about you?" Brian asked Larry.

"The Sunday before, like Leanne," Larry said.

"Can you tell us where you were the night before Rachel died?" Brian asked.

Leanne considered the question a moment and then said, "I had one of my headaches. I took some medicine and turned in for the night. It was about seven. That medicine always knocks me out. The next morning, I drove over to Rachel's to pick her up for church." Leanne teared up.

"That's true," Larry said without being asked. "That medicine always knocks her out. She was in bed early."

"And what did you do that night?" Brian asked Larry.

"I watched TV for about an hour after Leanne went to bed. Then I hit the sack," Larry said.

"And neither of you left that night?" Joe asked.

Larry shook his head. "Of course, Leanne was sound asleep by the time I got in bed, so I guess she can't vouch for me. But I can tell you with certainty she was sleeping next to me all night."

"What did you do after the funeral?" Brian asked.

Leanne frowned at Brian. "Excuse me?"

"After you left Rachel's funeral, what did you do that night?" Brian asked.

"We went home. Didn't go out again. There was a storm that night. I had a little too much to drink. Turned in early," Larry said.

"We both turned in early," Leanne said.

Brian and Joe asked a few more questions and then said goodbye. Pearl lingered a little longer, curious to see what the pair would say in private after the officers left.

"You lied to them," Leanne told her husband. "You left Saturday night."

"I didn't lie. I just didn't feel it was necessary to tell them I ran out to pick up a burger. If you hadn't gone to bed before fixing me dinner, I wouldn't have had to go."

"You could have told them the truth," Leanne said.

"No reason to complicate things. And if they really suspect someone killed Rachel, it's better for you to have a solid alibi."

"Why do I need an alibi?" Leanne asked.

"You inherited her house. And now she's dead."

TWENTY-FOUR

Danielle didn't bother crawling under the blankets while she read. They had made the bed that morning, and she didn't want to mess it up, so she lay atop the bedspread, leaning against the pillows piled along the headboard, while covered with a fleece throw blanket. That morning she'd dressed in yoga pants and an oversized T-shirt, which she still wore. Nearby, Walt sat at his computer, working. Max had been napping at the foot of the bed, but ten minutes earlier he had taken off and headed downstairs.

"How do you feel about reopening the B and B?" Walt asked, breaking the silence.

Danielle looked up from her book. "I can't believe you're asking me that. You never liked the B and B."

"That's not true. Not entirely."

"And with the baby coming? This surprises me." Looking at Walt, Danielle closed her book and set it on her lap.

Walt turned in his chair to face Danielle. "I'm not talking about reopening as a full-time business. I certainly wouldn't want to do that now that we're starting a family. But it's not like we don't use it as an inn when it suits us."

"You mean for charity," Danielle said.

"Yes. And I was talking to Adam and Chris a while back, and they mentioned it was too bad we had our license pulled, because if this was a licensed business, we could benefit from the tax deductions. It's not like we'd take reservations on a full-time basis, but we'd have the option to rent out rooms if it suited our needs. And you always enjoyed it."

"True. Except for the times our guests tried to murder me."

"We just won't let any of Chris's family stay with us," Walt said with a smirk.

Danielle laughed and then said, her tone no longer teasing, "You're serious, aren't you?"

"It's something we should consider."

"Funny you bring this up now. Earlier, Pearl asked me if we were going to reopen the B and B."

"There you are!" The subject of Danielle's last remark suddenly appeared, standing atop the foot of the mattress. Instead of a solid apparition, Pearl reminded Danielle of an image on an old television tube that needed its rabbit ears adjusted.

"What did we say about popping into bedrooms unannounced?" Danielle chided.

Pearl fine-tuned her apparition, and the next moment, it looked like a living woman standing on the bed. A moment later, she floated down to the floor.

"It's not my fault," Pearl explained. "Marie wasn't in the room downstairs, and I can't find Heather."

"Marie took a break to attend a movie with Eva, and I imagine Heather's at work," Danielle said, suspecting Pearl hadn't overheard her comment about reopening the bed-and-breakfast.

"You need to tell Chief MacDonald Larry Hodge is the killer!" Pearl insisted.

"I already talked to the chief about it. He sent Joe and Brian over there to interview the Hodges."

"Yes, yes, I was there." Pearl then told Danielle and Walt what she had overheard at the Hodges' after Brian and Joe left.

THE THREE BUSINESS partners sat around the table at Lucy's Diner: Ruby, Sam, and Andy. Frederickport often saw Sam with Ruby. He had worked for her at the Seahorse Motel for years and was known for his fierce loyalty toward his boss. Perhaps not loyalty exactly. Some speculated it was more fear based. Ruby might be small in stature, but there was something about her that made people uneasy.

"I'm just glad I like to drink and gamble." To prove his point, Andy took a swig of his beer.

"You really think they were looking at you for Rachel's murder?" Sam asked.

"Damn right. And Pearl's too. No secret how I felt about her. A constant thorn in all of our sides," Andy said before taking another swig of beer.

"Careful," Ruby warned. "Never a good idea to speak ill of the dead—especially the victim of an unsolved murder. And who said Pearl was murdered? I heard it was an accident."

"Murder or accident, I have an airtight alibi. Vegas and jail. And to think my mama told me gambling and drinking would lead to no good." Andy let out a snort before finishing his bottle of beer.

"Maybe you didn't do it yourself," Sam teased. "You hired someone."

Andy glared at Sam. "Yeah, well, you and Ruby had as much motive as I did. Ruby had more."

"I don't know. I haven't killed you yet," Ruby told Andy.

"Are you suggesting we had something to do with their murders?" Sam asked.

"You're the one who just asked if I hired a hit man. And if the police talked to me, they're probably going to talk to both of you."

"None of us killed anyone," Ruby said. "And while this has worked out in our favor, we need to be careful what we say outside of the three of us."

"You're serious?" Sam asked.

"Rachel's death solved an immediate problem. But Pearl's took care of an ongoing one," Ruby reminded them. "But from what I understand, the coroner feels it was an accident. She slipped on the stairs. It happens. No one murdered her. But we don't need to go around town expressing our relief that she's gone. No reason to get the police to ask if her death wasn't an accident."

"They're already asking that question. They asked where I was the night she died," Andy reminded them.

"If the police interview any of us, we need to make them understand that while Rachel blocking our petition stopped our plans for turning the house into a B and B, we always understood that was possible. And we had a plan B, put the property into a vacation rental program—which does not require that type of permit—or flip the property for a profit. So we had no reason to resort to murder."

"That's not entirely true," Andy grumbled.

With narrowed eyes, Ruby glared at Andy. "Just remember, you might have an alibi, but I'm sure it would be easy enough to prove you paid someone off to do your dirty work. After all, you were the one who had words publicly with both Rachel and Pearl. Not Sam or me. And you have a history with Pearl. Didn't you steal from her?"

LEANNE SAT with Brian and Joe in her living room. She fidgeted with her hands.

"Larry should be home in about thirty minutes. He's at the hardware store."

"We have some information that suggests your husband left your house on Saturday night before you found Rachel. You said he was home all night with you," Brian began.

"Actually, my husband said that. I went to bed, remember?" Leanne reminded him.

"And you never woke up during that night?" Brian asked. "Please carefully consider before you answer that question, because information has recently come to light that contradicts what your husband told us."

Leanne closed her eyes briefly and let out a sigh. "Okay, I woke up to use the bathroom. I remember looking at the clock, and it was around eleven. Larry wasn't here. I was just going back to bed when he walked in."

"Did he say where he had gone?" Brian asked.

"He went to get something to eat. Because of my headache, I hadn't cooked dinner that night. He was hungry."

"THE POLICE WERE HERE," Leanne told Larry when he returned home.

"Why did they come back?" he asked.

"I don't know how they knew, but they knew you left that night.

One of the neighbors must have seen you leave in the car. I bet they talked to the neighbors. And since I walked out on the back porch when you came home, I think they saw me up, too."

Larry stood there a moment, considering what his wife had just told him. "I got to go," he said abruptly.

"CHIEF, there is a Larry Hodge who insists he needs to talk to you. He says it's about the Rachel Moore case," the person at the front desk called to tell Chief MacDonald.

"Okay, send him back," the chief said.

A few minutes later, Chief MacDonald sat alone in his office with a nervous Larry Hodge.

"I didn't kill Rachel Moore," Larry announced.

The chief, who hadn't bothered standing up, motioned to a chair and told Larry to sit down.

"Anyone accuse you of killing her?" the chief asked.

"I told your officers I never left the house on Saturday night. I didn't see the point of telling them I had gone anywhere. After all, I didn't kill anyone."

"But your wife knew?"

"Yeah, she woke up to use the bathroom when I came home. Kinda surprised me because she usually sleeps like a rock when she takes that medicine. When I told your men I hadn't gone anywhere, Leanne didn't contradict me. But after they left, she asked why I didn't say anything, and I told her I just didn't see the point in making a big deal over it. It's not like we had anything to do with Rachel's death."

"Why did you feel you needed to talk to me now? My people already spoke to your wife."

Larry let out a sigh and said, "Because she told you I left to get something to eat. I figure they're going to check out the story, and when they do, they're going to find out I wasn't there. Hell, there are cameras everywhere now."

"Where were you?" the chief asked.

"Please don't say anything to my wife."

The chief arched his brow.

"It's just a little harmless fun. She's a woman from our church. A widow. And sometimes she needs male companionship, and I like to help her out. When Leanne takes her headache medicine, she's normally dead to the world until morning. You don't need to embarrass the poor woman or upset Leanne. But I don't want you to wonder if I had anything to do with Rachel's death just because I was trying to keep a little extracurricular activity a secret from my wife."

INSTEAD OF CALLING DANIELLE, the chief called Heather, who had just gotten home. He asked her if she could find Pearl for him; they needed to talk. Thirty minutes later, Heather sat in her living room with the chief and Pearl.

"I don't think the killer is Larry Hodge," the police chief told Heather and Pearl.

"Why?" Pearl asked. Heather conveyed the question, to which the chief gave the reason given to him by Larry Hodge.

"Impossible!" Pearl shouted after the chief finished.

"Pearl doesn't buy your story," Heather said dryly.

"Why?" the chief asked.

"Because I can't imagine any woman having an affair with that man," Pearl said.

After Heather conveyed Pearl's sentiments, the chief said, "We already spoke to the woman. While she was about to die from embarrassment, she confirmed his story."

"Who was this woman?" Pearl demanded.

"I really can't say," the chief said.

Heather stood up. "I'm going to get some tea. While I'm gone, you can tell Pearl who the other woman is. She can find out anyway. All she has to do is follow this Larry dude for a while."

When Heather left the room, the chief gave Pearl the woman's name.

A few minutes later, after Heather returned, Pearl said, "Tell the chief I suppose Hazel is the one woman in Frederickport who might actually have an affair with that man."

"Um, I don't think you were supposed to say her name. That was sort of the point of me leaving the room," Heather said.

"Well, you don't know who she is, do you? I didn't mention her last name."

"True. I never met Hazel, and you didn't say her last name." Heather glanced over to the chief.

"You can also tell the chief, if Hazel Stone would fool around with Larry Hodge, she could also be his accomplice. He should keep an eye on poor Leanne. Those two might bump her off next," Pearl said.

TWENTY-FIVE

Brian sat with the chief in his office.

"I suppose I'm not surprised he has an alibi," Brian said. "After we spoke to the restaurant and realized he had lied about going there, I still couldn't figure out how he could have poisoned Moore. She already told Heather she had been alone all day Saturday. We've already tested the food in her pantry for signs of poisoning. Nothing. Even the pills in her medicine cabinet show no sign of tampering. It would be different if Heather hadn't already talked to Moore's ghost."

"Unfortunately, we still have to go through the normal stages of an investigation. We can't shortcut even though we understand it will probably lead to a dead end," the chief said.

"How did someone get the cyanide into Moore? Now, if Leanne had been the killer, I'd suspect she had tampered with the melatonin capsules we found in the medicine cabinet, and when she got there that morning, she would have flushed the remaining capsules before calling the police," Brian said.

"Which Rachel's spirit would have seen," the chief said.

"Exactly."

"Rachel herself told Heather everything she consumed that day. None of which we could link to the poisoning."

"Now what?" Brian asked.

"Rachel's spirit has obviously moved on. So we can't learn more from her. We do what we did before we could interrogate victims of a homicide. Keep digging and find out as much as we can about Rachel Moore, and who would want her dead. And then figure out how they did it."

The chief's desk phone rang. He answered it while Brian quietly waited for him to finish the call. The chief picked up a pen from his desk and began writing on a pad of paper.

"That was about the church's missing money," the chief said as he hung up the phone.

"And?" Brian asked.

"It seems Rachel Moore opened a new bank account in Astoria, a week before her death. That's where she moved the money from the bank here."

"Did she get upset at the local bank? I assume the church is the beneficiary of that account too," Brian said.

The chief shook his head. "No." He glanced at what he had just written on a piece of paper. "The beneficiary is a Tammy Morgan. I have an address in Portland, Oregon."

TAMMY MORGAN LIVED in a one-bedroom rental house in an older Portland neighborhood. According to the information Brian had on the woman, she had never married, had turned sixty on her last birthday, and currently worked for the local school district in the cafeteria.

He wondered briefly if the strawberry birthmark covering the right side of her face had something to do with never being married. Heather had once told Brian, "Men are more superficial than women." The conversation, in part, had started when discussing Brian's past choices and their age difference. Heather told a story about a boy who had burned off half his face when playing with fireworks in his garage and the fireworks came in contact with a can of gasoline. "Women loved him. Half of his face was handsome; the other half was pretty much gone. Tell me men would feel that way about a woman," Heather had challenged.

Tammy had just gotten home from work when he arrived at her house. The two sat together in her living room.

"I have no idea who Rachel Moore is or why she made me beneficiary on her bank account. It must be some mistake, but I've been told it's not. I haven't touched the money or the account. I'm afraid once I do, then I'll find out it was all a mistake, and then I'll owe someone all that money."

"You've never met Rachel Moore?" Brian asked.

Tammy shook her head. "Not that I can remember."

"Have you ever been to Frederickport?" Brian asked.

Tammy smiled at the question. "Yes. I go every summer and stay two weeks at the Seahorse Motel. Such a lovely place. They told me Rachel Moore lives in Frederickport, but I've never met her."

"Are you sure?" Brian asked.

"I would assume if someone left me that much money, I would have some memory of them if we actually met. Although, I suppose it could have been someone I met when I was there, and don't recall. But I just don't understand why they would leave me anything. The entire thing is perplexing."

Brian removed his cellphone from his pocket and opened his photos app. He located an image he had of Rachel. He reached across the table and handed the phone to Tammy. "Does she look familiar at all?"

Tammy stared at the photo a minute and then said in surprise, "Yes, I recognize her. I don't remember her name." She looked up at Brian with a frown. "Are you saying this is Rachel Moore? The one who left me all that money?"

Brian nodded and took back the phone. "Yes."

Tammy slumped back in her chair and shook her head. "This is all so crazy."

"Do you know where you met her?" Brian asked.

"Yes. Ruby introduced us," Tammy said.

Brian cocked his brow. "Ruby?"

Tammy nodded. "Yes. Ruby Crabtree. She owns the Seahorse Motel. Ruby and I have gotten friendly over the years. Like I said, I spend two weeks there each summer."

"How did Ruby happen to introduce you to Rachel Moore?"

"It was at her church. She invited me to go with her. I normally go to church on Sundays when I'm home. I met many people that day. But… well… I remember her because…" Tammy didn't finish her sentence.

"Go on," Brian urged.

Absently, Tammy touched the right side of her face. "She kept staring at my birthmark. And then she asked all sorts of personal questions. She made me uncomfortable."

"What kind of questions?"

Tammy shrugged. "Random and personal. She wanted to know my life story, I suppose."

"What do you mean?"

Tammy wrinkled her nose while composing her words. "She seemed fixated on my birthmark. And I suspect she wondered what it was like for someone like me, living with it. She asked me if I had ever been married. Like she wondered if a man would ever find me attractive."

Brian felt a wave of guilt for his previous thoughts when he first saw her.

"When she spoke of marriage, she clearly meant between a man and a woman. But the truth is, I'm not really interested in men. I didn't bother sharing that with her." Tammy flashed Brian a smile. "I lived with my partner, Barbara, for almost thirty years, but she died five years ago. I have to wonder, did Rachel Moore leave me the money because she pitied me because of my birthmark? She seemed especially troubled by it. I suppose she assumed I'd been alone all those years because when she asked me about a husband, I never told her about Barbara."

WHEN BRIAN GOT BACK into Frederickport on Wednesday evening, he stopped at the Seahorse Motel, where he found Ruby in the lobby, talking with Sam.

"Of course I know who Tammy Morgan is," Ruby told Brian. The two sat alone together on the sofa in the lobby, while Sam remained behind the counter on the computer. "Why do you ask?"

"Do you remember introducing her to Rachel Moore?" Brian asked.

Ruby frowned at Brian. "Don't tell me you're dragging Tammy into this murder investigation. She only met Rachel once, briefly. How did her name even come up? It's been a couple of months since she was even in Frederickport."

"I just need you to tell me what you remember about their meeting," Brian asked.

Ruby let out a sigh and leaned back on the sofa. "Not much to tell. You could also ask Millie Samson, Pastor Chad, and Herman Shafer. They were all there that day. I invited Tammy to attend church with me that Sunday. After the service, we were in the fellowship hall, having coffee and cookies, when I introduced Tammy to Rachel and the others. They were all there. But Rachel was the only one staring at Tammy's birthmark. It was embarrassing. In fact, Millie told me she later chided Rachel for staring like that."

"Tammy mentioned Rachel plied her with personal questions."

Ruby chuckled. "To be honest, I think Rachel was just doing that because she felt she had to say something since she couldn't take her eyes off the woman."

"You don't think Rachel really cared about the answers to the questions?" Brian asked.

Ruby shrugged. "I don't think so. Some people just start rambling on when they feel they need to fill up the silence. Kinda reminded me of that. It gave her an opportunity to keep staring at Tammy while she waited for her to answer the questions."

"How did Tammy take her encounter with Rachel?"

"She wasn't so upset that she plotted two months to enact her revenge and kill her." Ruby laughed at the idea. "I think she was a little annoyed, but mostly embarrassed."

"After that, did Rachel ever talk to you about Tammy?"

Ruby frowned at the question. "No. Why would she? And I certainly never brought up the subject with Rachel."

"How did you like Rachel?" Brian asked.

Ruby arched her brows. "Oh, are you wondering if I killed Rachel because she was blocking our license for a B and B on her street?"

"Did you kill her?" Brian asked.

Ruby laughed again. "No. We were aware there was a chance we'd be denied. Look what happened to Marlow House. I never thought it was a for-sure thing. None of us did."

"It's my understanding you purchased that property with Sam and Andy," Brian said.

"Yes. I realized, after Marlow House closed, how they filled a special niche in our community. Some of our visitors prefer a motel, some a vacation rental property, like Adam Nichols handles. And others want a different experience, like a B and B. I had a little money to invest, but I didn't have enough to buy the house myself.

And I didn't want to take out a loan or borrow on the motel. Sam mentioned he had some money to invest, and one thing led to another."

"How did Andy become a partner? He's your cousin, right?"

"Yes, but not first cousins. I only met him after he moved to town, and he introduced himself."

"How did he become a partner?"

"Sam and I were discussing our options, and one day went over to look at the Presley House property. If that house hadn't burned down, it would have made a great B and B." Ruby let out a sigh. "And the lot is in an ideal location."

"Were you considering building on the property?" Brian asked.

"We bounced around different ideas. When we stopped to look at the property, Andy was in his yard, and he came over to see what we were doing. One thing led to another, and it turned out he had some money to invest too. We ended up buying the house across from Rachel's. Paid cash. But we all agreed if the B and B didn't work out—like we all understood was possible—we would flip the property for a profit or put it in a property management program. So you see, there was never a reason for any of us to do Rachel harm. We simply did not have a motive. Now tell me, why were you asking me about Tammy meeting Rachel?"

TWENTY-SIX

Exhaustion overwhelmed Brian; he wanted to call it a day. But there was one more person he needed to talk to, Millie Samson. Before pulling out of the Seahorse Motel parking lot, he called the museum. It turned out Millie was still there, working late in the back office.

Ten minutes later, Brian stood in the museum gift store with Millie Samson. They were the only two people in the building.

"Oh yes, I remember that. So embarrassing. I don't know what Rachel was thinking, staring like that. It really wasn't like her. I told her so later."

"What did she say?"

"She seemed embarrassed yet wanted to know if I knew anything about the woman. Which I didn't, of course. The only time I had ever met her was earlier that day."

"Were you close to Rachel?" Brian asked.

Millie let out a sigh. "Is it true? Is her death being investigated as a murder? Because I can't imagine anyone would want to hurt Rachel. I mean, why?"

"We are looking at everything," Brian said. "Can you tell me what you know about Rachel? Were you close?"

"Not really. We attended the same church. But Rachel kept to herself. She only let a few people in. Now, if Marie Nichols were still alive, I imagine she could tell you all about Rachel. They had been friends back in high school. But I think they drifted apart in later years."

"HAVE YOU SEEN MARIE?" Brian asked Heather when he arrived at her house on Wednesday evening.

"Well, hello to you too," Heather said, opening her door to let him in. "Tell me first; did you bring food? Maybe Chinese takeout? Pizza?"

Brian frowned as he paused in the open doorway. "I didn't think we'd see each other tonight."

"You're the one standing in my house." She looked down at his feet still in the doorway. "Well, not in my house exactly. I just figured if you showed up unexpectedly, you'd be bringing food."

Brian smiled wearily at Heather and stepped into her house. "Sorry. Still in work mindset. I just left Millie Samson at the museum, and she mentioned Marie might have known Rachel well. I was hoping you could play interpreter for me."

"Then will you feed me?" Heather asked.

Brian chuckled. "Sure."

"Marie went to a movie with Eva, but she might be back. I know she wanted to finish her painting project. Let me call over there and see."

BRIAN DIDN'T HAVE to take Heather out for food. Danielle had a pot of chili on the stove and invited the couple to join her and Walt for dinner. The four sat around the kitchen table with Marie, eating dinner while the mediums played interpreter.

"So Brian wants to find out more of what I know about Rachel. I take it they don't have any good leads in the case and want to learn more about her, see what secrets pop up that might be responsible for her murder?" Marie asked.

"Something like that," Heather said with a shrug.

"Rachel was always a private person," Marie began. "She married young, her high school sweetheart. He was friends with my husband. They had two children right away, two girls. The youngest died of measles when she was in grade school, and then her oldest child was killed when she was just entering high school. It was a car accident. So sad. Her husband came down with measles at the same time as the daughter, and I suspect after that, he was sterile. They never had more children. And in those days, there wasn't much in the way of birth control."

"What happened to him?" Danielle asked.

"He died fairly young. Rachel was just in her early thirties. While my husband had been friends with her husband, Rachel and I were never close. She was difficult to get close to. But she started seeing a man about a year after her husband's death. He was much older, and frankly, I think she needed someone older, steadier. She didn't have any family."

"What happened to him?" Heather asked after repeating for Brian what Marie had just said.

"They dated for about six months when he died suddenly of a heart attack."

"Crap, couldn't poor Rachel get a break?" Heather asked. "Her kids die, her husband dies, her lover dies, and then someone murders her."

"I suspect she felt the same way back then. Everything she loved seemed to die. That's when she decided she needed to get away for a while. She closed up her house and left for about a year and a half," Marie said.

"Where did she go?" Danielle asked.

Marie shrugged. "I heard Europe. Not really sure. But when she came back, she continued to keep to herself. Her social life included church and the quilting guild. She seemed content. But quiet. Always quiet and liked to keep her personal business to herself."

Danielle repeated for Brian what Marie had just said.

"Marie, do you have any idea why Rachel would leave her money to a stranger?" Brian then explained what he had learned that day.

"Perhaps you should tell me where I can find this Tammy. Let me see what she says about Rachel when she doesn't think the police are listening in," Marie offered.

Heather chuckled. "Brian, I think Marie wants to go eavesdrop on Tammy."

"WOW, MARIE COULD BE A PROFESSIONAL PAINTER," Brian said after Danielle and Walt showed him and Heather to the master bedroom on the second floor.

"Before she was married, she dated a house painter," Danielle explained. "Marie says he taught her a few tricks."

"And he also taught her how to paint," Walt added.

They all laughed, and Danielle gave Walt a playful swat on his shoulder and said, "You're awful."

"Marie is the one who said it," Walt reminded her.

"She didn't say that exactly," Danielle said.

"Close enough." Walt chuckled. He wrapped an arm around Danielle and pulled her close before giving her cheek a quick kiss.

"So how you feeling, Little Mama?" Heather asked.

"I wasn't grossed out by the smell of the chili, so that's a vast improvement." Danielle looked over to Brian and said, "But Brian there looks like he is about to fall over."

"It's been a long day," Brian said. "One interview after another, a fast trip to Portland. Pearl is keeping me busy."

"I keep wondering how someone like Pearl became such close friends with someone like Rachel," Heather said.

"What do you mean *someone like Rachel*?" Danielle asked.

"According to Marie, Rachel is private, keeps to herself. Doesn't have any family. Lived by herself," Heather explained.

"Sounds like you're describing Pearl," Walt said.

"Agreed," Brian said.

Heather frowned. "Really? Hmm… now that you mention it, you're right. I guess they had a lot in common. Although Rachel is older than Pearl."

"Have you made any progress in this case?" Walt asked.

Brian updated the three on all that they had learned so far, telling them much more than he normally would tell a civilian. They left the bedroom and returned to the kitchen table, where Danielle served dessert.

"I was thinking about how someone could have poisoned Rachel. And I keep coming back to those Tylenol poisonings," Danielle began.

"That was before your time," Brian said.

"Yeah, my mom told me about them. About a year or so before she was pregnant with me. Said it really freaked her out," Danielle said.

"Fortunately, now we have tamperproof bottles," Heather said. "Helps keep those wackos from screwing with the meds."

"True, but that doesn't mean someone can't come into your medicine cabinet and tamper with your drugs that are already open," Danielle reminded them.

"The only problem with that," Brian said, "while we found an open bottle of melatonin capsules in Rachel's medicine cabinet, and her doctor told us she normally took one before bedtime, none of the capsules in that bottle had been tampered with."

"Unless someone tampered with just one, and she took it," Heather suggested.

"That's always possible," Danielle agreed. "The killer might not have been in a hurry and was willing to wait until she got to the tainted capsule."

"Or risk someone else getting it," Brian said.

"I don't think they had much to worry about in that respect," Walt said. "From what I'm hearing about this Rachel, she didn't have people coming and going in her house, and who would she be loaning medication to?"

Brian let out a sigh. "True. Which would mean whoever planted it could have done it at any time."

"Unfortunately. And unless someone confesses, or Rachel comes back in a dream hop, I doubt you'll find out who had access to those pills," Danielle said.

Brian looked at Danielle. "So she could come back in a dream hop and answer more questions?"

Danielle smiled at Brian. "I wouldn't count on it. She's moved over to the other side, finally with the daughters and men she lost."

"Ahh, both men? Her husband and her lover?" Heather asked.

Danielle shrugged. "Who knows? People who remarry after losing a spouse often wonder what happens after they die. Who will they be with in the afterlife?"

"Like with you and Walt?" Heather asked.

"I certainly will not be with Angela," Walt said with a snort.

Danielle flashed Walt a grin and then said, "I was thinking about your interview with the Hodges. While someone could have tampered with those pills at any time—assuming that's what happened—it is also possible that either Leanne or Larry could have done it on Saturday despite their alibis."

"Why do you say that?" Heather asked.

"At first, they assumed Leanne had been out all night because of the meds she had taken. But she admits she got up to use the bathroom about the time her husband returned. It's possible she snuck over to Rachel's that night while he was gone and somehow swapped the meds. Did Rachel have one of those pill organizers?"

Brian frowned. "Pill organizer?"

"You know, with the days of the week on it. Fill it up on Sunday so you remember to take your pills every day. If someone got in her house that week after she filled her organizer, they could have switched one pill. They could even pick which day of the week to kill her. No reason to tamper with the pills in the bottle."

"We didn't find one," Brian said. "And according to her doctor, she wasn't on any prescription medication."

"That's pretty impressive for someone that age," Heather noted.

"According to her doctor, the only thing she took was a daily vitamin and the melatonin," Brian said.

"It's possible Rachel put her pills in a little cup or dish each day so she knew she took them. My mom used to do that with her thyroid pill. Before she'd go to bed each night, she'd put a thyroid pill in a little bowl and set it on her nightstand. That way, she would remember to take it when she first got up in the morning," Danielle suggested.

"Rachel said she was alone that day. No one came over," Heather reminded her.

"But Leanne has a key. She could have slipped into the house unnoticed and swapped the pills. Heck, even her husband could have done that. He could have taken the key from Leanne's purse and used it before going to his girlfriend's. Pearl could be right, and those two are in it together, planning to get rid of Leanne for the house Rachel left her," Danielle said.

"That would make more sense than Leanne doing it because they only have one car. Leanne would have had to have walked over to her house," Brian said.

"How far is it?" Danielle asked.

After Brian told her, she said, "It's possible she walked there and back."

"It all sounds pretty farfetched," Heather said.

"I have to agree," Brian said.

"I never said that's what happened." Danielle reminded them.

"I just meant, even with both their alibis, they could have possibly done it."

"At this point, alibis are useless to mark a suspect off the list, because her pills could have been tampered with at any time, assuming that's how it was done," Brian said.

"Alibis aren't useless in Pearl's case," Danielle reminded him. "We know when the killer was at her house, and whoever killed Pearl probably killed Rachel."

TWENTY-SEVEN

On Thursday morning, Danielle opened her front door to get the newspaper and found Adam Nichols about to ring the doorbell. In his hand, he held the newspaper.

"Are you delivering that or stealing it?" Danielle teased.

Adam laughed and handed her the newspaper. "You caught me!"

Danielle flashed him a grin and opened the door wider for him to come in. "What are you up to this morning?" she asked.

"I came over to check out your neighbor's house and thought while I was in the neighborhood, I might as well steal your newspaper. But since you caught me, how about a cup of coffee?"

Danielle shut the door behind Adam. "Sure. Come on in the kitchen. Walt's in there getting the coffee going."

"How you feeling?" Adam asked as he followed Danielle. "Mel said you were doing a lot of puking. Sounded gross."

Danielle chuckled. "I'm feeling pretty good now. Your grandmother once told me some women never experience morning sickness, some have it for a long time, others for a short time. I'm hoping I fall into that latter category."

"You talked about morning sickness with Grandma?" Adam asked.

"Yeah, we talked about a lot of stuff." *We still do*, Danielle added silently.

"I miss her. She would have loved to help us plan the wedding. Of course, she'd probably be upset to learn we wouldn't be giving her any great-grandchildren."

"I think your grandma only wanted you to be happy. She would get used to the idea you and Mel don't want children." *I think she already has*, Danielle thought.

Ten minutes later, Adam sat at the kitchen table with Walt and Danielle, drinking coffee and sharing an Old Salts cinnamon roll.

"You probably shouldn't eat that thing, being pregnant and all," Adam said, eyeing Danielle's share of the cinnamon roll.

"I wouldn't try taking it from her," Walt warned. "She might break your arm."

Adam chuckled and flashed Danielle a wink.

"Are you going to try getting the listing for Pearl's house?" Danielle asked. "Is that why you're going over there?"

"Do you know if they're planning to sell?" Adam asked.

Danielle shrugged. "I don't even know who it belongs to now. Do you?"

Adam shook his head. "No, I haven't heard. But I figure whoever inherits the property, chances are they will end up selling it or putting it in the rental market. I can help with either. It would be nice to check out its current condition."

"What's happening to Rachel's property?" Danielle asked.

"According to Mel, it has to go through probate, which she says will take at least four months. The Hodges aren't thrilled," Adam explained.

"Any idea what they want to do with the property?" Walt asked.

"He wants to sell. I went to talk to him about it, but he made it clear he intends to do an FSBO. Typical," Adam said.

"What's an FSBO?" Walt asked.

Adam turned to Walt. "Wow, when you lost your memory, you even forgot what you knew as a Realtor. I didn't realize it worked like that. What else did you forget?"

"That's the thing about forgetting something; you never know what you forgot," Walt reminded him.

Adam shrugged. "True."

Danielle looked at Walt and said, "FSBO is an acronym for 'For Sale By Owner.'"

"I talked to Herman, who's the executor. He's a little annoyed

Rachel wouldn't set up a trust to avoid probate, but she didn't want to spend the money," Adam said.

"I guess with Rachel gone, Mel will get a B and B across the street," Danielle said.

"It looks that way." Adam sipped his coffee and then grinned at Walt and Danielle.

"What?" Danielle asked.

"Mel's agreed to let me list her house. I'm going to list mine too. We want to buy something together," Adam explained.

Danielle smiled. "That's great. But if you sell both your houses without finding something first, you might be homeless."

"We'll figure out the logistics of it all before listing. I asked Mel what she wanted, and she said something like Chris's or Ian's."

"You mean beachfront?" Walt asked.

"Yeah. Shoulda kept Grandma's house," Adam said. "Actually, Mel would love to be on this street. With or without an ocean view."

"Didn't you hear, our street is cursed?" Danielle said. "That's what June Bartley told Ian and Lily. She wants them to buy a house on their street."

Adam laughed. "Yeah, right. I still get nightmares about the property I sold them."

"Whatever was going on there, I think the spirits moved on," Danielle promised.

"I hope you're right," Adam said.

"If Mel really does like Beach Drive, there is always Pearl's house," Danielle reminded him.

"You mean the house with dead bodies in the backyard?" Adam asked.

"They're gone now," Danielle said. "And isn't that why you're here? To check out Pearl's house?"

"Sure, but as a listing. Not to move into myself," Adam said.

Walt chuckled.

"Oh, I have been meaning to ask; you guys considering reopening Marlow House as a B and B? With Pearl gone, you probably can," Adam asked.

"We were just discussing that the other day," Walt said.

"If we did, it would be only part time," Danielle said. "Walt was telling me you and Chris told him it would be a good tax write-off."

"It's definitely something to check out with your accountant," Adam said.

"We might," Danielle said.

"Are you still thinking about moving into the bedroom on the second floor if you decide to reopen?"

"Yes. Because it would be on a smaller scale. Even with the nursery, there will be two bedrooms to rent out," Danielle said.

"Did you ever find someone to paint the bedroom?" Adam asked.

Walt and Danielle exchanged quick glances before Danielle said, "Yeah. In fact, it's done. We're going to move in this weekend when Joanne gets back."

"Back from where?" Adam asked.

"She's on a trip with a couple of her friends."

"Can I see the room? Want to see how good a housepainter you are," Adam said.

"I'm a horrible painter. And we don't know if Walt can paint or not."

"Because he forgot?" Adam asked at the same time Walt said, "Because I forgot."

"WOW, this looks great. So who did you get to do it? I know it wasn't Bill," Adam said, checking out the trim.

"Oh, they aren't from around here," Danielle said.

"I remember Bill told me Lily got someone named Marie to paint Connor's nursery. That always struck me as so funny. Did you know my grandma could paint?" Adam asked. "I'm not talking about painting pictures, house painting."

"Umm… yes. She mentioned something to me about it once," Danielle said.

Adam looked at Walt and said, "You never met Grandma. She was a character. Always my champion, even when I didn't deserve it."

"You were a good grandson," Danielle told him.

Adam looked around the room and said, "Whoever painted this, they knew what they were doing. Back when Grandma was still getting around well, I used to tease her about putting her to work, painting my rental houses. She said I couldn't afford her." Adam laughed at the memory.

"She sounds like someone I'd like," Walt said.

Adam smiled. "I should probably get going. I wanted to go next door, look around. You don't have a key, do you?"

Danielle arched a brow. "Seriously? Like Pearl would give us a key."

Adam shrugged. "It was worth a shot. Think she left a key under a rock somewhere?"

"Aren't you afraid of getting shot?" Danielle teased.

"If Pearl were still alive, yeah. I could see her shooting me if I stepped on her property," Adam said.

"I'll go with you; maybe a door is unlocked," Walt suggested.

"Okay, guys, while you're snooping over there, try not to get shot," Danielle said.

WHILE WALT WASN'T afraid Adam would get shot while snooping around Pearl's house, he wasn't sure what might happen if he ran into her spirit, considering she had managed to harness energy. The two men started down the street to Pearl's.

"I'm curious to see what the inside looks like now. Think we might find a key?" Adam asked.

"You never know," Walt said, thinking he would simply use his telekinesis to unlock a door.

"No one has come over to check out the house? Someone connected to Pearl's estate? Someone from her family?" Adam asked.

"I haven't seen anyone over there." Walt had been tempted to ask Pearl who would inherit the house. But it seemed too soon to broach the subject, considering her death had not been a natural one.

Walt's cellphone rang right before they reached Pearl's front gate. He paused, took the phone out of his pocket, and looked at it. "It's Danielle," he said with a frown.

"Dang, you haven't even been gone five minutes," Adam teased.

"Hello?" Walt answered the call.

"Just wanted to let you know, I just talked to Heather, and Pearl is there, driving her nuts. I told Heather Adam wanted to check the house out and you were taking him over, and I asked if she could keep Pearl at her place."

"What did she say?" Walt asked.

"Her exact words, 'No problem. I think she's my new roommate.'"

"Everything okay?" Adam asked when Walt got off the phone.

"Danielle reminded me that when they found Pearl, Brian mentioned the lock on her back door didn't always catch. If we're lucky, we can get in that way." Not only had Danielle not told Walt that, Pearl had mentioned the faulty lock to Walt, it wasn't something Brian had mentioned.

When they reached the kitchen door, Walt focused his energy on the lock, just in case the police had secured the door after removing Pearl's body. He then reached out and tested the doorknob. It turned.

"It's unlocked?" Adam asked hopefully.

"Yes," Walt said with a grin, pushing the door open.

A moment later, both men stepped into the house. When they did, they heard a crashing noise from upstairs. They froze and looked at each other.

"Someone is here," Adam whispered.

Footsteps ran overhead on the second floor.

"Sounds that way. Perhaps we should leave?" Walt suggested.

Adam nodded, and both men quickly backed out the door. Once outside, they glanced up at the second floor and spied a shadow run across the window.

"I THINK you scared them off before they got anything," Brian said when he and Joe stepped out of Pearl's house after walking through it. "Looks like they were going through the drawers in her bedroom when you interrupted them."

"They jumped out a back window," Walt said. "I think they saw us when we stepped back outside. They were parked in the alley, but I didn't see their car. We just heard it race off."

"What were you doing in the house?" Joe asked.

"I just came over to look around, in case the new owners wanted to sell," Adam said.

"You always break in houses to do that?" Joe asked. "I didn't know Realtors just let themselves in stranger's houses uninvited."

"That's not what happened," Walt interrupted. "I walked over here with Adam. We had no intention of going inside. But I noticed the door was open. I figured you guys didn't lock up when you were here," Walt lied. "I started to close the door, and that's when we heard something upstairs."

"But you just said they saw you when you stepped back outside," Joe reminded him.

"When Walt realized the door was unlocked, we felt we needed to make sure everything was okay," Adam said. "It's a good thing we did, or they might have ransacked the entire house."

TWENTY-EIGHT

"Someone broke into my house?" Pearl said after Walt told her what had happened. Adam had left thirty minutes earlier, not long after Brian and Joe. Before going to Heather's, Walt had gone home to get Danielle to go with him.

"If you would have stayed home, this wouldn't have happened," Heather said.

Pearl frowned at Heather. "How would my being home have prevented a break-in?"

"You've learned to harness your energy," Heather reminded her. "I doubt burglars could have gotten up the stairs with you there."

Danielle groaned. "Please don't encourage her, Heather. We don't need another haunted house in Frederickport, and certainly not on Beach Drive."

"Haunted house?" Pearl perked up. "Oh, it is almost Halloween. I've never been much for Halloween or haunted houses before, but I've never been a ghost before. Interesting…"

Danielle groaned again and plopped down on a chair in Heather's living room.

With a shrug, Heather took a seat next to Danielle and said, "Well, it beats her hanging out here."

"I'm not hanging out," Pearl said, sitting down on the sofa. "But I need to find out who killed Rachel and me. And unfortunately for both of us, you are one of the few people I can communicate with, and your boyfriend is investigating my case. I need you to communicate with him. I wonder if the killer is whoever broke in."

"Both Brian and Joe don't feel it's connected to the murder. People heard you've died, lived alone, and no one's staying at your house, but your stuff's still in it," Danielle said. "An easy mark for burglars. Especially since no one's been at your house since we found you."

"Speaking of which," Walt began, taking a seat next to Danielle. "Who inherits your house?"

Pearl frowned at Walt. "That's not really any of your business."

"If you want the police to capture your killer, it might help if you told us who benefited financially from your death," Danielle said.

Pearl scoffed. "My death is connected to Rachel's. It has nothing to do with who inherits my property. If Andy didn't push me, then Ruby or Sam did. Rachel was stopping their little B and B venture. And after they got rid of her, they realized I would be a problem."

"Yeah, because you threw such a fit at the funeral. Perhaps you'd still be alive if you weren't such a b—" Heather began, only to be cut off by Danielle.

"Okay, Heather," Danielle interrupted. "I don't think it was Sam or Ruby. They didn't have enough motive. They had other plans for the property if the B and B didn't work out."

"Then it was Larry Hodge. He understood that with me still alive, he wouldn't be able to push his wife around," Pearl said.

"What do you mean?" Heather asked.

"Leanne is a sweet woman, but her husband easily manipulates her. She might bend to her husband's will instead of carrying out Rachel's wishes. If I were around, I would have helped her stand up to that no-good husband of hers."

"Rachel's wishes?" Danielle asked.

"I've said enough." Pearl stood. "I respect Rachel's privacy. This is none of your business, but if Leanne isn't able to do the right thing, then we'll know who killed us. Larry Hodge." With that, Pearl left.

"What is she talking about?" Danielle asked.

"I have no idea. But I hope she doesn't come back," Heather said.

"One more thing," Pearl said when she suddenly reappeared.

Heather groaned and slumped back in her chair.

"I'm going to Rachel's. I want to make sure no one has burgled her house." Pearl vanished again.

PEARL MOVED through Rachel's front door, into the entry hall. She stood there a moment, listening to the steady ticking of the wall clock.

"Rachel, are you here?" she called out, momentarily hoping Heather had been wrong and her friend's spirit hadn't yet traveled on in her journey. She needed to talk to her. When there was no response, Pearl moved through the house. She came first to Rachel's sewing room. Instead of trying to use her energy to open its door, Pearl stepped through it. Once inside the room, she looked around and thought how it all belonged to her now—technically. Pearl wondered what would happen to all Rachel's quilting supplies. Would they go to Pearl's estate and then be sold?

With a sigh, Pearl continued through the house. Nothing had been disturbed. It looked like the last time Pearl had come to the house, hoping to find her friend's spirit, but instead, she'd found a ghost child.

When Pearl arrived in Rachel's study, she spied the photo albums on a shelf. Rachel had shown them to Pearl once, sharing the pictures of her beloved daughters and husband. Pearl smiled, thinking her friend was probably with them now. Moving closer to the shelf with the albums, Pearl wondered if her energy could move one of the books—perhaps open it?

She focused on one album, not sure how this all worked. The next moment, the album flew from the shelf, in the same way Joe Morelli's plate had flown from the table in the diner. And like the plate, the album landed on the floor.

"Oh my," Pearl stammered, afraid she might have damaged the book. It landed open on the floor with photographs scattering from its pages. Pearl leaned down to try using her energy to gather up the fallen photos, put them back in the book, and return it to the shelf. But when she got closer to the photographs, her gaze fell on one of a little girl with blond curls. The same little girl she had seen with the golden Lab. A little girl ghost.

Pearl let out a gasp—she remembered. Focusing her energy on the photographs scattered on the floor, they moved several inches to the right and then the left, allowing her to see more of each one. One was a black-and-white picture of a large dog. Along the white border on the picture, someone had written in ink, *Charger*.

With a sigh, Pearl stood and refocused her energy. But as much as she tried, she seemed unable to convince the photographs to return to the album, or for the album to return to the shelf. Each time she tried moving the album, thinking she would then focus her energy on the photos, another album fell from the shelf, until there were a dozen photo albums scattered along the floor at the base of the bookshelf.

"Oh my," Pearl muttered. "Rachel would not be happy. I need to get someone to help me put this right. But first…"

"I KNOW WHO SHE IS!" Pearl shouted when she barged back into Heather's living room, making its occupants—Heather, Walt, and Danielle—jump in surprise.

"Dang, Pearl, you scared the crap outa me!" Heather grumbled.

"You have to stop making entrances like that," Danielle said.

Pearl winced. "Oh, I'm sorry. I forgot you're pregnant."

"I'm not pregnant, and I don't like it either," Heather snapped.

"But I know who she is!" Pearl repeated.

"What are you talking about?" Walt asked.

"The little girl ghost," Pearl said, turning to Walt. "I told you I recognized her. Now I remember why. Rachel once showed me her picture. It's her daughter. The youngest one, the one who died of measles."

"Are you sure?" Heather asked. "If she died of measles, then why didn't her spirit have any rash?"

"She died a long time ago," Danielle reminded her. "Which makes her more adept at managing her image. And how we see ourselves is not always how others see us."

"And the dog," Pearl continued. "It told me its name was Charger. I found a photograph at Rachel's, it's of the dog, and someone wrote Charger on the picture. That's the ghost dog."

"So the spirit of one of Rachel's daughters never moved on?" Danielle asked.

"Oh no!" Pearl sat down in a chair, looking dejected. "Rachel moved on without her. How does that work? She so missed her girls.

I assumed now, now she'd finally be with them. But if we saw the girl…"

"It's possible she moved on after the last time any of us saw her," Heather suggested.

Leaning back on the sofa, Walt shook his head. "I don't think so."

They all turned to Walt, noting his thoughtful expression.

"Why do you say that?" Danielle asked.

"The first time we saw them—well, we didn't see the girl; we just saw the dog. That was before Rachel's death. According to Evan, the girl and dog were playing. How Evan described her, she was happy, even mischievous. But the other times we saw her, she appeared lost and looking for something—or someone."

"When we saw her at the beach, she was calling out, but we couldn't hear what she was saying," Danielle said.

Walt looked at Danielle. "Was she calling for her mother?"

"Are you suggesting Rachel's youngest, her spirit stuck around all these years with her mother, and then, when her mother died, she didn't know it? And Rachel left without her?" Heather asked.

"It's possible," Walt said. "It's obvious the child sometimes left her mother to play with her dog."

"The girl told me she was looking for me," Pearl said. "I remember now. I don't understand why she was looking for me."

"Her spirit could have been with her mother when you and Rachel visited," Danielle suggested. "She saw you as her mother's friend. And then when she couldn't find her mother, she went to your house, wanting to see if she was with you."

"Oh no," Pearl moaned. "I told her the woman who lived at Rachel's house was murdered. But I didn't understand she was Rachel's daughter at the time. Is it possible the poor child thought her mother was still alive, and I went and told her she was murdered?"

"I wonder what else she might have seen," Walt mused.

"What do you mean?" Heather asked.

"I can understand a child who passes young staying with its mother instead of moving on," Walt began. "And if that child's pet stays with the child when it dies, instead of moving on, I imagine they would play together, as they did in life."

"We know they did," Danielle said. "Evan saw them. We saw the dog."

"So when the child and pet are off playing, they may not be there when the mother dies or moves on," Walt said.

"Rachel left with her body to go to the morgue," Heather said. "So if that's when her daughter came home after playing with her dog, Rachel wouldn't be there."

"Correct," Walt said with a nod. "And if Rachel returned to the house before moving on, it might have been a time when the daughter was out looking for her."

"This is horrible," Pearl moaned.

"But what did you mean? What else she might have seen?" Danielle asked Walt.

"The chief speculates the killer might have tampered with Rachel's melatonin capsules. It's possible the daughter witnessed this. Maybe she doesn't even realize what she saw," Walt explained.

TWENTY-NINE

"I can't believe you broke into Pearl Huckabee's house," Melony told Adam Thursday afternoon. They sat in her kitchen, having a cup of coffee and a slice of double fudge chocolate cake from Old Salts Bakery. "Oh, what am I saying? Of course I can."

"We didn't break in exactly," Adam said. "And Walt's the one who opened the door. I just followed him inside."

Melony shook her head and speared another bite of cake with her fork. "Someday you're going to land yourself in jail."

"Been there, done that," Adam reminded her. "But now you know the real reason I'm marrying one of the best criminal attorneys in the Pacific Northwest."

Melony rolled her eyes. "You're incorrigible."

Adam shrugged and took another bite of cake.

"By the way, I heard they're having Pearl's funeral on Saturday," Melony said. "At the church. She'll be buried next to her grandmother at the local cemetery."

"Wasn't she married?" Adam asked.

"I guess so. She wanted to be called Mrs. Huckabee," Melony said.

"I wonder why she's not being buried near her husband. Who told you about the funeral?" Adam asked.

"Millie Samson called me. Pearl went to her church." Melony picked up her cup of coffee and took a sip.

"Millie didn't say what was going to happen to her house, did she?"

"I asked her. She didn't know who Pearl left the house to. I guess Pearl made funeral arrangements with Paster Chad and the funeral home a while back. So it's not her executor making the final arrangements, like in Rachel's case."

"Hey, Mel," Adam asked in a quiet voice.

Melony looked up at Adam. "What?"

"Do you ever regret not having a funeral for your mom?"

"She didn't want one," Melony reminded him.

"True. But they say funerals are for the living, not the dead."

"Some people see funerals as a closure," Melony said. "But with the issues I had with my parents, I wasn't about to get closure at a funeral. It was more complicated than that."

Adam nodded. "We both kinda got shortchanged in the parent department."

"At least you had your grandma," Melony reminded him.

Adam smiled. "Yeah. I always wondered how Dad turned out like he did with a mom like Grandma. But then I remembered his dad and figured it takes just one parent to screw up a kid."

Melony chuckled. "Well, we won't have that problem."

"You think you'll change your mind?"

Melony shook her head and smiled at Adam before saying, "Hey, I already have you. One kid is enough for me."

Adam laughed, leaned across the table, and dropped a kiss on Melony's lips.

HERMAN SHAFER PULLED his car into Rachel's driveway, parked, and turned off the ignition. He sat in his vehicle a moment, looking at Rachel's house, not in a hurry to go inside. An hour earlier, Police Chief MacDonald had called to tell him someone had broken into Pearl Huckabee's house. They suspected it was someone targeting empty houses—specifically the empty house of someone who had recently died. If Rachel had simply put her house into a trust, the property would have already passed to Leanne Hodge, and it would be her problem now, not his.

Grumbling, Herman opened the car door, grabbed his cane from the passenger seat, and climbed out of the vehicle. Determined, he hobbled up to the front door and, with the key Rachel had given him, let himself in. He didn't expect to find anything amiss, but he felt it his duty to check out the house. Everything looked fine until he got to the study and found the photo albums strewn all over the floor. He froze.

He needed to call the police, but he had no intention of doing it while standing in the house. For all he knew, the robbers could still be inside. With haste, Herman left the house. Instead of going to his car, he headed next door to Melony Carmichael's house. Her car was in the driveway, as was Adam Nichols'.

"HERMAN, HI," Melony greeted him in surprise when she opened the front door.

"Someone broke into Rachel's house; I need to call the police. Can I come in?"

"Certainly," Melony said, opening the door wider and glancing to the house next door. Melony assumed Herman wanted to use her phone, but after he walked in and she closed the door behind her, he pulled out his cellphone.

"I'll be in the kitchen," Melony whispered to Herman, leaving him alone to make the call.

"Who's here?" Adam asked when Melony walked into the kitchen.

"Herman Shafer. Umm… you didn't break into Rachel's house too, did you?"

"YOU READY TO COME BACK TO the office on Monday?" Chris asked Heather when she opened the door for him late Thursday afternoon. "They finally finished with the electrical in your office."

"Yes! I never thought I would be so happy to leave this house and get back to the office!" Heather said as Chris walked inside. A few minutes later, he stood in the kitchen with Heather, helping himself to a slice of her homemade sourdough bread.

"I take it Pearl has been hanging around?" Chris asked as he slathered soft butter on his slice of bread.

"I swear she's taken up residence here. Hopefully she won't follow me over to the office, considering all the people there."

"How are she and Bella getting along? Have they been having long chats, working out their differences?" Chris asked, only half teasing.

"Bella has been hiding in my bedroom ever since Pearl showed up. She's not a fan."

Chris glanced around. "Pearl's not here now, is she?" He took a bite of bread.

Heather told Chris about her day while the two sat at her kitchen table.

"Sounds like you didn't get a lot done for the foundation, working at home today." He took another bite of bread.

"Blame Pearl." Heather reached over and tried to snag a hunk of Chris's bread.

He pulled it out of her reach. "Get your own."

Heather started to do just that, but her cellphone rang. She sat back down at the table and picked up her phone. "It's Brian," she whispered before taking the call.

"It's Brian," Chris repeated in a snotty middle school mocking sort of way.

Heather ignored him and answered the call.

Chris silently finished the piece of bread while listening to Heather's side of the conversation. Finally, she said, "Umm, Brian, I don't think Rachel's house was broken into. That was Pearl."

Chris looked up at Heather and arched his brows. A few minutes later, after she was off the phone, she said, "Herman Shafer called the police to Rachel's house. They thought someone had broken in. They found the albums on the floor."

Chris chuckled. Heather had already told Chris about the pictures Pearl had found, and how she could not put the albums back on the shelves.

"I thought that might be a problem," Chris said, "when you told me she knocked them down but couldn't put them back."

"Pearl is turning out to be a bull-in-a-china-cabinet sort of ghost," Heather said, tossing her cellphone back on the kitchen table.

"Poor Herman and most of the police department think someone broke into the house," Chris said.

"At least the chief and Brian know the truth." Heather shrugged and added, "Well… the chief will after Brian tells him."

"Who do you think broke into Pearl's? Doesn't thrill me having burglaries on our street," Chris said.

"Why, is that worse than one of our neighbors getting murdered in the middle of the night?" Heather asked.

Chris let out a sigh. "You have a point."

"Brian doesn't think Pearl's break-in had anything to do with her murder. Unless she's holding back, and she's really a diamond smuggler who double-crossed her partners and now they're coming back for their loot."

Chris stared at Heather a moment and then shook his head. "You're a weirdo. You know that?"

IT TOOK little for Melony to convince Adam to spend the rest of the afternoon with her. He didn't have any appointments, and Leslie was at the office.

"I really don't think you have anything to worry about," Adam said as Melony peeked out her window, spying on Rachel's house. "It was probably teenagers screwing around. What self-respecting house burglar starts with the family albums?"

"It just kinda creeps me out. I could have been here when whoever it was broke in next door, and wasn't even aware what was going on. I could have gone out to get my mail, seen something they didn't want me to see, and then I'm the target."

"Hello? What did you do with my Mel?" Adam called out. He sat on a recliner in the living room, watching Melony, who continued to stand by the window, hiding behind the curtains from the outside world while peeking out.

She turned to him. "What?"

"Seriously, Mel, you used to live in New York. And now you're freaking out in Frederickport?"

"I expect stuff like that to happen in New York. But police think someone killed my ninety-five-year-old neighbor, and now her house is being broken into."

Melony turned away from Adam and looked back out the window. "Adam! Someone is lurking over at Rachel's."

Adam frowned. "What do you mean, lurking?"

"Someone is out there, all dressed in black. Black pants, black hoodie, and they are going up the walk to her front door."

Adam laughed. "So? Maybe it's someone selling magazine subscriptions. Really, Mel, calm down."

Ignoring Adam, and still peering out the window at her neighbor's, she gasped, "They're going inside! They're inside!"

Adam pushed the recliner footstool down, sat up straight, and put his feet on the floor. "What do you mean, they're inside?"

Melony turned to Adam and frowned. "What is there about that sentence you don't comprehend?"

"How did they get into the house? Climb through the window, down the chimney, what?"

Melony rolled her eyes and turned back to the window. "The front door."

Adam stood up from the chair. "What kind of car are they driving?"

"They didn't come in a car. I noticed them walking up the street, all lurker-like, with their head down and hands in their pockets."

"Well, in all fairness, it is cold out."

"I think we should call the police," Melony said.

HERMAN SHAFER MET THE POLICE, but he didn't park in Rachel's driveway. He pulled up in Melony's. He gave Brian the key to Rachel's house and stayed with Melony and Adam while Brian and Joe headed next door to investigate what Melony had claimed to see.

Cautiously, Brian entered first, followed by Joe. The house was quiet, with no lights on, yet there was enough afternoon sunlight streaming in the windows to illuminate the room. They started toward the hallway when they heard something coming from behind one of the closed doors. A toilet flushed. Both officers stopped and looked at each other.

"Our intruder is using the bathroom?" Joe whispered.

The next moment, a door swung open, and a person clad in dark pants and a black hoody stepped out into the hall. Unable to see who it was in the dim lighting, Joe called out, "This is the police; stay where you are and put your hands in the air."

The person froze and then immediately complied.

"This is my house," came the timid voice.

LEANNE HODGE STOOD in the kitchen of Rachel's house with Brian Henderson, Joe Morelli, and Herman Shafer.

"I told you, it is not your house until it goes through probate," Herman said after Leanne repeated what she had said to the police.

"I just wanted to check on it. I didn't think there would be a problem. I have a key," Leanne said.

"Where is your car?" Brian asked.

"Umm, I walked over. We only have one car, and Larry had taken it to go to the hardware store. I just wanted to check and make sure everything was okay."

THIRTY

The friends on Beach Drive held an impromptu potluck at Marlow House on Thursday evening. Lily made macaroni and cheese in her Instant Pot, and Ian picked up a bottle of wine. Heather brought over two loaves of homemade sourdough bread, along with Brian, who picked up a case of beer. Danielle baked brownies and a giant chocolate chip cookie in her cast-iron skillet. Walt and Chris picked up ribs and chicken from a new restaurant in town, along with a selection of salads.

They arranged the food on the buffet in the dining room, along with paper plates, napkins, silverware, and pitchers of lemonade and iced water. Walt insisted on serving Danielle, who he claimed had been on her feet too long baking her brownies and cookie. She didn't argue. She figured she'd enjoy the spoiling while it lasted.

Connor sat in his highchair next to Danielle, eating macaroni and cheese, while all the others filled their plates and came to the table.

"Do we have any ghosts here?" Lily asked as she took a seat next to her son.

"Nope," Danielle said. "Pearl is off with Marie and Eva, looking for Rachel's daughter."

"That entire thing is so weird," Lily said as she gingerly picked up a rib with her fingers and inspected it before putting it on her plate.

"Something wrong with the rib?" Chris asked from across the table, food piled high on his plate.

Lily shrugged. "Just checking it out. It's from that new place, right?"

"Yeah. Walt and I thought their food looked pretty good," Chris said.

Lily picked the rib back up, gave it a little sniff and then took a nibble. Chris chuckled and then scooped up a spoonful of mac and cheese. He primly gave it a sniff and then barely scraped his teeth over the end of the spoon as if hesitantly sampling the mac and cheese.

Lily scowled at Chris. "Stop being a jerk."

Chris laughed and shoved the spoonful of mac and cheese in his mouth.

Heather looked over at Chris and shook her head. "And he wonders why he can't get a girl, even with all his money and stupid good looks."

Chris frowned at Heather. "There is a compliment in there… somewhere."

"What I was saying, before someone so rudely mocked me," Lily said while flashing a grin at Chris, "Do you think Rachel's daughter is still here? She was for a while after her mother died, but when Pearl told her Rachel was dead, wouldn't she have moved on to be with her mom?"

"The only problem with that, we all saw the little girl after Pearl told her about her mother. The child seemed to be looking for Rachel," Danielle explained. "After talking with Eva when they first met, and Eva explained things to Pearl, well, I think Pearl is worried Rachel's daughter might get trapped on this plane, and then Rachel might never see her again."

"Is that possible?" Brian asked.

Danielle shrugged. "I'm not sure."

Brian's cellphone rang. He stood and took it out into the hallway to answer the call. When Brian returned to the room a few minutes later, he said, "It seems they have a lead on whoever broke into Pearl's house."

"What kind of lead?" Heather asked.

"One of your neighbors saw a car parked behind Pearl's house and took a picture of it with her phone. She read in the paper Pearl had died and wasn't sure the car should be there. It was around the time of the break-in."

"Does this mean you know who the person was?" Heather said.

Brian looked at Heather for a moment and said, "If I did, I couldn't tell you." He grinned.

Heather narrowed her eyes, glaring at Brian. "The next time you want me to go to the morgue with you to talk to a spirit, ask someone else."

Brian let out a sigh and said, "I don't know who it is yet."

Heather grinned. "That's what I thought."

Thirty minutes later, after the friends finished dinner, Walt and Danielle took them upstairs so they could see Marie's handiwork.

"I like the new color," Chris said. "Marie did a great job."

"I'm not even going to say how strange this all is," Brian murmured, walking around the room.

"You kinda just did," Heather said.

Brian gave a shrug and added, "But she does good work."

"When are you guys moving into the room?" Lily asked.

"Before Joanne gets back, Walt's moving all our things in here," Danielle began.

"Yeah, and I bet it will be a lot easier than when I had to move my parents' furniture," Ian grumbled.

"I offered to help," Walt reminded him.

"And Joanne will organize and put everything away. Walt says he doesn't want me doing any manual labor," Danielle said.

"It might be worth getting pregnant to get spoiled like that," Heather said with a sigh. "Almost."

Walt wrapped an arm around Danielle and pulled her closer to him, kissing the top of her head.

While the others walked around the room, commenting on Marie's work and asking Danielle how she planned to decorate the room, Lily wandered over to the window overlooking the side yard. Looking outside, her gaze drifted to Pearl's house. She noticed a light going on in one upstairs bedroom.

"Umm, Danielle, does Pearl's harnessing energy powers extend to turning on lights?" Lily asked.

"It's possible," Danielle said. "Why?"

"Because either Pearl's gotten home and is turning on lights over at her house, or our burglar is back."

They all moved to the side window and looked toward Pearl's house.

"I don't think it's Pearl," Brian said.

"Why do you say that?" Heather asked.

"Because I see someone over there," Brian said.

The next moment, Brian pulled his phone out of his pocket and made a call.

IAN, Walt, and Chris followed Brian over to Pearl's house. By the time they got there, Joe, who was covering for a fellow officer on vacation, pulled up in the squad car and parked behind another car in front of Pearl's house.

"That car wasn't there when we walked over to Marlow House," Ian noted. The five men stood on the sidewalk outside Pearl's front gate.

"If it belongs to whoever is in the house, they aren't trying to be inconspicuous," Brian noted.

"I recognize that car," Chris told Walt and Ian after Brian and Joe walked through Pearl's gate and were out of earshot. The three residents of Beach Drive stood on the sidewalk, waiting.

"DID you get the name of who broke in earlier?" Brian asked Joe in a whisper as they walked up to Pearl's front door.

"Yes, but whoever's inside can't be Andy Delarosa. He's down at the station right now in holding," Joe told Brian.

Brian paused at the front door and looked at Joe. "Delarosa?"

"That's whose car was in the picture."

They didn't need to try the door. Whoever had entered the house had left it ajar. Joe entered first. They could see lights on in the entry and living room. They knew someone was in the kitchen. Whoever had broken in whistled a tune.

Joe and Brian paused a moment and exchanged frowns. "What do we have, the whistling bandit?" Brian asked in a whisper.

They didn't continue to the kitchen. The next minute, whoever had been whistling stepped out into the living room. The man, in his fifties wearing gray slacks and a dark blue down puffer jacket over a white shirt, froze in his tracks and stopped whistling when he saw he was not alone. When his glance moved to Joe, who wore a police uniform, the man visibly relaxed and flashed the two officers a smile.

"Dang, you about gave me a heart attack," the man said.

"What are you doing here?" Joe asked.

The man glanced around the room before looking back at Joe and said with a smile, "In a way, I'm the new owner." He stepped to Joe and extended his hand. "I'm Brandon Purnell."

"BRANDON, I thought that was your car," Chris said when Joe and Brian walked outside with the man they had found in Pearl's house.

"Chris, I remember you said you lived on this street." Brandon walked to Chris, who now stood inside Pearl's gate, and shook his hand while Brian and Joe trailed behind him.

"What are you doing in Pearl's house?" Chris asked.

"It looks like this is your new neighbor," Joe explained.

Chris frowned at Brandon, who gave him a smile. "I won't be moving in," Brandon explained. "But Pearl Huckabee left her estate to our foundation."

"What foundation is that?" Walt asked, wondering for a moment if Brandon worked for Chris, yet finding it hard to imagine Pearl leaving anything to the Glandon Foundation.

Chris introduced Walt and Ian to Brandon and then said, "Brandon founded a dog and cat rescue organization, which the Glandon Foundation has partnered with on many occasions."

"That's actually how I met Pearl," Brandon explained. The other five men gathered around him, listening. "Pearl attended the Pit Bull Rescue Adoption Event we had in Portland. She told me pit bulls always terrified her, but that one saved her life once, and she realized she had misjudged the breed. After that, she was a regular donor, but always insisted she did not want any public acknowledgment. She was a private person."

"And she left your foundation her estate?" Ian asked.

Brandon nodded. "She set up a trust, asked me to be the trustee, and gave me a key to her house. I'd been in Colorado attending a wedding. When I got back, I heard she had died, and I thought I'd better get over here and check on her house. It's not wise to let a house sit unattended after someone has passed." He looked to Joe, smiled and then added, "But fortunately the Frederickport police are on top of things. I hadn't been in the house fifteen minutes when they were ready to arrest me." He laughed.

"There was already a break-in," Chris said.

Brandon nodded. "Yes, they told me. But I understand they've apprehended the culprit. So once again, the local police are on top of things." Brandon grinned.

"Unfortunately, Pearl's death may not have been an accident," Brian said.

Brandon frowned. "What do you mean? I thought she fell down the stairs during the night. That's what I read in the newspaper."

"Perhaps you could come down to the station tomorrow? I'm sure the chief would like to talk to you," Brian said.

THIRTY-ONE

After Joe finished with Brandon, he said his goodbyes and drove off. Brian offered to help Brandon finish checking out the house and lock up. He accepted the offer, and Chris, Ian, and Walt joined them.

Brandon cleaned out Pearl's refrigerator and medicine cabinets, and Ian helped gather up all the household garbage while Chris checked the bathrooms and flushed the toilets. Brian checked to see if all the windows and doors were locked, and Walt offered to take the trash out. Before preparing to leave, Brandon gathered up all Pearl's mail and put it in a drawer. "I'll come back later and deal with that," he said.

All the men went outside, and Brandon used his key to lock the front deadbolt while Chris asked, "When did you get back from Colorado?"

"About thirty minutes before I came over here. I got home and started going through my mail and noticed the article about Pearl in the newspaper. I can't believe it might have been a homicide." Brandon shook his head.

"They think it may be connected to the murder of her friend," Chris said.

"That's what Officer Morelli told me," Brandon said right before his stomach grumbled.

"Is it trying to tell you something?" Chris teased.

"I haven't had anything to eat since I left Colorado. I planned to stop and get something after I checked out Pearl's house. I needed to make sure everything was alright."

"If you haven't had anything to eat and are hungry," Walt offered, "come back to Marlow House with us. We have a ton of food left over."

"Oh, I don't want to impose," Brandon said.

"Ah, come on. I was planning to have seconds myself," Chris said. "Don't make me eat alone."

"Come," Ian urged.

Brandon smiled. "I have always wanted to see inside Marlow House. My sister was really sorry when it closed. She'd planned to stay there the next time she came to town."

"Maybe she still can," Walt said. "Danielle and I are considering reopening."

"You are?" Brian asked.

Walt shrugged. "Thinking about it."

They chatted briefly about the bed-and-breakfast as they headed toward Marlow House, but then Chris said something about Ian's pen name being Jon Altar, to which Brandon claimed he was a big fan. Chris, Brandon, and Ian chatted while Brian and Walt trailed some distance behind them on their way back to Marlow House.

"You know," Brian said in a whisper, "you and Danielle reopening the B and B might put you on the suspect list."

Walt glanced over to Brian and arched a brow, flashing him a smirk-like grin. "Ahh, and I could have used my telekinesis to push her down the stairs without even being there."

Brian frowned. "How?"

"From one of the upstairs windows at Marlow House," Walt suggested. "Like tonight, I could have given Brandon a shove when you saw him."

"He wasn't on the stairs," Brian reminded him.

Walt shrugged. "Minor details."

"You think you could move something from that far away?" Brian asked.

"I have no idea."

Brian let out a sigh. "But I can't figure out a motive for Rachel Moore."

"Meh, maybe I'm just a homicidal maniac," Walt suggested.

Brian laughed and then said, his tone now serious, "There was a time I might have put you and Danielle on the suspect list."

"And now?" Walt asked.

"Like Heather always tells me, the last thing a medium wants to do is bump off someone they dislike. She tells me I don't have to worry; she'd never pull a Bev Klein."

Walt chuckled and said, "She has a good point."

BRANDON HAD ALREADY BEEN INTRODUCED to the rest of the dinner party and had taken a seat at the table with a plate of food, while others joined them, either having seconds or dessert, when Pearl suddenly appeared.

"Oh," Pearl said in surprise. "Brandon Purnell is here."

The mediums glanced over to Pearl, who stood at the head of the table—actually, she stood in the head of the table; the tabletop, giving the illusion of cutting her body in half.

With her gaze meeting Pearl's, Heather said to Brandon, "I still can't get over the fact Pearl left her estate to your organization. I remember a time she demanded poor Hunny be arrested."

Upon hearing her name, Hunny, who had been napping in the corner with Sadie, lifted her head and looked toward the table.

Pearl looked at Hunny and said in a childlike voice, "Oh, don't listen to what that naughty girl is saying. Who is my Hunny bunny?"

Hunny, who hadn't understood what Heather had said other than recognizing her name, looked to Pearl and wagged her tail, but didn't get up. Heather suppressed an eye roll at Pearl's baby talk.

Brandon, who had missed the entire exchange, said, "Yes, Pearl mentioned that to me. She had been terrified of pit bulls. Honestly believed they would rip out your throat if given half a chance. But then, when one saved her life, she began seeing things differently."

"It was that pit bull over there," Heather said, nodding to Hunny. "Chris's dog saved Pearl's life."

Brandon arched his brows in surprise. "Really? She never mentioned it was Chris's dog. That surprises me."

"Why?" Chris asked.

Brandon shrugged uncomfortably and glanced around the table.

"What is it?" Danielle urged.

"We don't need to get into this," Pearl said, moving out of the table and taking a seat on one chair that had been left pulled out.

"I just got the impression Pearl wasn't close to her neighbors. I knew Chris lived on her street, but I didn't know it was his dog who saved her life."

"It was at Christmas," Danielle explained. "She was up on a ladder, fixing her Christmas lights—"

"Which she had absolutely no business doing," Heather interjected, earning a scowl from Pearl.

"She fell and was there for a while when Hunny found her. She came and got us and then returned to Pearl and kept her warm until help arrived. It was a really cold night that night," Danielle said.

"Yep. She could have frozen like a popsicle," Heather chirped.

"Well, the poor woman is dead now," Brandon said uneasily.

Heather smiled sweetly, her complexion looking especially pale this evening with her heavy black eyeliner, black lipstick, and ebony-colored hair straight and falling past her shoulders, making her look like a cast member from *The Addams Family*. "Ahh, but I feel like she is still with us."

Worried Brandon might misread Heather's humor and get the wrong impression, Danielle shifted the subject by saying, "I doubt you heard, but Pearl's murdered friend, Rachel Moore, she left Pearl all her quilting supplies, the entire contents of her sewing room. I understand it's considerable. I heard Pearl was quite touched when she found out."

"Really? Not sure what we would do with it. I suppose Rachel's estate could keep it," Brandon said.

"No!" Pearl blurted. "The house isn't going to someone who quilts. It will all end up in a thrift shop or trash. Rachel wanted me to have it because she knew I'd take care of it and use it. It must go to someone who appreciates it."

"I have an idea." Heather spoke up.

"Oh, what, burn it?" Pearl snapped.

Ignoring Pearl, Heather said, "From what I understand, Rachel Moore had some really nice quilting supplies. I assume a special sewing machine, pricy quilting hoops, books, all kinds of stuff. As Pearl's trustee, take ownership of the inheritance from the Moore estate, and then have a raffle—raffle off all the quilting supplies to one winner—and the money raised can go to your charity. That way, whoever gets Pearl's inheritance from Rachel will probably be someone who loves to quilt. I would even be willing to help organize the raffle. I think it's something both Rachel and Pearl would want."

Pearl stared at Heather. "Oh my, I love that!"

"Humm, sounds like a good idea," Brandon said.

"Herman Shafer is the executor of Rachel's estate," Chris said. "You'll probably want to get in contact with him."

"I don't know who he is," Brandon said.

"I can give you his contact information," Chris said. "I understand Rachel's estate was not in a trust, and it has to go through probate, but I'm not sure how it's going to affect any of the smaller bequests."

"What are you planning to do with Pearl's house?" Lily asked.

"It will be sold," Brandon said. "Since Pearl created a trust, we won't have to go through probate, so I'd like to list it as soon as possible."

"Do you have a Realtor already?" Danielle asked.

"No. To be honest, this is the first time I've had to deal with this," Brandon admitted. "We've had small cash bequests before, but never someone's entire estate."

"Have you considered keeping the property as an investment and renting it out?" Ian asked.

"No! We don't want renters in the house!" Pearl scoffed.

"No." Brandon shook his head. "Pearl wanted her house to be someone's home. She told me she had fond memories of it growing up and made me promise to find a good owner for it when she was gone."

"If you need a Realtor, I work with Adam Nichols," Chris said. "I don't think anyone knows the local real estate market as well as he does."

"I've heard of him, but we've never met," Brandon said.

"That's Marie's grandson," Pearl muttered. "I suppose that would be alright."

"If you want, I can take you over there tomorrow and introduce you to him," Chris offered.

"Yes, I'd like that. Thank you," Brandon said.

Forty minutes later, after Brandon said goodbye and left, Danielle sat in the kitchen, watching Walt and Chris clean up. Connor had gotten fussy twenty minutes earlier, and Ian and Lily had taken him home. Heather had offered to help clean up, but Walt and Chris told her they could handle it. Pearl had also made her departure, wanting to spend a few remaining nights in her house before potential buyers started arriving.

"You know, Chris," Danielle began, "Brandon doesn't really need you to take time to go introduce him to Adam."

Chris chuckled. "Come on, it's always fun to watch Adam light up when he gets a new client."

"One thing you can say about Adam, even after inheriting his grandmother's estate, it hasn't curbed his appetite for more clients." Danielle snickered.

Walt chuckled and shook his head while he dried the now clean brownie pan.

"I have to say, I am rather impressed with Pearl. She gave her money to a good cause," Danielle said.

"I wonder how her relatives will feel about it," Walt asked.

"From what I understand, she doesn't really have anyone," Danielle said. "Aside from the cousins who sold her the house, which there doesn't seem to be any love lost there. And Ruby."

"Brandon told me tonight, one of those relatives is the one who broke into Pearl's house," Chris said.

"Seriously?" Danielle asked.

"Which one?" Walt asked.

"Andy Delarosa. Joe told Brandon after he realized who he was. I guess he figured the owner of the property was entitled to the information on the break-in," Chris explained.

THIRTY-TWO

Joe Morelli didn't have to go into work until later Friday afternoon, so he took Kelly out to breakfast at Lucy's Diner before going in. He had worked a double shift the night before, and they hadn't shared a meal together since Wednesday. The two sat across from each other in one of the smaller booths next to the window, each reading through the breakfast menu.

After a moment, Kelly set the menu on the table and looked over at Joe, who continued to read his. "I thought you knew that thing by heart," she said.

He closed the menu and set it on the table atop Kelly's. "I do. But I'm just trying to decide what I want."

A moment later, the server came to the table, took their order, and refilled their coffee cups. When they were alone again, Kelly said, "So when is Pearl's house going on the market?"

"He didn't say, but I suspect soon," Joe said.

"I was thinking, we've been talking about selling your place and buying something that would be ours," Kelly began.

"I understand you'd like to live close to your brother, but I can't afford that neighborhood," Joe said.

"Maybe you can't, but we could. And if it's going to be our house, then I need to contribute too."

Joe studied Kelly. "You're talking about that money your grandmother left you?"

"Yes. I think buying a house would be a wise use of that money."

"Kelly, that's your savings, your nest egg. There is no reason to spend it if we already have a perfectly good place to live."

Kelly let out a sigh and leaned back in the booth, staring across the table at Joe. "Yes, when my grandmother left me that money, I told myself it would be my nest egg. It would enable me to try pursuing my dream without having to take a job I hated. I was lucky, I only borrowed from it once, and then I paid it back. And I supported myself doing what I loved, without getting a job I hated. I feel blessed. But now, I'm confident enough to use that money in another way. Investing in real estate rather than letting it sit in my savings account would be a smart move. With my money and your equity, we'd have a low house payment. I already figured it out."

"You don't know what they're going to list the house for," Joe reminded her.

"True. But I did some research, seeing what other houses on that street sold for. And since it's not on Ian's side of the street, it won't be as much."

"What about your parents?" Joe asked.

"What about them?"

"Your mom seems to think Beach Drive is cursed," Joe reminded her.

Kelly laughed. "Yeah, that might be a problem, but I think she will get over it."

"It doesn't bother you about the bodies they took out of the backyard?" Joe asked.

"It doesn't thrill me. But they aren't there now. And those poor people died a million years ago."

"I don't know…"

Kelly reached across the table and rested her hand on one of Joe's. "But can we at least consider it?"

WHEN ART TEACHER Elizabeth Sparks sat down at a table for two in Lucy's Diner, she noticed Officer Joe Morelli sitting with his fiancée on the other side of the restaurant. Over the years, she had lent her talent to the local police station as a police sketch artist. It had been a field she had once considered pursuing, but when she realized computers would replace sketch artists, she changed her mind. Instead, she settled in her hometown of Frederickport, where she taught private art classes, worked for the local school district and, on rare occasions, filled in as a sketch artist for the Frederickport Police Department. Joe Morelli had been one officer she had worked with over the years, and she considered him a friend. She told herself she would have to stop by his table and say hi before leaving.

"Sorry I'm late." A voice broke Elizabeth's train of thought. She looked up and smiled at the woman now standing over the empty seat at her table. Connie Hodge had been a childhood friend of Elizabeth's, who now lived in Salem, but when she visited Frederickport, she and Elizabeth tried to get together for breakfast or lunch. Elizabeth stood up, the two women exchanged hugs and greetings, and then they sat down at the table together.

"I just got here myself. So are you staying all weekend?" Elizabeth asked, picking up a menu.

Connie shook her head. "No, I'm taking Mom out for an early birthday dinner; then I have to head back home."

"Is your dad going?"

"I hope not, but probably," Connie said as she picked up a menu.

"I'm sorry."

Connie shrugged and said, "Hey, it is what it is. Charlie doesn't understand why I even try." Charlie was Connie's live-in boyfriend.

"I take it Charlie didn't come with you?" Elizabeth asked.

"No. Ever since Dad pulled a gun on him; he avoids my parents."

"You should have reported it to the police," Elizabeth said.

"Probably, but Mom has enough to deal with. Although, did you hear about her inheritance?" Connie asked.

"What are you talking about?"

"A friend of hers from church died and left Mom her house. It has to go through probate, but after it does, I guess Dad says it's worth a lot of money. I don't know how they always manage to do that." Connie shook her head in disgust and tossed her menu on the tabletop.

"What do you mean?" Elizabeth asked.

"Mom's always making friends with these lonely little old ladies, and they end up leaving her something in their will."

Elizabeth arched a brow. "Really?"

"There was at least three other times over the years. I guess it's probably the good Lord's way of rewarding Mom for taking them under her wing while she has such a jerk of a husband."

AFTER LEAVING home on Friday morning, Adam stopped by the pharmacy and then headed for Lucy's Diner to have breakfast with Mel before going to the office. When he walked through the door to the restaurant, he spied her already at a table. En route there, he gave a hello nod to Joe and Kelly.

"Guess who I have an appointment with this afternoon," Adam said as he sat down across from Mel.

"Who?" She poured cream in her coffee.

"The trustee for Pearl Huckabee's estate. He wants to talk to me about listing the property." Adam reached for his coffee cup and found it already filled with hot coffee.

"Really? Is it some relative of Pearl's?" Melony asked.

"No. She left her estate to a nonprofit organization. In fact, the guy is a friend of Chris's. Chris is bringing him over this afternoon to introduce us."

"Oh sweet! Umm, and maybe you might already have a buyer for the house?" Melony asked with a grin.

"You seriously want to live on Beach Drive?" Adam asked. "I thought you wanted to live right on the beach?"

"You told me there was no beachfront property currently on the market. And her house still has something of an ocean view. Plus, if a tsunami hits, we wouldn't be as close."

Adam laughed. "If a tsunami hit, we'd be toast."

Mel shrugged. "True, but I was trying to look on the bright side."

"Before we go making an offer, we need to check out the property. When I was over there the other day, I didn't get much of a look. And frankly, after what we experienced over at the Marymoor property, I'm not sure I'd feel comfortable moving into a place that used to have bodies buried in the backyard. Bodies of murdered victims." Adam shivered at the idea.

"I suppose you have a good point." Melony let out a sigh. "But I'm still interested. We'd have great neighbors."

"WHAT'S GOING to happen to the guy who broke into Pearl's house?" Kelly asked. "Isn't he the same one who ripped out her rosebush?"

"He was never charged. Nothing we could prove. But yeah." Joe picked up his English muffin and took a bite.

"So, what's going to happen to him?"

"I doubt much of anything. He claims the only reason he broke in was to see if Pearl had anything that should go back to the family. Delarosa figured she had left her house to her church."

"I thought you said she left it to some animal rescue group," Kelly asked.

"She did. But he didn't know that. He said the church wouldn't care about anything of a personal nature that had belonged to Pearl's family. He claims he took nothing, because when he looked outside, he saw Adam and Walt, and he figured he needed to get out of there."

"Assuming someone murdered Pearl, and it wasn't an accident, don't you think his breaking in has to be related? Wasn't he the one who had issues with both murder victims?" Kelly asked.

"Yes. But there is no way he killed Pearl. The night she died, he was in lockup. I think the only reason the chief kept him overnight, he was trying to shake him up a bit for being such an annoyance. We really don't need this BS in the middle of a murder investigation."

"He could still be the killer," Kelly insisted. "After all, they aren't sure when Pearl died. It might have been Thursday after he got out of jail. Is the coroner really sure she died Wednesday night? Can they really call it that close? Her poor body was there for a few days before they found it. And just because Danielle saw someone that night, it could have been Pearl. I wouldn't cross Andy Delarosa off your suspect list. Especially since the guy broke into Pearl's house."

"THEY FOUND out who broke into Pearl's house," Adam told Melony after the server brought their food.

"You mean besides you and Walt?" Mel asked.

"Ha ha. But yeah. Andy Delarosa," Adam said. "One of the cousins who used to own Pearl's house."

"Really? He was the one who had a confrontation with Pearl at Rachel's funeral. I wasn't there yet, but Danielle told me about it."

Adam nodded. "Andy confessed to the break-in, but he claimed he was just looking for family heirlooms that he didn't want the church to get. And he said he left before he took anything."

"She didn't leave it to the church."

Adam shrugged. "No, but that's what he assumed she'd do. And he has a solid alibi for the time of Pearl's death. But then, there are always his partners. But I can't imagine Ruby or Sam killing anyone."

"I don't really see the motive. Like Ruby said, they always understood they might not get the permit, and vacation rental was still an option."

Adam cringed.

Melony frowned. "What?"

"I ran into Carla this morning at the pharmacy. She mentioned Andy's arrest. She dated him for a short time. According to Carla, a while back he came into Pier Café and bragged about how the B and B on your street was just the beginning. They had all these plans for a franchise B and B, starting in Frederickport. Supposedly, they had lined up investors. But then later, after Pearl got Rachel to block the license, she asked Andy about it the next time he came in. I guess he was pretty pissed and said he'd like to wring Pearl's neck."

THIRTY-THREE

"Have you made any progress in Rachel's case?" Herman Shafer asked Chief MacDonald early Friday afternoon. The elderly man sat on a chair facing the chief, who sat behind his desk.

"Unfortunately, no. It might help if we found out why Rachel moved her money from the bank here to Astoria and named Tammy Morgan as her beneficiary."

"Like I told you, I don't know who this Morgan is, or why Rachel left her the money," Herman said. "What have you found out about Morgan?"

"She doesn't have a record aside from one traffic ticket. She never lived in Frederickport, but vacationed here, and admits to meeting Rachel once, which I told you about. Aside from that, I couldn't find anything to connect her to Rachel. She's made no attempt to touch the money. She told me she thinks it's a mistake and doesn't want to cause problems for herself by taking the money," the chief explained.

Herman leaned back in his seat and let out a sigh, his right hand holding the top of his cane as it stood by his chair. "Rachel was a peculiar bird. Always felt sorry for her, losing both her daughters like that. I know how that feels to lose a child. No worse pain. Then she lost her spouse; I also know how that feels." Herman gave the chief a sad smile and said, "And so do you."

"You mentioned she called you while you were on your trip," the chief said.

"Yes, she asked me when I was coming home and told me she needed to see me when I returned. She didn't mention any changes to her estate, but I figured that's what she wanted to talk about. It's not like we ever got together and just visited."

"If she wanted to change her will, wouldn't she just contact her attorney?" the chief asked.

"After Carmichael passed away and Renton took over, Rachel asked me to recommend an attorney. She never cared for Renton," Herman said. "I introduced her to someone I trusted, and that's who she used. When Rachel wanted to change her will, I'd contact the attorney and arrange an appointment, and we'd go together. She always wanted me to go with her, felt it was important that I understand her wishes since I'm the executor. I tried to get her to appoint someone else as executor, reminding her she wasn't much older than I was. But I'm afraid she grew rather dependent on me after her husband died. If she moved her money to another bank and assigned this Morgan woman her beneficiary, I assume that's what she wanted to talk to me about."

"Did Rachel change her will often?" the chief asked.

"Probably more than most. Every few years, she would change her mind and move things around. For a while she had all her money going to a nonprofit and then changed it to another one. Then there was a scandal with the organization, and she changed her will again and left everything to the church. But she was never that keen on leaving everything to a church. So when she got close to Leanne Hodge, she decided to leave her the house, but give the church the money in her savings account."

"Why not just set up a trust and avoid all that?" the chief asked.

Herman chuckled. "She didn't want to pay to set up a trust. Said she would rather have the money there for her to use if needed, and when her time came, her beneficiaries should just be happy she put them in her will; they could wait."

"WHERE'S HEATHER?" Pearl asked Danielle when she appeared in the master bedroom on the second floor of Marlow House.

"Hello to you, too," Danielle said. She stood alone in the now empty room. "She's probably at her office. Chris said something about them both going down there today for a couple of hours."

Pearl glanced around and frowned. "Where did all the furniture from this room go?"

"Walt took it out. We're rearranging things," Danielle explained. The next moment, the king-size bed from upstairs floated through the open doorway, followed by Walt, who trailed behind the bed.

Pearl's eyes widened. "I still can't believe he can do that. But it explains a lot. And I should be furious with you."

Ignoring Pearl, Walt focused on the bed, placing it where he and Danielle had already decided it should go.

Danielle frowned at Pearl. "Mad at me, why?"

"For gaslighting me all this time. Making me think I was going crazy. I don't suppose any of what I saw ever had anything to do with that marijuana medication my doctor urged me to try. No wonder he looked at me like I was a crazy old woman when I told him how it made me hallucinate."

"What were we supposed to do, tell you the truth about everything? You think you would have believed us?" Danielle asked.

With the bed now in place, Walt looked over to Pearl and Danielle, waiting for Pearl to answer the question his wife had just asked of her.

Pearl let out a sigh. "I suppose not."

"Why did you want to see Heather?" Danielle asked.

"I wanted to find out when she'll be starting on the auction for the quilting supplies," Pearl said. "And I wanted her to talk to Brian and find out what's happening with that criminal cousin of mine."

"I assume you mean Andy?" Danielle asked.

"Of course."

"I don't think you should bother Heather today. If you want her to do the auction like she volunteered, she needs to first see to her responsibilities at the Glandon Foundation. I tell you what, I'll take you over to the police station myself, and we can go to the top. I'll find out from the chief what is going on with Andy, and you can be there and hear for yourself," Danielle offered.

"When?"

"Let me get dressed, and then we can go," Danielle offered. "Walt doesn't need me here to move the furniture."

"I'll meet you in the kitchen," Pearl said before vanishing.

"Why did you offer to take her to see the chief?" Walt asked.

Danielle turned to Walt. "I spoke to the chief this morning on the phone, asking him how the investigation is going. He'd really like to find out why Rachel left her money to a virtual stranger. I think Pearl knows."

"I agree, but she keeps changing the subject when we ask. How is this going to get her to open up?" Walt asked.

"It's one thing if we ask her, but it might be another if it comes directly from the chief. She claims the only reason she hasn't moved on is because she wants to find out who murdered her and Rachel. I understand this might be a total dead end, and it may have absolutely nothing to do with the murders, but it might be important. And if Pearl realizes that, understands that her keeping quiet might impede the investigation, then maybe she'll open up. The bottom line, I don't think she wants to do anything that protects her killer."

CHIEF MACDONALD SAT behind his desk, looking at Danielle, who sat in the same chair Herman Shafer had used earlier that day. He understood there was someone else in the room—the spirit of Pearl Huckabee. Danielle pointed to where Pearl sat in the office.

"Your cousin didn't kill you," the chief said. "He was in lockup that night."

Pearl studied the chief curiously, her head tilting slightly to one side. "Is it strange talking to someone you can't see?"

Danielle let out a sigh and turned to Pearl. "He can't hear you either. Do you understand what he is telling you?"

Pearl turned to Danielle and waved her right hand dismissively. "Yes, yes, I'm not stupid. But I find it so fascinating the chief of police is sitting right there talking to an empty chair."

"It's not empty. You're sitting in it," Danielle reminded her.

"I know that." Pearl huffed indignantly. "But if anyone walked in here, they would think he was talking to a chair. All of this… it changes my perspective on everything. Nothing is really as I assumed it was all these years. Fascinating."

"What is she saying?" the chief asked.

"She's rambling," Danielle said.

"I am not rambling. I just find this all so fascinating."

"Yes, you've said that before," Danielle said.

"I have no idea what you two are talking about," the chief said, "but, Pearl, it would help the investigation if you would tell us what you know of Tammy Morgan. She's the woman Rachel left her money to."

Pearl looked at the chief and said, "Yes, I know who Tammy Morgan is. She had absolutely nothing to do with Rachel's death or mine. Why would she? Frankly, she had no motive, just the opposite. It would have been much better for Rachel to die next month instead of last week. Just leave the woman alone; you're wasting your time."

"Why did Rachel leave her that money?" Danielle asked.

Pearl turned a scowl to Danielle. "It really is no one's business. That was between Tammy and Rachel, and it is not my place to say. It would be best if Rachel were to do it in her own words. That's what she wanted."

"Rachel is dead," Danielle reminded her.

"Yes, but Rachel wrote Tammy a letter explaining everything. And while it may take a little longer now, this is what Rachel wanted."

"What letter?" Danielle asked.

"I've said enough. I'll wait for you in the car." Pearl disappeared.

"She's gone," Danielle said.

"What just happened?" the chief asked. Danielle repeated all that Pearl had said.

The two sat in silence for a few minutes, considering what Danielle had just told the chief. Finally, he said, "Is she saying there is a letter somewhere in that house that explains why she left Tammy her money?"

"That's what it sounded like," Danielle said.

"I need to call Herman and see about going through her house again," the chief said.

LATE FRIDAY AFTERNOON, Adam sat in his front office with Brandon Purnell, going over the real estate listing for Pearl Huckabee's house. Chris had been there earlier to make introductions, and then left the men to return to the Glandon Foundation. Leslie had taken the afternoon off, which was why Adam met with Brandon in the front office instead of his private office in the back.

"I don't know what condition the house is in, structurally, that is," Brandon said just as Herman Shafer walked into the office.

"Herman," Adam greeted him.

"Sorry to bother you, Adam, but I was looking for Melony. She wasn't at home or her office, and I tried calling her," Herman explained.

"Mel's in court this afternoon. Always turns off her phone when she's in court," Adam explained. "But now that you're here, there is someone you should probably meet."

After introductions, Herman said, "I was wondering what I was going to do about Pearl Huckabee." Herman looked at Adam and said, "Actually, that's why I wanted to talk to Melony. I wanted to see if she could pick up that trunk this weekend with the quilts." He turned to Brandon and said, "And maybe you could clean out that sewing room this weekend, get everything out of there? I'd really like one less thing to worry about."

"What about probate?" Adam asked.

"I don't think the courts really care about a couple of quilts, an old trunk, and quilting supplies. I just don't want to be responsible for them. After all, the house was already broken into, and Leanne has a key. I don't want anyone coming back later and saying something is missing."

THIRTY-FOUR

Police Chief MacDonald was about to call it a day when Elizabeth Sparks came knocking on his office door. "Elizabeth? This is a welcome surprise."

He stood up from behind his desk and was about to walk around and greet her when she said, "Chief, I was hoping we could talk a moment?"

"Why, certainly. My door is always open to you." He waved to a nearby chair for her to sit down. Before she took the invitation, she shut the office door.

The chief cocked his brow at the gesture and asked, "Is this serious?"

"I would just prefer no one overheard what I have to say, because it might mean nothing."

Both Elizabeth and the chief sat down.

"So, what can I help you with?" he asked.

Elizabeth leaned forward and said, "This is about Rachel Moore's death. I understand it's being investigated as a murder, yet other than speculation, no one has mentioned the cause of death."

"I'm not at liberty to say at this time. Do you know something?"

Elizabeth let out a sigh and leaned back in her chair, dropping the purse she had been holding on the floor by her feet. "I don't know. Maybe…"

"What do you think you might know?" he asked.

"I understand Rachel left Leanne Hodge her house. Is that right?"

The chief nodded. "Yes. What about it?"

"I've been friends with Leanne's daughter, Connie, since we were in second grade. I know the family."

"And?" the chief asked.

"Her father used to beat the crap out of her when she was a kid."

"I checked out both of the parents, and they've never been turned in for child abuse," the chief said. He failed to mention the various complaints made by neighbors, accusing Larry Hodge of threatening behavior.

"No. Because her mother would cover for him, make excuses for her husband. In fact, I never realized what was going on in that household back them. Connie told me after she moved out of the house and left town. I know she was in therapy for a while."

"What does this have to do with Rachel's murder?"

"I saw Connie this morning. She came into town to take her mother out to dinner for her mother's birthday. They are her parents, and despite everything, she keeps trying. At least with her mom. Anyway, I met her for breakfast, and she told me about her mother inheriting Rachel Moore's house. Then she told me something interesting. She said it's not the first time something like this has happened, where some person her parents befriended ended up leaving them something in their will."

The chief nodded. "Yes, I'm already aware of that."

Elizabeth's eyes widened. "You are?"

"Once we suspected there might be foul play, we naturally checked out anyone who benefitted financially from her death. We learned the Moores have inherited money from other elderly women. Women they met in other churches they attended over the years."

"So you know? Maybe her father did something to these women?" Elizabeth suggested.

"From what I found out, Mrs. Hodge was always the sole beneficiary, not her husband," the chief said.

"Yes, but he still benefits," Elizabeth reminded him.

"True. But we interviewed the different churches those other women attended, and we kept coming up with the same consensus."

"Which was?" Elizabeth asked.

"That Leanne Hodge was a nice woman who liked to help people. That it was a shame she stayed with her husband, yet they felt she did so because Leanne believed it was her duty."

Elizabeth let out a sigh and said, "Connie once told me, before she moved out of the house she asked her mother why she stayed with him. Her answer, she had taken a vow before God. That it would be a sin to leave him."

"Also, none of the women who mentioned Leanne in their wills died under suspicious circumstances. And each person I spoke to felt Leanne deserved to be mentioned in the wills, because she had gone out of her way to help the women, and most of them had no family."

"Well, I suppose there was no reason for them to kill her off, anyway, considering her age. It's not like they would have to wait a long time for an inheritance from a ninety-five-year-old woman. Not the best motive. Why risk killing her and facing murder charges when all you had to do was wait. According to Connie, her parents have plenty of money from all those other inheritances. Not like they needed it in a hurry. I suppose I really didn't need to come in here today. You already knew everything," Elizabeth said.

"I'm glad you came in. I appreciate any information you might have."

When Elizabeth said goodbye and left his office ten minutes later, the chief didn't leave immediately. Instead, he sat down in his desk chair and thought about what Elizabeth had said, about waiting for Rachel to die of natural causes. It was true; they didn't need the money, considering what he'd discovered they had in the bank. Yet he understood someone's wealth didn't mean they wouldn't kill for more money—look at Chris's uncles. Plus, waiting until she died might not have been an option—not if she intended to change her will. After all, she had virtually written the church out when she'd moved the money to another bank and named a new beneficiary. Perhaps she was going to make more changes when Herman returned from his vacation. But how would Larry Hodge have known of Rachel's intentions?

WALT AND DANIELLE intended to eat leftovers from the potluck for dinner on Friday night. But Chris called and asked them to meet him, Heather, Adam, and Melony at Pearl Cove for dinner. Danielle thought that sounded much better than leftovers, and since she hadn't been plagued with morning sickness for the last few days, she found she had a craving for Pearl Cove's clam chowder.

"Where's Brian?" Danielle asked after she sat down with Walt at the table at Pearl Cove. Chris, Heather, Melony, and Adam were already seated.

"He had work tonight. So Chris is my date," Heather chirped.

"I am not your date," Chris said.

Heather frowned at Chris. "Does this mean you aren't paying for my dinner?"

Chris rolled his eyes. "Yes, I'm paying."

Melony chuckled and then asked, "I thought Ian and Lily might join us?"

"Ian's family is going over there for dinner tonight," Danielle said.

The server came to the table and took their drink orders. When she left the table, Chris said, "Guess who listed Pearl Huckabee's house today."

Danielle looked at Adam and said, "Ray Collins? I heard he's fantastic."

"Wasn't he the listing agent for the Marymoor property?" Walt asked.

"Yes, and your wife knows he didn't get the listing," Adam scoffed.

Danielle flashed Adam a grin. "Congratulations."

"I have Chris to thank for the new listing," Adam said, raising a glass of water in toast to Chris, since the server had not yet brought their cocktails.

"I know someone who might be interested in the house," Melony said with a shy smile.

"Wow, you have a line on a buyer already?" Heather asked. "Way to go, Adam."

Adam glanced at Melony and sighed. He looked back at Heather and said, "Mel wants the house."

"Really? I'd love to have Mel as a neighbor," Heather said.

"Me too," Danielle agreed. She looked at Adam and said, "Oh, wait, are you two still getting married?"

"Come on, wouldn't you like me as your neighbor?" Adam asked.

"I'd like Mel as a neighbor," Danielle said. She smiled at Melony and asked, "Are you guys seriously thinking about it? It honestly would be great, even if you bring Adam with you."

"Adam is a little reluctant. Something about those bodies that were buried in the backyard," Melony said.

"After what we saw at Marymoor, do you blame me?" Adam asked.

"If it makes you feel any better, we've never seen anything—Halloween-like—over there," Walt told him.

"Yeah, says the guy who lives in a haunted house," Adam said.

"Oh, fiddle, nothing wrong with living in a haunted house," Danielle said. "As long as you have friendly ghosts."

"Yeah, well, yours hurled a croquet set at me," Adam grumbled.

"Are you guys still thinking of reopening the B and B?" Mel asked.

"Sure, change the subject," Adam muttered under his breath.

"We are," Danielle said. "But I think we'll wait until they solve Pearl's murder before we see about getting our license reinstated."

"Yeah, I could see that getting you on the top of the suspect list." Adam chuckled.

"I think Pearl's cousin still holds that spot," Mel reminded him.

"I don't think so," Danielle said. "According to the police, Andy was in lockup the night Pearl died."

"It could have been an accident, and she simply fell down those stairs. It happens. But if it was murder, Andy might have had someone do it; there was a lot at stake," Melony suggested.

"What do you mean?" Danielle asked.

Adam then recounted what Carla had told him.

"Have you said anything to the chief?" Danielle asked.

"I'm sure he knows," Adam said.

The next moment the server arrived with the cocktails for everyone but Danielle, who had a virgin bloody Mary.

"Danielle, are you doing anything tomorrow?" Heather asked after the server took their order and left the table.

"Just Pearl's funeral. And then do some stuff around the house. Why?"

"Herman Shafer asked Brandon if he could get all the quilting stuff out of the house this weekend," Heather began. "Since I volunteered to do the auction, I need to go over there and box it all up, do an inventory, and I wondered if you might go with me. I'm not really a quilter, but you mentioned your mom liked to quilt, so I was hoping you could help me. I was thinking about going over there after the funeral."

"You're going to Pearl's funeral?" Adam asked. "Didn't think she was your favorite neighbor."

Heather shrugged and said, "She did live next door to me. I think I should go."

"That's really nice you volunteered to help her estate with the quilting auction," Melony said.

"It's for a good cause," Heather said.

"Sure, I can go with you," Danielle said.

"As long as she lifts nothing heavy," Walt said.

Danielle patted Walt's knee and said, "I promise I won't pick up anything heavy."

"Herman also asked if I'd pick up the trunk tomorrow. But Adam's working all weekend, and I don't think I can move it myself," Melony said.

"I'll move it for you," Walt offered. He looked at Chris and added, "Chris will help me."

"Sure. I'd be happy to," Chris said, knowing there would be no heavy lifting involved.

"I have an idea. After Danielle and Heather go through the quilting supplies and box them up, Chris and I can go over there and move the trunk for Melony and then pick up the rest of the things," Walt suggested.

THIRTY-FIVE

Edward MacDonald stood at his kitchen counter, dipping slices of sourdough bread into an egg mixture before setting them on a hot skillet. When home on Saturdays or Sundays, he enjoyed fixing his boys something other than cereal for breakfast, and today French toast was on the menu.

Behind him, Eddy Jr. and Evan set the table while discussing video games, baseball, and plans for the weekend. Glancing over his shoulder at his sons, he couldn't believe how fast the boys had grown. Now officially a teenager, Eddy looked like Edward had at that age. People always said the boy was his mini-me, tall, stocky with blue-gray eyes. Eddy junior had the same brown hair as his father, before his father began turning gray. His younger son, Evan, favored his late wife, Cindy.

Removing the now cooked French toast from the skillet and placing them on a platter, Edward told his boys to sit down as he brought the food to the table. Setting the platter of French toast on the center of the table, he said, "According to the weather report, no rain this weekend. So, what do you boys want to do this morning?" Edward sat down at the table.

"Some of the guys were talking about meeting at the park and shooting some hoops," Eddy junior said. "Is it okay if I go? Evan can go with me if he wants."

"Sure." The chief looked at Evan. "You want to go with Eddy?"

"Yeah, but I don't want to play basketball. Can I take my skateboard?" The nearby park had a small adjacent skateboard park.

"As long as you wear your helmet and check in with your brother every fifteen minutes or so," the chief said.

"Do you have to go into the station today?" Eddy asked his father.

"No. But I have that funeral I have to go to, remember? So I want you both to be back by one, okay?"

AFTER BREAKFAST EVAN and Eddy helped their father clean the kitchen before returning to their bedrooms to make their beds, pick up any dirty clothes from the floor to put in the hamper—along with some clean clothes that just happened to fall off hangers. It seemed easier to shove them in the hamper rather than rehanging them.

As Evan gathered up his skateboard and helmet and Eddy scoured the house for his missing basketball, Edward reminded both boys to brush their teeth before going, telling them the syrup from breakfast would rot their teeth, and he couldn't afford another trip to the dentist.

Eddy got to the bathroom first, brushed his teeth, and then resumed looking for his basketball. By the time Evan finished brushing his teeth, his brother had found the basketball, and the two boys said goodbye to their father before taking off for the park.

HALFWAY DOWN THE STREET, one of Eddy's friends showed up. The two older boys started talking, excluding Evan from the conversation. Evan stopped for a moment while the other boys kept walking. He secured his helmet on his head and dropped his skateboard to the sidewalk. He wasn't supposed to use the skateboard on the sidewalk or on the street. His father said he could only use it at the skateboard park. But he figured he wasn't going to really ride it, just push it along, slow like.

Evan stepped on the skateboard with one foot, using the other one to gently push it along. After a few minutes, Eddy looked back and saw his brother on the skateboard. They were a good twelve feet apart.

"Hey, don't fall off that thing and hurt yourself, or we'll have to carry you to the park so Dad will think you hurt yourself there," Eddy called out. Both older boys laughed, then turned around and kept walking toward the park.

Humming, Evan kept pushing himself along when a flash of gold flew by in front of him, straight through Eddy and his friend. Evan stopped immediately and looked toward whatever had just gone by. His eyes widened when he saw her. The girl ghost and the ghost dog.

Unlike the last time, she wasn't throwing the ball for the dog. In fact, the dog was not holding a ball in his mouth. The girl talked to the dog, but she was too far away from Evan. He couldn't hear what she had said. The girl pointed in another direction, and the dog ran off.

"Evan, hurry up!" Evan heard his brother shout. Evan looked to Eddy and his friend and saw they had gone a considerable distance ahead of him since he had stopped to watch the girl and her dog.

But Eddy and his friend were not the only ones looking at Evan. The girl, after hearing Eddy's shout, looked at Evan. The two locked gazes, staring at each other.

"Come on poky-slow!" Eddy shouted.

Evan reluctantly looked away from the girl to his brother. "I'm coming," he called out while reaching down and picking up his skateboard. Holding the skateboard under one arm, he started walking while glancing back to the girl and then to his brother. Eddy shook his head, annoyed at his little brother, but turned around, his back again to Evan, as he and his friend once again started walking toward the park while talking amongst each other.

The next moment, the little girl appeared by Evan's side and said, "You aren't afraid of me."

"Why would I be afraid of you? You're just a girl," Evan said, his voice a whisper so the older boys wouldn't hear.

"I'm not just a girl," she said, now walking along beside him.

They walked in silence for a few minutes. Finally, Evan said, "I'm sorry."

She frowned and looked at him. "For what? You didn't do anything."

"Umm… because… well… because you're not just a girl."

"You mean because I'm dead?" she asked.

Evan nodded. "I wasn't sure you knew. They don't always know."

"They? You've seen others like me?" she asked.

"Haven't you?" Evan asked.

She shrugged. "A couple others, like my dad and sister. I like to stay home. But sometimes I take Charger out to play ball, but we never saw anyone like me."

"You might have, but didn't know," Evan said.

She frowned at Evan. "You think so?"

Evan shrugged.

They kept walking yet fell silent. Finally, she said, "My name's Cindy Moore."

Evan turned to her. "Really? That was my mom's name, Cindy."

"Was?"

"She died a long time ago," he explained.

"But you still see her, right?" she asked.

He shook his head. "No. She moved on."

Cindy let out a sigh. "Like my dad and sister."

"My name's Evan MacDonald."

"Nice to meet you, Evan. The only one I ever talk to is Charger. When he died, it surprised me we could talk to each other. But… but he doesn't talk exactly."

"I understand," Evan said with a nod.

Still walking, she studied Evan's profile. "You do?"

Charger returned and started trotting along with them. Cindy looked down at the dog, silently telling him all that had just happened.

"Umm, how did you die?" Evan finally asked.

"I got sick. They called it measles."

"How long ago?" Evan asked.

"I'm not sure exactly. But a while after I died, our next-door neighbors had a baby girl. Her name was Melony. I used to go over there and visit her. She was so cute. For a while, I was sure she could see and hear me. When she cried, I would talk to her, and she stopped. But I must have been mistaken, because she didn't seem to see me when she got older. Unless she was ignoring me. I watched her grow up. She left for a while but came back. A lot older. Like the age my mom was when I died. So I figure I must have died a long time ago."

"Why didn't you move on? You said your dad and sister did." After Evan asked, he heard his brother calling his name. They had reached the entrance of the park. Evan stopped talking, and he and Cindy continued to the park entrance, where Eddy and his friends stood, waiting.

"Looked like you were talking to yourself," Eddy said with a laugh. He turned to his friends and said, "My brother likes to talk to himself."

Evan gave a shrug and told his brother he was going on to the skateboard park.

"Make sure to be back here by twelve thirty. I don't want to have to go find you," Eddy called out as he and his friends headed to the basketball court.

Instead of going into the skateboard park, Evan took a seat on a park bench under a large tree, away from the other visitors to the park. Cindy sat next to him.

"Do you think you could help me?" Cindy asked after she sat down.

"Help you how?" Evan asked.

"I'm trying to find my mom. I think she might be dead, too."

Evan looked at Cindy. "Have you been looking for her all this time?"

"You mean since I died?"

Evan nodded.

Cindy smiled. "No."

With a sigh, Cindy leaned back on the bench and told Evan her story. "After I died, my mom was so sad. She cried all the time. I just couldn't leave her like that. She couldn't see or hear me, but I felt she needed me, anyway. Then one day, Charger died. I was so happy when he could see me, and shocked that we could… well…"

"Communicate?" Evan finished for her.

"Oh yes! It was so nice to talk to someone again." She paused a moment, let out a sigh and then continued, "As time passed, I watched my sister get older and start high school. But then, she was in a car accident, and she died. Mom cried again."

"But your sister didn't stay?" Evan asked.

Cindy shook her head. "No. I saw her, and she wanted me to go with her. She was ready to move on. But I wasn't. And then Dad, he got sick and died and was happy when he saw me. But when he heard my sister had moved on, he felt he needed to go to her. I told him I wanted to stay and wait for Mom. So I did."

"But now you can't find her?"

"I left to play ball with Charger. We stayed out later than normal, watching the stars. We like watching the stars. When I came home, Mom was in the bathroom, with the door shut. I always know when she's getting ready to go to bed, because she puts a pill in a little cup on her nightstand and sets her clothes out for the next day. She had already done that, so I knew she was in the bathroom, getting ready to turn in for the night. By the clothes she had laid out, I knew she was going to church the next day. I just figured there was no reason to stick around. She was going to bed anyway. So Charger and I left to play some more. But when I got back the next night, she wasn't there."

"And you've been looking for her?"

Cindy lowered her head. "I think she's dead. I went to one of her friends, looking for her, and her friend, she could see me."

"She was like me?" Evan asked.

Cindy shook her head. "She was like me. I knew she was because I saw her body. She had fallen and died. And later, I saw her in our house, and she said my mother had been murdered."

"Murdered?" Evan squeaked.

Cindy nodded. "And I saw another one of my mother's friends there, too. She went through mother's things and found what looked like a letter. I watched as she took it to the bathroom, tore it into pieces and then flushed it down the toilet. Someone else came, a man. He told her she shouldn't be there."

THIRTY-SIX

On her way to Marlow House, Heather spied Lily crossing the street. She gave a little whistle, Lily looked her way and waved, and a moment later, the two women met on the sidewalk in front of the side gate into Marlow House.

"You going to Pearl's funeral?" Heather asked.

"Yeah, Ian and I thought we should. She might have been a pain, but we were still neighbors." Lily paused a moment, cringed, and then looked around guiltily. "Don't tell me she's here?"

Heather laughed. "Nah, you're good. She's not here. In fact, I haven't seen her, which is why I want to talk to Danielle."

"Is there a problem?" Lily asked as the two walked through the gate and headed for Marlow House's back door.

Heather shrugged. "Not a problem. More curious."

When they arrived at the door, they knocked, walked in, and found Walt and Danielle sitting at the kitchen table, eating lunch.

"What are you two up to? Want a sandwich?" Danielle asked, holding her sandwich up briefly.

"No, thanks," Heather and Lily said in unison before joining Walt and Danielle at the table.

"Have you seen Pearl today?" Heather asked after she sat down.

Danielle shook her head. "No. But I imagine she'll be at her funeral."

"Maybe not. I'm wondering if she moved on," Heather said.

"Why do you think that?" Danielle asked.

"I haven't seen her since Thursday night, not a peep or boo," Heather said. "Kinda unusual, considering I felt she was haunting me. I even stopped by her house this morning; she wasn't there."

"Ahh, you miss her?" Lily teased.

Heather looked at Lily and said with a shrug, "I think maybe I did, in a perverse sort of way."

"We saw her yesterday," Danielle said. "In fact, she was looking for you, but I told her she needed to let you get your work done for the Glandon Foundation."

"I'm certain she's still here," Walt said. "She's probably already down at the church."

"Hmm… strange," Heather murmured.

"What?" Lily asked.

"I was a little sad when I thought she already moved on, and now I'm not thrilled she's still here," Heather explained.

Walt, Danielle, and Lily laughed at Heather, and then Danielle looked at Lily and asked, "You still going to the funeral?"

"Yeah. Ian's mom is staying with Connor," Lily said.

"How was dinner last night?" Danielle asked. "You had the whole family over."

"We actually had a good time. How was Pearl Cove?" Lily asked.

"It was nice, but we missed you," Danielle said.

"Thanks. Anyway, I'm over to see if you guys wanted to drive to the funeral with Ian and me." She looked at Heather and added, "You're welcome, too."

"Thanks, but after the funeral I'm going with Heather to help her pack up the quilting supplies, and then Walt and Chris are coming over later to help us move everything," Danielle said.

Before anyone could comment, glitter fell from the ceiling. Everyone but Lily looked up.

"Hi, Eva," the mediums said, moments before the spirit materialized.

"Ready for a funeral?" Eva asked cheerfully.

THE IDEA of observing one's own funeral was not a foreign idea to Pearl. While she had always thought it a possibility, she hadn't seriously considered it was something she might one day do. Yet here she was, standing at the head of the church, next to her closed casket, waiting for Pastor Chad to give the signal to open the doors and let the mourners enter. She wondered—would there be any?

"Ah, you're here." A familiar voice broke Pearl's concentration. She turned to find the spirits of Eva and Marie hovering nearby.

"You came?" Pearl asked in surprise.

"Yes, we couldn't let you do this alone," Eva said. "For some spirits, their funeral can be quite traumatic."

"It's also an excellent opportunity to do a little snooping, pick up some hints on who might have been responsible for your death," Marie said. "On TV, the detectives always go to a victim's funeral, believing the guilty party won't be able to stay away."

"Perhaps, but one thing I've learned, in my brief experience with death, unless the killer has an accomplice, they probably won't be chatting to others or themselves about their dastardly deed," Pearl grumbled.

"That's true," Eva agreed.

"I stopped by Andy's house, and he was alone and not prone to talking to himself. I went to Ruby's, and she wasn't alone. She was with Sam. If either of them did it, they are keeping it from the other one. Then I headed over to Larry Hodge's house. If he's responsible, his wife is totally clueless. She's sweet, and I have probably been too hard on her. She's coming to the funeral and dragging her husband along. He doesn't want to come, but she kept telling him I was her friend, and as her husband, he needed to be by her side if she needed him. Leanne told him she had just lost two dear friends in a very short time, and he could at least be supportive. She called me a dear friend." Pearl smiled sadly.

"Are you planning to move on after your funeral?" Eva asked.

"No. I need to find out who is responsible for Rachel's and my deaths," Pearl said stubbornly.

The next minute someone opened the doors to the church, and mourners started drifting in.

Twenty minutes later, Pearl remained standing at the front of the church, now next to Pastor Chad, as he began the service. Eva and Marie had taken a seat in imaginary chairs at the back of the church, while the mediums from Beach Drive kept looking from Pastor Chad to Pearl. Police Chief MacDonald was also there, as was officer Brian Henderson.

When the service ended, Eva and Marie returned to Pearl's side.

"That was a lovely service," Eva said.

"I must say, there were more people here than I expected," Pearl said, sounding pleased.

Marie kept quiet but told herself funerals of murdered people tended to get more mourners—curious lookie-loos and those spectating on who in attendance might be the killer. Although Pearl's death had not been ruled a homicide, and from what Marie had overheard, the chief feared it would eventually be ruled an accident, considering his only evidence proving murder had come from a ghost. She chose not to share that information with Pearl. The three spirits watched as Danielle, Walt, and the others from Beach Drive filed out of the church.

"It was nice. All your neighbors came," Eva said after the church emptied and most of the lights had been turned off.

"Yes, I suppose," Pearl said with a sigh. "And I'm afraid Heather might be another one, like Leanne, who I was a little hard on. She volunteered to arrange an auction of the quilting supplies Rachel left me and give the money to charity. She didn't have to do that."

"Heather does a lot of charity work," Marie reminded her.

"Pearl, I stopped by Marlow House before coming here today," Eva began. "They tell me you are still holding back on what you know, which might help find your killers. You say you want to help, but why all these secrets?"

"They want to know why Rachel left the money to a virtual stranger. But that's not going to help them. She had nothing to do with any of this. She didn't even know who Rachel was," Pearl insisted.

"It may not matter, but it might. Why the secret?" Marie asked. While Marie had found Tammy Morgan, her brief time eavesdropping on the woman had revealed no insight into why Rachel had left her any money.

"Because I keep my promises. I made a promise to Rachel to never tell a living soul until she was ready to do it herself."

Eva and Marie stared at Pearl for a moment. Finally, Eva said in a calm voice, "Then tell us."

"I just told you, I promised Rachel that I would never tell a—" Pearl didn't finish her sentence. She looked from Marie to Eva, who continued to stare at her.

"Neither one of us is a living soul," Eva reminded her. "You can tell us."

Pearl didn't immediately respond, but looked from Eva to Marie, back to Eva. Finally, she let out a sigh and said, "Tammy Morgan is Rachel's daughter."

"Her what?" Marie squeaked.

Pearl sat down on the lid of her casket and let out another sigh. "About a year or more after Rachel's husband died, she was bereft. The poor woman had lost her children and then her beloved husband. Out of loneliness she became friendly with an older gentleman, who, well, he provided comfort. A widower, much older than Rachel. They weren't together long, yet long enough for her to get pregnant. Neither of them knew she had gotten pregnant when he died suddenly of a heart attack. And she was alone again."

"But she had a child coming," Eva reminded her.

"Like I said, she didn't realize she was pregnant. After he died, she felt overwhelmed and just needed to get away from everything. So she closed up her house and intended to do some traveling. She had only been in Europe for a few weeks when she realized she was pregnant. While she returned to the States, she didn't go home. Rachel was too embarrassed, a grown woman, coming back to town like a pregnant teenager. She thought she should have known better.

"Rachel also felt she was too old to raise a child alone. There was no family to help her, and she worried that if she died, it would end up in foster care. She believed it was in the baby's best interest to be placed with a young, loving couple who wanted a child. So she made arrangements to give the baby up for adoption, but insisted on holding the baby after delivery so she could say goodbye. That's when she saw her daughter had a severe birthmark on the side of her face. She feared the child might grow up believing her birth mother gave her up because of the birthmark."

"But she did give her up," Marie said.

"Yes, but not because of the birthmark. She wrestled with it, but decided it was still for the best. It was a decision she came to regret, especially considering she lived long after the girl entered adulthood. She wouldn't have been alone."

"How did she find her daughter?" Eva asked.

"I suppose you might say Tammy found her mother. They met at the church; Ruby introduced her. The moment Rachel saw the birthmark, she thought of the child she had given up. She asked

Tammy questions, trying to determine if she was the right age, anything that might tell her. When she went home, she decided it couldn't be her daughter. But she couldn't stop thinking of her, and eventually she hired a private detective. A week before Rachel's death, she learned her hunch was right, she was her daughter. Tammy had no idea."

"Was she planning to tell her before she was killed?" Marie asked.

Pearl shook her head. "No. She didn't want Tammy to feel she expected anything from her. Rachel didn't believe she had the right to just barge into her life, expect a relationship. But she wanted to leave her something."

"Money and a mystery," Marie scoffed.

"It wasn't supposed to be a mystery. Rachel had written a letter explaining everything. She intended to give the letter to her executor. He would give the letter to Tammy at the reading of the will. But Rachel died before he came back from vacation, and she couldn't give it to him. But it's in the house, and when it's found, she'll know the truth," Pearl said.

"Hopefully it will be found," Marie said.

"I've heard how Leanne has been caught in Rachel's house several times despite the executor telling her she shouldn't be there," Pearl said. "But I'm sure Leanne is simply looking for the letter, because like me, she wants to honor Rachel's wishes."

"How is that honoring Rachel's wishes?" Eva asked.

"Rachel wanted to tell Tammy in her own words why she gave her up for adoption. That letter is there, and Leanne will find it. And if for some reason she can't, then, unfortunately, she will have to tell Tammy herself," Pearl explained. "And then she'll let the executor know Tammy is to inherit the house, not her."

"She left the daughter her house?" Marie asked.

"She intended to change the will when her executor returned to town. Rachel naturally assumed she had enough time. He was coming back the next week. And she explained everything to Leanne, who more than understood."

"So Leanne knew she was being cut out of the will?" Eva asked.

"Leanne never wanted the house," Pearl insisted. "She said it often enough. In fact, at Rachel's funeral, I asked her if her husband was going to be a problem after he found out about the inheritance and then learned she wasn't keeping it. She told me she would handle him. And that's when I told Leanne I was there for her. That I'd help her stand up to her husband if needed so we could carry out Rachel's last wishes. That's why I think Larry might have been the one to kill us.

"Larry is always snooping around. He could have found out about the inheritance and then overheard Rachel and Leanne discussing changes to the will. He needed to get rid of Rachel before she left the house to Tammy. And then, after the reading of the will, Leanne must have told him she wouldn't be keeping the house and why. And she probably told him I knew everything. He realized it would be easier to bully her into doing what he wanted if I was out of the way. After all, he couldn't touch the inheritance without Leanne's permission."

"If Larry did kill you and Rachel over the inheritance, and you believed Leanne might cave to her husband without your moral support, why in the world haven't you let the police know all this?" Marie asked.

"Because if Leanne is looking for that letter, like I believe she is, it means she's planning to carry out Rachel's wishes despite her husband. I heard her standing up to him, telling him they needed to go to my funeral. And while I initially worried Leanne might be in some danger herself, I no longer believe he would do anything to her now; it would be too risky, not with the police investigating Rachel's murder and learning about Larry's infidelity," Pearl explained.

THIRTY-SEVEN

Danielle ended up driving Walt and Heather to the funeral in her Ford Flex instead of taking Walt's Packard. After the service, Walt hitched a ride home with Ian and Lily, while Danielle drove Heather over to the Glandon Foundation offices to pick up some empty boxes. Chris had driven to the service in his own car and told Danielle and Heather he would meet them at the office to help them load the boxes. But when he finally got there, they had already loaded everything into the car.

"You show up at the right time," Heather snarked as she slammed the vehicle's back hatch shut.

"I'm sorry," Chris said, walking from his car to the Flex. He peeked in the window and saw they had put the back seat down to make room for the boxes. "But I got talking to the chief in the parking lot after the service."

"Anything new?" Danielle asked.

"Aside from his son seeing the girl ghost again and having a conversation?" Chris asked.

"Really? When?" Danielle asked.

"This morning, at the park near their house," Chris explained. The chief had arrived at the service right before it started, so while he'd sat not far from Danielle and Walt in the church, they'd had no opportunity to talk. After the service, Danielle and Heather hadn't lingered. Instead, they'd headed to the foundation offices.

"Anything interesting?" Heather asked.

"Pretty much what we already knew; she was Rachel's daughter. One interesting thing, she mentioned Mel and watching her grow up, and how when she was a baby, she thought she could see her," Chris said.

"I imagine that is more common than we realize," Danielle said.

"Looks like she stuck around with her mom after she passed away, but she was off with her dog when her mother was killed and when her mother's body and spirit left the house. She's looking for her," Chris explained.

"Poor girl," Danielle murmured.

"The chief also told me they searched Rachel's house again during the service. Not sure what they were looking for, but he said they would be gone before you got there."

"CAN I use the bathroom before we leave?" Danielle asked Heather after Chris drove off.

"Sure, Little Mama." Heather used her key to get back inside the building.

After Danielle headed to the bathroom, Heather sat at her desk and began surfing on her cellphone. She had been looking at her phone for just a few minutes when a large snowflake landed on her phone's screen.

Heather looked up. She didn't see anyone, but another snowflake fell from the ceiling. "Eva?"

"How did you know?" Eva asked when she materialized a moment later.

"It doesn't normally snow inside," Heather said, setting her phone on her desk.

"Where is Danielle?" Eva asked.

"Where she usually is these days, in the bathroom."

"I heard that," Danielle said when she walked into the room the next moment. "Hello, Eva. Marie didn't come with you?"

"She stayed with Pearl; the funeral home picked up the casket and is taking it to the cemetery," Eva explained. "I'm going over there, but Marie and I felt I needed to let you know what Pearl told us, and you can pass the information on to the police. Not sure how much it's going to help."

Eva then told Danielle and Heather about Rachel's connection to Tammy. When she finished the retelling, she said her goodbyes and left for the cemetery. After Eva left, Danielle phoned the chief and retold the story.

"What did he say?" Heather asked when Danielle finally got off the phone.

"That letter Pearl told Marie and Eva about, he suspected there might be something like that at the house. Remember when Chris said the chief told him he had his people search the house this morning? That's what they were looking for. Herman Shafer let them in. But they found nothing," Danielle explained.

"If he is the killer, I don't think he did it by poisoning one of her vitamins and waiting for her to take it. Sounds like he needed to get rid of her before Herman Shafer got back from his vacation," Heather said.

"Yeah, that's what the chief said too."

"But if he got into her house to poison something he knew she'd take, then it is possible he removed the letter," Heather suggested. "So what now?"

"I have no idea." Danielle glanced at her watch and then looked back at Heather. "But we need to get over to Rachel's house. Did you remember to bring the key?"

"Of course."

EMPTY CARDBOARD BOXES filled their arms, so Heather and Danielle left their purses in the locked car, shoved under the front seats. After setting the boxes she had been holding on the porch, Heather unlocked Rachel's front door and opened it for Danielle to enter. Heather gathered up the boxes she had set on the porch and then followed Danielle into the house.

Still holding the boxes, Heather nudged the front door closed with her hip and looked around the room. "It's kind of creepy in here."

"I don't know, just an empty house," Danielle whispered.

"Then why are you whispering?"

Danielle chuckled. "I don't know. Okay, where did they say the sewing room was?"

"That way," Heather said, nodding toward the hallway.

No lights were on in the entry hall or living room, yet enough sunlight made its way into the house along the edges of the curtains to see while walking toward the hallway. But when they reached the hall, they found it illuminated by an overhead light fixture. Danielle assumed Herman had left it on, knowing they would be there this afternoon.

Still carrying the empty boxes, they made their way down the hallway and easily found the sewing room, its door wide open. Once inside, Danielle and Heather stacked the boxes along one wall. When they finished, Heather let out a little curse.

"What's wrong?" Danielle asked.

"I need to go back to the car and get my purse."

"Why?"

"I put a pad of paper and pen in there. I want to inventory the items while we're boxing them up."

"I bet there's some paper and a pen in here we can use," Danielle said. She walked to a small desk in the room's corner. Just as she opened a drawer, the sound of footsteps from overhead made her freeze. Both she and Heather looked up at the ceiling.

"Someone's here," Heather whispered.

"Umm… no one is supposed to be here."

"Tell that to whoever is upstairs," Heather said.

"Perhaps the chief was wrong, and his people didn't finish going through the house," Danielle suggested.

"Then wouldn't there be a police car parked out front?" Heather asked.

Danielle cringed. "We should probably call someone."

Heather glanced around the room and then whispered, "I don't see a phone in here, and my cellphone is out in the car in my purse."

"Mine too," Danielle said. "Maybe we should just get out of here."

"Leanne! Where are you! I'm going to kill you!" a man's voice shouted. It sounded like he was down the hall from them.

"Crap," Heather muttered, looking around the room for a place to hide. They had left the door to the room wide open, and whoever was in the hall could walk by the open doorway at any moment and see them in the room.

"The closet," Danielle whispered. Together, Heather and Danielle rushed toward the set of louvered doors along the far wall.

When they pushed open the doors, they found several quilts folded neatly and piled on the floor. Stepping inside, they tried closing the doors behind them, but the doors refused to shut all the way, leaving about a three-inch opening. Both women leaned to opposite sides of the closet to avoid being seen through the gap.

"Leanne, are you in here?" the voice demanded. He had entered the sewing room. "I should kill you, you know. I think I might."

Moving slowly, to avoid making any noise, Danielle wrapped herself in a quilt in a feeble attempt to hide should he open the doors. Heather did the same. Tempted to look out the opening to see who had come into the room, both women resisted. Yet Danielle had already surmised the man's identity: Larry Hodge.

"Leanne, come out, come out, wherever you are!" Larry taunted. "Are you in the closet?"

Huddled together in the dark closet, Danielle and Heather held their breaths while Larry Hodge approached, all the while calling for his wife. He did not try opening the doors, but he put one eye against the opening, trying to see inside. Both Danielle and Heather, each pressed up against the back wall, wrapped in a quilt, peered out through their blanket, and watched as the eye of Larry Hodge attempted to see inside the closet. After a moment, he stood abruptly and turned his back to them.

"I know you're here somewhere! Don't think you're going to get away from me! You are my wife, and I won't take your insolence! Don't push me, Leanne, I could easily break your neck!" Larry yelled before marching out of the room.

Now trembling, Heather reached down and took hold of Danielle's hand, giving it a squeeze. Danielle squeezed her back. Neither woman made any attempt to leave the closet. Instead, they listened for the sound of Larry's voice while their rapid heartbeats filled the momentary silence.

"Leanne!" they heard him shout.

"I think he's upstairs," Heather whispered.

"Sounds like it."

"I could make a run for it, get to the car and call the police. You hide here," Heather suggested.

They heard Larry shout again.

"Sounds like he's in the living room now," Danielle said.

"Damn, he gets around," Heather grumbled. "But I might be able to outrun him."

"It's not safe," Danielle argued.

"This isn't good for you," Heather insisted. "If I can just distract him so you can get out."

Danielle turned to Heather and frowned. "Are you trying to protect me?"

"Well, yeah," Heather said, giving her hand another squeeze. "I can't let anything happen to Little Mama."

Danielle gave Heather's hand a final squeeze and then released it while saying, "We are in this together. You don't need to protect me or put yourself at risk for me. We just need to stay hidden until Walt gets here."

Heather let out a sigh and gave Danielle a nod. The two women settled back in the dark closet, still wrapped in the quilts, the only sound the beating of their hearts. Larry called out for Leanne again. It sounded like he was still downstairs. The next minute, they heard a door opening and closing. All went silent.

At least fifteen minutes had passed when Danielle whispered, "I think he's gone."

"I think you're right. Let me peek out the window," Heather suggested.

Just as they opened the closet doors, Leanne Hodge walked into the room. She halted when she saw the women, her eyes wide.

THIRTY-EIGHT

"Leanne, did you just get here?" Danielle asked.

"What are you doing in there? You scared the bejesus out of me!" Leanne blurted.

"We all need to get out of here before he comes back," Danielle said.

"Before who comes back?" Leanne asked. "And you didn't answer my question. Why are you in my house?"

"Herman Shafer gave me the key so I could remove the quilting supplies Rachel left Pearl," Heather explained.

Leanne frowned. "Why?"

"We really need to get out of here. You're in danger," Danielle said. "We all are."

Leanne refused to budge. "I don't know what you're talking about. Why did Herman give you a key to my house? How long have you been here?"

"Maybe twenty minutes. We just came to remove the quilting supplies. This is the only room we've been in. But you need to listen to us," Danielle urged.

Leanne visibly relaxed. "Why are you taking the quilting supplies Rachel left for Pearl? Pearl didn't even like you."

"Please listen," Danielle begged.

Before Danielle could say another word, Larry Hodge stormed

into the room, his angry glare focused on Leanne. "There you are! I'm going to kill you!"

Unable to contain herself, Heather let out a gasp, drawing Larry's attention from his wife to Heather and Danielle. He frowned and looked at the two women in surprise, as if he hadn't realized they had been standing there the entire time. "What are you doing here?"

"You are the one who isn't listening," Leanne snapped, still looking at Heather and Danielle and ignoring her husband. "Why would Herman Shafer think it was alright to let you take Pearl's inheritance? And to come into my house without asking me?"

Larry turned from Heather and Danielle and faced his wife. "Look at me, Leanne!" Larry shouted. "Stop ignoring me! I swear, I am going to break your miserable neck!"

Wide eyed and speechless, Danielle and Heather stood together in front of the open closet doors, looking from Leanne to Larry, neither able to fathom Leanne's casual dismissal of her clearly enraged husband.

"Are you going to answer me?" Leanne demanded, still focused on the two women.

When Larry leapt on his wife a moment later and attempted to strangle her, they finally understood why Leanne seemed unfazed by her husband. She couldn't see him.

Leanne continued to demand answers from Heather and Danielle while Larry tried unsuccessfully to grab hold of his wife's neck. His hands kept moving through her body as if it were air. Fascinated by the bizarre sight, neither Heather nor Danielle could look away, and both remained speechless.

Frustrated by his inability to grab hold of his wife, Larry stopped trying. Standing next to Leanne while she now demanded why Heather and Danielle refused to answer her, he looked down at his hands, staring at them for a moment while turning them from side to side, trying to understand.

"Your husband is dead," Heather muttered. To confirm it, Heather picked up a throw pillow from a nearby chair and tossed it at Larry. It fell through his body.

"Why did you do that?" Leanne asked, looking down at the pillow on the floor.

"Oh my god, I am dead. You killed me!" Larry shouted at Leanne.

"You killed your husband?" Heather blurted without thought.

Danielle cringed at Heather's careless comment. The next moment, Leanne pulled a revolver from her purse, pointing it at them. Larry vanished.

"Get into the closet," Leanne demanded; her hand holding the revolver shook precariously.

"Umm… I think there has been a misunderstanding," Danielle stammered. "We just came here to get Pearl's inheritance so her estate can auction it for charity."

"I… I need to call the police. Yes, that's what I need to do. Go back in the closet, and sit down, now, while I call the police." Leanne stammered. Her right hand continued to quiver as she held onto the gun. She wiped the back of her left hand over her now perspiring brow.

"Leanne's not going to call the police," Larry said when he suddenly appeared. "If she does, they are bound to find my body upstairs in Rachel's bathroom, where she left me."

"Do not repeat any of what he just said," Danielle quickly warned Heather.

Leanne frowned, pointing the gun now directly at Danielle. "What are you talking about?"

"Please don't point that gun at her. She's pregnant, and the stress is not good for her or the baby," Heather said. "Like Danielle said, this is all a misunderstanding. Please call the police, and they can tell you it's okay we're here."

"In the closet. I need to think." Leanne motioned to the closet with her gun.

When the two women climbed back into the closet, they were not alone. Larry went with them, insisting on sitting in the middle, and Leanne shut the doors. When the doors refused to shut all the way, like they had for Danielle and Heather, Leanne gave them a firm shove. They shut. They heard Leanne moving something against the closet, locking them in.

After they heard Leanne leave the room, Heather leaned forward and tried moving the doors; they would not budge. "She's locked us in here," Heather whispered.

"She needs time to think. That's what she does. Wants everyone to get out of her sight so she can think," Larry said, leaning back in the closet, crossing his arms over his chest. They then heard the sewing room door shut and, a minute later, the sound of footsteps going up the stairs.

It wasn't totally dark in the closet. Light coming in the window made its way around the ill-fitting edges of the closet doors. Danielle looked to Larry and said, "You're not locked in here."

Larry shrugged. "I just need a little quiet time. This seems as good a place as any. I'm a little annoyed myself. My wife killed me. Damn. I never thought she would do something like that."

"Was it because she found out you killed her friend?" Heather asked.

"Me?" Larry scoffed. "I didn't kill anyone."

"Then why did she kill you?" Heather asked.

"Was it because she found out you were cheating on her?" Danielle asked.

Larry groaned. "Why do women have to get so upset over something like that? We are men; we can't help it. It's what we do. I never expected her to overreact like that."

Heather let out a grunt.

"I have a question," Larry said.

"What?" Danielle asked.

"I'm dead, right?" he asked.

"As a doornail," Heather grumbled.

"Never understood that phrase," Larry said.

Heather shrugged. "It's been around over seven hundred years, and you haven't figured it out by now?"

"I take it you're used to this," Larry said.

"What, being locked in a closet with a ghost?" Heather asked. "While his body is upstairs, and his wife is running around with a gun?"

"No. I mean used to seeing ghosts. That's what I am, right?" he asked.

"Perhaps we can discuss this later, we really need to get out of here, and I'm hoping you can help us," Danielle told Larry.

"How can I help you? I couldn't even strangle my wife," he grumbled.

"You can go get help for us," Danielle said.

"She's right," Heather agreed.

"Okay," Larry said before disappearing.

"Come back!" Danielle cried out. "We need to tell you who to get!"

"He just left?" Heather groaned. "What a jerk."

Danielle reached out and tried opening the closet doors. They still would not budge.

CHRIS PULLED his car up behind Danielle's and parked. He looked at Walt, who sat in the passenger's seat, unfastening his seatbelt.

"You want to move the trunk over to Mel's before we load up the boxes?" Chris asked.

"I know why you want to do it first," Walt said with a laugh.

Chris grinned. "Well, if we do it now, before Mel gets back, it'll be much easier. And she gave me her key."

"Easier on you," Walt teased.

"True." Chris unfastened his seatbelt.

Several minutes later, the two men walked up to Rachel's front door. When they got there, they found it unlocked. Chris walked in first, followed by Walt.

"I guess we should tell Heather and Danielle we're here before we move the trunk," Chris said.

"Where is the trunk?" Walt asked. "You can go tell them we're here, and I can start moving it."

"Mel said it's upstairs, in the master bedroom, first door on the right. It's the only trunk in the room, at the foot of the bed," Chris explained.

Walt started up the stairs while Chris headed to the sewing room. Chris got to the sewing room first. When he did, he didn't see Heather and Danielle, just the boxes they had brought, still empty and stacked along one wall.

"It doesn't look like they've done anything," Chris said aloud.

"Who's there?" a voice called out.

"Heather?" Chris said, walking to the closet. Once there, he noted someone had shoved a pole through the handles of the closet doors, locking them in place.

"Is that you, Chris?" Heather called out. "Help! We're locked in the closet!"

"What the—" Chris said as he quickly removed the bar holding the doors. The next moment the closet opened, and a relieved

Danielle and Heather rushed out, throwing their arms around Chris.

"Thank god you're here!" Danielle said. "Where's Walt?"

"How did you guys get stuck in there?" Chris asked.

"God, I'm glad to see you!" Heather cried, giving Chris another hug.

"Everyone put your hands up, now!" Leanne demanded, now standing in the open doorway, the revolver in her hand, pointed at Chris, Heather, and Danielle.

"What's going on?" Chris asked, yet quickly shoved his hands in the air when Leanne repositioned the revolver so that it pointed at his head.

"This will not do," Leanne stammered. "Not at all. I think we need to take a little trip to the basement. Yes. I think that would be a good idea."

The next moment Larry appeared, standing next to his wife. He shook his head emphatically. "No, I don't think that would be a good idea. Bad idea. You really don't want to go to the basement with her."

Chris glanced over at Danielle and Heather, his hands still up in the air. "Is that…"

Danielle nodded, and Heather whispered, "I think the rest of him is upstairs."

"Now, get moving. Or I will have to use this gun," Leanne demanded.

They started moving toward the door, yet intentionally at a slower pace, trying to buy time.

"I'm not in the mood, faster!" Leanne shrieked; her hand clutching the pistol shook.

Larry cringed. "Yeah, it's never pretty when she gets like this."

Together, the three, all with their hands in the air, trudged toward the doorway. Once in the hall, Leanne trailed behind them, giving them directions to the basement. Larry disappeared again.

THE CEDAR CHEST FLOATED OVERHEAD, making its way down the upstairs hallway, Walt following behind, directing it as one might a remote control airplane, yet without the remote. As he started down the staircase, cedar chest overhead, Walt looked to the first floor and froze when he saw his wife, Heather, and Chris, all with their hands in the air, while a woman pointed a gun at them.

With Walt's attention diverted from the trunk, it began to fall. Downstairs, the woman holding the gun glanced up when she noticed motion overhead. She screamed in terror as the cedar chest hurled toward her. Walt regained control of the truck just seconds before it landed on the woman, like the house landing on the wicked witch in *The Wizard of Oz*.

THIRTY-NINE

Heather wanted to kick Chris for being so nice to Leanne. The woman deserved to be in handcuffs, not helped up from the floor and gently led to the sofa. After diverting the trunk so it didn't land on the crazy lady's head, Walt had confiscated her gun. Danielle borrowed Walt's cellphone to make a quick call to the chief, and then handed it to Heather, who wanted to call Brian.

Brian arrived at Rachel's house at the same time as the chief. The moment the two police officers walked into the living room and Leanne saw them, her tears stopped, and she stood up. Her abrupt transformation from hysterics to calm outrage gave Danielle pause.

"I'm glad you're here. These people have broken into my house," Leanne accused.

"You pulled a gun on us, locked us in the closet, and you wanted to take us to the basement," Heather snapped.

"It's only because you broke into the house, and I wanted to hold you for the police," Leanne insisted.

"They did not break into the house," Police Chief MacDonald told her. "I know for a fact the executor to Rachel Moore's estate asked them to come and remove what Mrs. Moore had left for Melony Carmichael and Pearl Huckabee. Pearl Huckabee's trustee was also aware of the arrangement and was working with Ms. Donovan."

"They about killed me." Leanne pointed to the cedar chest now resting quietly at the base of the staircase. "That trunk Rachel left to Melony, it about fell on me. He must have just thrown it over the banister upstairs."

"He would have to be pretty strong to do that. Pick it up, and then toss it over the banister?" Brian said. He and the chief exchanged glances and then looked to Walt, who responded with a shrug.

When Brian and the chief looked back to Leanne, she said, "The property has not gone through probate yet. I don't think anything should be taken from the house until it goes through probate."

"From what I understand, you aren't supposed to be letting yourself in here," the chief told Leanne while the others silently listened to the exchange.

Leanne raised her chin defiantly and said, "I just wanted to check on the house, see if everything was okay. I assumed if I didn't remove anything, it wouldn't be a problem. I suppose that's why I got so upset when I thought they were trying to remove things." She looked at Heather and Danielle and said, "I guess it was all a mistake. I apologize." She looked back at the chief and asked, "Can I go now?"

"I think we should go upstairs first," Danielle said.

"You don't have any reason to go upstairs. If you must take the contents of the sewing room, then do it. But that's on the first floor. You don't need to be going through my house," Leanne said.

"I think it might be a good idea if we walked through the house just to make sure everything is okay," the chief said calmly.

"Fine, but I need to go home." Leanne walked toward the door, but the chief called her back.

"No. I would like us all to go together," the chief said.

"This should be fun," Larry said when he appeared a moment later. Walt startled at the ghost's sudden appearance.

"It's the dead husband," Chris whispered to Walt.

BOTH THE CHIEF and Brian knew what they might find on the second floor as they started through the house. Danielle had told the chief on the phone, while Heather had told Brian. The chief led the way, with Leanne by his side and behind them Brian, followed by the others. Danielle watched Leanne and the officers, thinking the two men reminded her a little of two herding dogs, keeping Leanne moving along, not allowing her to step away into a room so she could disappear out a window.

When they reached the master bedroom, Leanne hesitated by the doorway, reluctant to go inside. Danielle knew Walt had been in the room to get the trunk and had seen nothing. But she remembered Larry mentioned his body was in the bathroom, off this bedroom. Danielle looked to Larry.

"Yes, I'm in there. Dead to the world. Just because of one itsy-bitsy indiscretion."

A few moments later they all stood in the bedroom. Leanne dropped her silent demeanor and said, "Okay, let's get this over with so I can go home. Everything is obviously fine." She marched into the bathroom ahead of the police chief.

A moment after entering the bathroom, Leanne let out a scream. "Larry, oh Larry! What have you done?"

ONCE AGAIN SITTING on the living room sofa, Leanne sat stoically, dabbing the corners of her eyes with a tissue. The responders had already arrived and were upstairs, yet the body had not yet been removed. Brian stayed upstairs with those processing the scene while the chief stood by the sofa with Leanne. In his hand, he held the suicide note they had found.

On the other side of the room, Heather, Danielle, Walt, and Chris sat quietly. The chief looked over to them and said, "Danielle, can you come here, please. I think I may need your help."

Leanne looked up at the chief and frowned at the odd request while Danielle gave him a nod, stood up, and walked to the chief. When she got to his side, he whispered in her ear, "Is the husband's ghost here?" Danielle nodded yes in reply.

"Find out how she did it, and repeat everything he says," he whispered.

Leanne hadn't heard the whispered question and request, but she looked up curiously at the chief and Danielle.

"I'd like to read this letter out loud," the chief said.

"In front of her?" Leanne asked.

"Yes. She's my interpreter," the chief said.

Leanne's frown deepened, yet she didn't ask him what he meant.

Danielle glanced at the suicide note. "He typed it."

"Yes. It makes it easier to read," the chief said. "But he signed it." He pointed to the signature.

"I didn't write that thing," Larry balked.

The chief began to read: "I can't finish what I started, and I can't live with my guilt. I thought I wanted out of my marriage so I could be with Hazel. I knew Leanne would never give me a divorce, so I knew if I wanted to be with Hazel, I would have to kill Leanne. I also knew Rachel was leaving Leanne her house. I decided to kill Rachel, knowing Leanne would inherit the house, and then when I killed Leanne, Hazel and I would have the money from the sale of Rachel's house."

"Rather wordy suicide note," Danielle muttered under her breath.

"I told you I did not write that. I did not commit suicide."

The chief resumed reading the typed letter. "Leanne attended a church retreat with Rachel and told me how she had a habit of laying out her clothes for the next day and putting her vitamin in a cup by her bed while she showered. So I used Rachel's key and got into Rachel's house. I hid in a closet, waiting for her to take a shower. All I had to do was replace her vitamin with one filled with cyanide. But after Rachel died, I realized I could not kill Leanne. I still loved her. So I am ending my life as I ended Rachel's. Leanne, please forgive me. I love you, Larry."

"What a bunch of malarky," Larry grumbled.

"Foolish, foolish Larry," Leanne said with a sniffle.

"Larry didn't kill himself," Danielle said as she stepped closer to the sofa. "You killed him."

Clutching her tissue to her chest, Leanne looked up to Danielle and gasped. "What a horrid thing to say!"

"Larry, how did she do it?" Danielle asked.

"What are you talking about?" Leanne looked to the chief and said, "Chief MacDonald, why are you letting this woman talk to me like this? My husband has just died!"

"She asked me to walk over here with her. Said she wanted to show me something," Larry began. Danielle repeated his words and continued to do so as he told what had happened to him that day.

"As soon as we walked in the house, she pulled out a couple of my favorite cookies from her purse. Pumpkin spice from Old Salts.

She said she bought them before she picked me up for Pearl's funeral. Said they were my reward for going with her, since I didn't want to. The first one tasted kinda funny, so she gave me hers, and we walked upstairs. She said she wanted to show me something in Rachel's bathroom. When we got there, my stomach started hurting, and then she pulled a gun on me. She told me she knew about me and Hazel, that she had put up with me for all these years, but it was over because I was a cheater. Then she said she was going to kill me just like she had killed Rachel. I was hurting so bad by that time, I don't remember much after that. Not until I thought I had come to, survived, and found you in the sewing room."

Danielle repeated all that Larry had said, except for his last comment about finding Danielle in the sewing room. The chief, who had said nothing while Danielle relayed Larry's words, studied Leanne, noting her stunned expression. She appeared to be in shock and just stared at Danielle.

"Why did you push Pearl down the stairs?" the chief asked Leanne in a calm voice.

Still staring at Danielle, seeing in her mind her dead husband instead of the woman she'd held at gunpoint, Leanne heard the chief's question and, without thought, said, "She knew about Tammy. Rachel said I was the only one she'd told. I don't understand any of this."

With a heavy sigh, the chief said, "Leanne Hodge, you are under arrest for the murders of Rachel Moore, Pearl Huckabee, and Larry Hodge. You have the right to remain silent. Anything you say can and will be used against you in a court of law. You have a right to an attorney. If you cannot afford an attorney, one will be appointed for you. Do you understand?"

Leanne stared at the chief. "I understand what you just said, but I don't understand how she knew about the pumpkin spice cookies… about all that other stuff she said."

"Leanne Hodge, did you murder your husband?" the chief asked.

Dazed and confused, Leanne turned her face to the chief and cocked her head slightly. "I had to. He hurt me. I killed Rachel for him. If I hadn't done that, she was going to change her will and leave everything to a woman she didn't even know. She gave the woman life, wasn't that enough? So I killed her, and I killed Pearl to keep her quiet. But it was all for nothing. Larry didn't care about all my sacrifices for him. I am always the nice person, going out of my way for people. Helping people. Larry doesn't do that. And when they leave me their money, I always share it with him. The very least he could have done was show me loyalty. Was that really asking too much? A little simple loyalty?"

Leanne smiled up to the chief as she got to her feet and offered her hands to be cuffed. In a childlike voice she asked, "Will I be charged for the others too?"

"Others?" The chief frowned.

"Yes, the others I killed." Leanne smiled sweetly.

FORTY

Brian Henderson sat on the sofa in Marlow House's living room, Heather Donovan by his side. He curiously studied the people around him while wondering about those he couldn't see. A year ago, he would never have imagined himself here, with this group of people and under these circumstances. Heather called it a gathering of mediums and ghosts. Of the living currently here, only he and the police chief were not mediums.

Lily and Ian, who normally attended Marlow House gatherings, were absent, along with their son, who counted among the mediums. According to Heather, they had gone to Ian's parents' house for Sunday dinner, along with Joe and Kelly.

Sitting in the chair across from him was Danielle, whom he considered the grand dame among the local mediums, and by her side stood Walt, one of his hands resting on her right shoulder. Walt had once been in the ghost column yet had moved over to the living medium section. Brian wasn't sure he would ever get used to all this.

Chris sat on the fireplace hearth next to young Evan MacDonald, and Evan's father, Police Chief MacDonald, sat in a nearby chair.

Those he couldn't see included the ghosts of Marie Nichols, Eva Thorndike, Pearl Huckabee, Cindy Moore, and a ghost dog name Charger. There were also two live dogs in attendance, Chris's pit bull, Hunny, along with Lily and Ian's golden retriever, Sadie, whom

Danielle and Walt had offered to dog-sit while his humans were at Ian's parents. Plus, Danielle's cat, Max, and Heather's cat, Bella. Brian figured the living dogs and cats might as well be counted along with the mediums, since they not only saw the ghosts, they also communicated with them.

THE FOUR GHOSTS sat on an imaginary sofa in the middle of the living room, with Eva on one end, Marie on the other, and Pearl and little Cindy sitting between them. On the floor by their feet lay Charger, who seemed unconcerned by the curious stares coming from the living dogs and cats in the room.

Pearl cleared her throat and said, "I have something I must say."

All the mediums turned their attention to Pearl.

She cleared her throat again—which in reality was totally unnecessary, for Pearl no longer had a throat, only an illusion of one. She then said, "I want to say I misjudged you all. Just as I misjudged Hunny." Pearl looked to Hunny, who in turn looked back, her tail wagging. "Thank you all for finding out the truth."

"Are you ready to move on now?" Danielle asked.

Pearl nodded at Danielle and then looked at Cindy. "Yes, I'm going to take Cindy to her mother."

Cindy smiled up at Pearl and then looked at Evan. "And thank you, Evan, for all your help."

"Oh, I didn't really do anything," Evan grumbled shyly.

Cindy shook her head. "No. You did. You talked to me, listened. Do you know how long it's been since I had anyone to really talk to?"

"When you get there, will you tell my mom hi if you see her?" Evan asked.

While the chief could not hear the spirit's side of the conversation, he heard the request. With a sad smile, he studied his youngest son.

"Sure. I will," Cindy promised.

"What is going to happen to Leanne?" Pearl asked.

Danielle repeated the question for the chief.

"At the moment, she's under observation," the chief said.

"Do you think she killed her husband over the affair? It sounded like it wasn't the first time. Why kill him now?" Heather asked.

"I don't believe Leanne thought anyone would ever suspect Rachel had been murdered, considering her age. She assumed the poisoning would go undetected," the chief said. "But once we started investigating it as a homicide, she worried she might become a suspect, since she had access to Rachel's house and motive. I think her husband's recent infidelity made it easier for her to set him up as the scapegoat, and since he was not mentioned in the will, his murdering Rachel wouldn't mean Leanne couldn't inherit the house."

As the chief explained it was only a theory, Larry suddenly appeared. Oblivious to the new ghost's appearance, the chief continued to talk.

"I'm here!" Larry announced, waving his arm to emphasize the point.

"Larry, what are you doing here?" Pearl asked, now ignoring what the chief was telling her about Leanne.

"I heard you were leaving this gin joint and moving to the next side, and figured I'd tag along. After all, I've never been there before."

"Neither have I. And you can't go with us," Pearl snapped.

"Why not?" Larry frowned. "I don't want to go alone."

"That is not my problem," Pearl said.

He then noticed Eva, who sat on the other side of the little girl next to Pearl, staring curiously in his direction. Larry's eyes widened. "Wowzer, who are you?"

"That's Eva Thorndike," Pearl said.

"The Eva Thorndike? Wow, you're even more gorgeous than your portrait. Are you going to the other side too? Because if you are," he looked back to Pearl and said, "no offense, but if you don't want me to go, then I'll go with her." He looked back at Eva and flashed her a grin.

"You're not going anywhere with Eva," Marie said with disgust.

Larry turned to Marie and frowned. "Who are you? Hey, I think I know you."

"Yes, you do. Marie Nichols."

Larry frowned. "Dang. Marie Nichols. You never liked me."

"That has nothing to do with it," Marie said. "Eva has her own path, and it isn't escorting you to the other side."

Larry gave a pout but said nothing.

Pearl stood, her body hovering several feet above the floor.

"We've bothered these people long enough. Come on, Larry, you can go with us."

Larry perked up. "Really?"

"Yes, come on," Pearl said impatiently. She then turned a smile to Cindy and asked, "Are you ready, dear?"

"Yes. I can't wait to see my mom and dad, and my sister!" Cindy said excitedly.

Taking Cindy's hand, Pearl looked at Larry. "Well? Are you going with us?"

Larry glanced briefly at Eva and let out a disappointed sigh. He looked back at Pearl and said, "Okay."

"Thank you, everyone," Pearl said. She then looked at Hunny and added, "Be a good girl, Hunny bunny."

Cindy glanced down at her dog and said, "Come on, Charger. Time to go."

The next moment Pearl, Cindy, Charger, and Larry vanished.

AFTER HEATHER FILLED the chief and Brian in on what the spirits had said, Brian asked, "Why do you think Pearl agreed to take him with her?"

"I believe it was her way of trying to make amends," Marie said. "To help make up for how she acted toward everyone."

"You think so?" Heather asked after repeating Marie's words for Brian.

Marie nodded and then looked at Walt and Danielle. "She also told me that while she didn't enjoy living next to a B and B, she understands now she handled it wrong. Moving here, she was trying to recreate a memory, and having Marlow House as a B an B interfered with the illusion she wanted to create. She would have been happier if Marlow House had been empty, like when she was a child."

"Now she's on an entirely new journey," Heather said.

"Oh, I don't know about that," Eva said slyly. The mediums turned to her questioningly.

In response, Eva smiled back at them and said, "*What has been will be again, what has been done will be done again. There is nothing new under the sun.*"

DURING THE REST OF OCTOBER, many residents of Beach Drive turned their attention to preparing for Halloween. For Walt and Danielle, who didn't plan to open Marlow House as a haunted house this year, they focused on exploring the possibility of getting their license for a bed-and-breakfast reinstated. While they intended to scale back the hours of operation compared to when Danielle had initially opened the business, they liked the idea of being able to take guests again, along with the tax deductions Chris and Adam had pointed out.

Pearl's house hadn't gone on the market yet. After thoroughly inspecting the property, they discovered it needed a new roof along with other repairs. As a homeowner, Pearl had often procrastinated over expensive home maintenance, such as when she had ignored trimming the trees in the front of her property, which resulted in a tree limb almost falling on her neighbor's car. In retrospect, she should have invested in a new roof instead of purchasing a woodstove. Since there was enough money in Pearl's estate to make the repairs, her trustee decided they would do that before putting the house on the market.

Leanne, having confessed to the murder of her friend, could no longer inherit Rachel's house. Yet even if no laws prevented a killer from inheriting their victim's property, Leanne still would have lost the inheritance. Although little Cindy told Evan about witnessing Leanne tear up a letter at her mother's house and then flushing it down the toilet, Evan had failed to tell his father about that part of the conversation with the ghost. What little Cindy had seen Leanne flush had been a copy of the letter Rachel had written to Tammy.

What none of them knew, after Rachel wrote the letter to Tammy, she made a copy of it and then gave the original to Leanne after having Leanne sign the document as a witness. Rachel's trust in Leanne had been so misplaced, she had asked her to keep the original, signed document for safekeeping—should something happen to her before Herman returned.

While Rachel was wise to write the letter, she chose the wrong person to hold it for her. Fortunately, Leanne had only destroyed the copy Rachel had kept. The original Leanne hadn't yet destroyed, and the police discovered it when searching Leanne's house after her arrest. It looked as if the house, after going through probate, would now go to Tammy.

NOVEMBER ARRIVED and with it an approved business license for Marlow House Bed and Breakfast. Danielle ordered a wooden carved placard from the artist who'd made their sign for Marlow House. They intended to attach it to the existing sign.

Danielle and Walt had moved into the master bedroom on the second floor, and they had converted the attic bedroom into Walt's office. They put a hold on fixing up the nursery. For now, they could rent the room as before, and when Joanne left on vacation in the spring, Marie could paint the would-be nursery before they prepared it for the new arrival.

Joanne proved to be the happiest about the reopening of the bed-and-breakfast and offered to answer the phones when she was at Marlow House, to take reservations. With Lily now living across the street, with her own responsibilities, Danielle and Walt accepted her offer.

THE WEEK BEFORE THANKSGIVING WEEKEND, Danielle and Walt arrived home from lunch at Pier Café to an excited Joanne.

"We have our first reservations!" Joanne said excitedly.

"Really?" Danielle said. "That was quick. I just relaunched the website two days ago."

"When's it for?" Walt asked, suddenly apprehensive. When Danielle had first moved into Marlow House, he hated the idea of a bed-and-breakfast and bringing strangers into their home. But over time, it had become a love-hate relationship. While there were things he disliked about the business, some aspects he truly enjoyed. Now that it was about to become a reality again, he wondered if they had made the right decision.

Joanne glanced at her watch. "I really need to run. I have a dentist appointment, and I'm going to be late if I don't leave now. But I wanted to tell you; everything is in the appointment book."

After Joanne gathered up her purse and rain jacket and said a hasty goodbye, Danielle headed for the parlor to look at the appointment book, to see when their new guests would be arriving. Walt trailed behind her.

Once in the parlor, Walt watched as Danielle opened the reservation book. She glanced at the page and looked up at him. "It's over Thanksgiving weekend. Looks like two rooms." Danielle looked back to the page and read more, her forehead drawing into a frown.

"This can't be right," Danielle muttered under her breath.

"What's wrong?" Walt asked, looking over her shoulder. He read the open page and couldn't understand what the problem might be. Joanne had taken a reservation for a man and a woman, with a room reserved for each one.

Danielle looked up at Walt and said, "It's my mother-in-law."

"What do you mean?" Walt asked.

"The reservation for the woman, that's my mother-in-law. And not just someone with the same name; that's her address."

"Your mother-in-law?" Walt asked, now frowning.

"Lucas's mother, Walt. Lucas's mother is spending Thanksgiving with us."

THE GHOST AND THE MEDIUM

Return to Marlow House

The Ghost and the Medium

Haunting Danielle, Book 30

When Marlow House reopens as a bed and breakfast, one of its first guests is Danielle's former mother-in-law, who Danielle has not talked to since moving to Oregon.

The mother-in-law brings with her one of the country's top mediums. Or as Danielle calls him, one of the country's top con men.

NON-FICTION BY

BOBBI ANN JOHNSON HOLMES

Havasu Palms, A Hostile Takeover

Where the Road Ends, Recipes & Remembrances

Motherhood, a book of poetry

The Story of the Christmas Village

BOOKS BY ANNA J. MCINTYRE

Coulson's Wife

Coulson's Crucible

Coulson's Lessons

Coulson's Secret

Coulson's Reckoning

Now available in Audiobook Format

UNLOCKED HEARTS

Sundered Hearts

After Sundown

While Snowbound

Sugar Rush

Printed in Great Britain
by Amazon